A FLAWED SCOTSMAN

Clan Ross
Book Four

Hildie McQueen

Dragonblade Publishing, Inc. is an imprint of Kathryn Le Veque Novels, Inc.
P.O. Box 7968
La Verne CA 91750
ceo@dragonbladepublishing.com

Produced in the United States of America

First Edition September 2020
Print Edition

ARE YOU SIGNED UP FOR DRAGONBLADE'S BLOG?

You'll get the latest news and information on exclusive giveaways, exclusive excerpts, coming releases, sales, free books, cover reveals and more.

Check out our complete list of authors, too!

No spam, no junk. That's a promise!

Sign Up Here

www.dragonbladepublishing.com

Dearest Reader;

Thank you for your support of a small press. At Dragonblade Publishing, we strive to bring you the highest quality Historical Romance from the some of the best authors in the business. Without your support, there is no 'us', so we sincerely hope you adore these stories and find some new favorite authors along the way.

Happy Reading!

CEO, Dragonblade Publishing

CHAPTER ONE

THE BRIGHT SUN and clear sky did little to cheer Ruari Ross that morning as he collected items that he'd take on the short trip. Facing the past was something most could do without much thought. In his case, however, it meant revisiting the reason for losing his family.

He trudged from his rooms beside the stables to the main house to break his fast, admittedly prolonging each moment before his departure.

Once inside the great room, the joviality of the people inside grated at him and he sat at a back table hoping to eat without being bothered.

A maid hurried to him, placing a platter of food before him, her body much too close, pressing against his side as she leaned forward. "I will fetch ye some ale."

He thanked her and began to eat. The sooner the trip was over and done with, the faster he could get to the routine of his day. His life was monotonous, not much different from one day to the next since the battle of clans had ceased. To Ruari, it was fine. He preferred predictable.

For someone like him, a path clear of obstacles meant he could keep away from too many complications. One day, he'd marry a woman from the clan, perhaps build a home and start a family. It would be on his terms, with a woman that was loyal and devoted.

However, if fate decided he should remain alone, the idea did not bother him in the least.

>>>><<<<

"I DO NOT want yer charity." Ruari's mother peered down at the sacks of food and grain he'd brought. "We are well enough to provide for ourselves." She picked up a small sack of coins he'd placed on top of the sacks and weighed it in her palm.

The house was unkempt, the rushes old and smelly. It was the home he'd never been welcome to or had ever lived in. After his father disappeared, his mother had insisted on moving away from Ross Keep. The late laird had gifted the home to her and Ruari.

However, she'd refused to take him and snuck away without a word, leaving him behind to be raised by his uncle and aunt.

Ruari did his best not to allow bitterness to take hold in his heart as he met her cold gaze. Did she really not care for him one bit?

"Where is yer husband?"

She looked away, past him to the doorway. An obvious invitation to leave. "He is gone hunting."

"That is what ye said last time I was here."

Her lips curled into a snarl. "What do ye want? To gloat? Coming here pretending to care for me when it is all a show for them." She motioned outside. "Do not come here again. I prefer not to see ye ever."

The fact his mother did not love him was not new. For years, he'd tried to gain something from her, at least a small amount of affection, but had failed. Now, he did his duty to see about her and ensure she had food and coin.

"Ye should leave," she said in a tired voice. "I do not need the constant reminder of the man who abandoned me."

His mother claimed that because she'd become pregnant and given birth to Ruari, his father had left them. He'd yet to make up his mind about it. At first, when he was a young lad, he'd believed her, felt guilty. Now, as a man and studying her, he wondered why his father had married her in the first place.

Despite the fact that his uncle had insisted that it had nothing to do with him and was, in fact, a problem between his parents, he never would really know the truth. Over the years, he'd overheard mumblings. Elders who whispered that she'd, in fact, killed his father. After all, Conor Ross vanished suddenly and had never been seen or heard from again.

There were so many unanswered questions, but Ruari had stopped bringing up the subject long ago. His mother would fly into a rage, accusing him of spreading rumors about her when, in fact, she was the victim of the cruelty of life.

Now, her second husband was gone. He, too, had not been seen in an entire season.

"Ensure to send word if ye need anything." Ruari met his mother's gaze for a long moment. "Take care."

She looked away, effectively dismissing him.

Riding back to Dun Airgid, Ross Keep, where he'd lived since childhood, Ruari did his best to keep from allowing the encounter with his mother to affect him. And yet a lump formed in his throat that made it hard to swallow and his eyes brimmed with unshed tears.

It would be better to send someone else in the future and not subject himself to his mother's hatred. But perhaps it was his penance if he was truly the cause of his family's demise. Whether innocent or not, if he'd not been born, perhaps his parents would have remained together.

When Dun Airgid came into view, Ruari pulled his horse to a stop and dismounted. He walked slowly, pulling his steed along. "Sometimes I envy ye," he told the horse. "Ye do not have to wonder what yer birth caused."

Feeling foolish, he wiped the sleeve of his tunic across his face. He was a grown man. Taller and more muscular than most. And here he was sulking like a child over how his mother treated him.

⤜⤜⤜

"Since we were young, ye've always loved to be around animals," his cousin, Ewan Ross, mused, his gaze moving from the horse to Ruari.

Ruari nodded. "I have, but sometimes the unruly ones like this one make me wonder why." He tugged the strap he'd tied around the huge beast's snout and neck. The horse pulled backward and pawed the ground in warning.

"Fine," Ruari barked and released his hold on the strap. The angry horse shook its large head, its mane waving about its head and then it galloped in a circle around the enclosed corral.

"That horse will eventually be a great warhorse."

By the incredulous look on Ewan's face, he didn't believe him. Ruari smiled. He loved a challenge and, eventually, this particular horse would be his mount.

Although both he and the horse were stubborn, Ruari was sure that, eventually, he'd win the beast over.

They walked to the guard training area just as the daily practice ended. In groups of threes and fours, sweaty men dispersed and headed to either their homes in the village or to the guard quarters within the keep. The ones who lived in the keep would soon be washed up and at last meal, more than ready to fill their bellies with hot food.

The laird, Malcolm Ross, motioned for Ruari and Ewan to come with him. He and Ewan exchanged looks and followed their cousin.

Usually too busy for more than a few words, most days, Malcolm hurried from sword practice to greet villagers and visitors for any last minute business before inviting them to stay and eat.

Already in the great hall, servants rushed about preparing the tables and ensuring all would be ready for last meal. They barely stopped in their duties to notice the group of warriors as they walked through the room and then down a side corridor to Malcolm's study.

Every time Ruari entered the study, with its tapestried walls and shelves that held tomes and various gifts from other lairds, he expected to find his uncle at the front. The recent horrible killing of Robert Ross had yet to seem real.

They were joined by Malcolm's brother, Tristan, and the head of the archers, Naill Hay. It was unusual to meet more than once a day to discuss what was happening in the clan. Most days, they'd spend at least an hour in the morning ensuring every aspect was covered. However, from time to time, Malcolm would call a second meeting if something was amiss.

Ruari went over his duties mentally, deciding to bring up the fact that they were low a few warhorses. There was a breeder not too far to the south and he intended to go himself with a group so that he could pick the best ones.

"We will be sending a group of guardsmen in a sennight to replace the men at the northern border," Malcolm began and looked to Naill. "Do ye have an idea of who must go?"

Naill nodded, his long hair falling over his face. "I will go with a party of twenty archers and relieve Kieran and his men."

"What about ye?" Malcolm asked his brother, Tristan, who headed the warrior contingent of the clan's large guard unit.

"I'll be sending twenty or five and twenty as well. I have a few volunteers, others I will assign based on the last time they've gone."

Ewan lifted a hand. "I'll go and help at the border. May as well make myself useful in some way."

Everyone looked from Ewan to Malcolm.

Malcolm's right eyebrow rose. "So ye prefer going to the frigid north rather than returning home to the seaside. Interesting. I am curious to know who the wench is that sent ye running."

When everyone laughed, Ewan scowled. "I needed a change of pace, to decide what to focus upon. As third born, I have nothing to cause me to go back. My coming here has nothing to do with a woman."

When scanning the room, Ruari could see no one believed Ewan.

"There is another matter that must be discussed," Malcolm said while pulling a parchment out. "A messenger brought this two days ago. I've been mulling over what to do about it."

"What is it?" Ewan asked, always the impatient one.

Malcolm let out a breath. "It is a request from Laird Fraser, head of the small clan just south of here. He asks for an alliance."

"I do not see any problem with it. Is there?" Tristan asked.

"I am prepared for an agreement between the clans. There is a threat from the Mackenzie that has them on edge. As we are all aware, Laird Mackenzie wishes to take over every clan in this area, looking to grow his territory," Malcolm said.

Malcolm continued. "There is an issue which gives me pause. Laird Fraser prefers something more stable in the alliance and asks that our clans be joined by marriage."

Tristan huffed. "We've all married. Certainly, he is aware."

"Not everyone." Malcolm looked to Ruari and Ewan who exchanged round-eyed looks. "Do not worry. I am sure a marriage will not be demanded as I am sure he expected for either Tristan or Kieran to be the grooms to his daughter."

"However," Tristan interjected. "A marriage between the clans does mean a more stable alliance."

"I am not going to get married. Besides, I am not from this clan," Ewan said with a glower.

Ruari huffed. "What did ye just say about making yerself useful?"

Once the chuckling died down, Ruari noted everyone was studying him as if they were noticing what he looked like for the first time.

"Why do ye not have a woman?" Malcolm asked. "Ye have never been with anyone longer than a night...or two."

The blood in his veins ran cold. "I have seen a woman longer than that," he lied.

"Who was she?" Tristan asked, eyes narrowed.

Was he really having to defend himself against a marriage arrangement?

His throat became dry and he fought to breathe.

"What if I say no?" Ruari finally asked, scowling at his cousin. "When the time comes, I prefer to choose whom I marry. Not some woman who is forced into it."

"We do not know if she is forced or not," Tristan, ever the diplomat, stated. "Besides, I am sure there will be meetings and negotiations first. A marriage may not need to take place."

Malcolm stood and went to a side table where he poured a glass of whisky. "I have an idea."

At everyone's silence, Malcolm gave Ruari a pointed look. "Ye wish to buy horses. Why don't ye go to see Laird Fraser with that as a pretext? The laird's brother breeds the best warhorses in the area. Ye can then meet his daughter and see how it will go."

"Will I be expected to bring the laird some sort of message from ye?"

Malcolm nodded. "Aye, of course. A message that I agree to the alliance, but not to fight if they go to war against the Mackenzie. We will send warriors as a show of solidarity, but our clan will not join in battle. We've had enough of it."

"What about the marriage request?" Ewan, ever helpful, asked.

Lifting one shoulder, Malcolm dismissed the idea. "If he asks, tell him that my brothers are married, and we have few options."

The idea had merit. It would be a good trip there and back since the weather was warm as it was the middle of the summer season. The house was full of people now that his cousins were all married and fathering children. There was rarely a moment of peace and quiet.

Malcolm's wife, Elspeth, had recently given birth to a second son, which meant her family was currently visiting.

The keep was crowded between family, visitors and villagers who spent an entire day or two there when coming to meet with Malcolm.

"I agree to go see the horses, and to deliver the message. I will not marry the woman, so ye must find someone else who is willing."

"Do ye need anyone to go along with ye and help bring back horses?" Tristan asked.

"No. If I choose more than two, they can bring the rest when they visit." Ruari was not about to give up the opportunity for time alone. Despite it being two days each way, he did not mind the idea of sleeping outside while heading to visit the Fraser.

They continued to discuss other things that pertained to everyday life in the clan. There were farmers and villages to visit and collect taxes from. There were elders that had to be checked on and widows who often required help of some sort. Ruari went over the list of responsibilities mentally.

"Tomorrow, Ian and I will ride out to the Stuart farm and take care of making sure all is well there," Ruari told the group.

"Very well," Malcolm said. "When can ye depart to visit Fraser?"

"In three days, if that is acceptable."

Once Malcolm nodded, Ruari left the study and walked back to the stables. He'd have to speak to one of his stable hands about the rebellious horse. Then he stopped and looked at the animal, considering if he should ride it. It would be a good opportunity to tame the animal. Besides, no one else would be able to go near unruly beast.

In the corral, the horse had stopped circling and now nudged the far end of the enclosure several times with its nose. Moments later, the horse moved a few feet away and repeated the gesture. The animal was intelligent and tested the fencing for weaknesses.

A lad who worked for him neared. "He is going to escape."

"If he sets his mind to it, aye. I might just have to ride him when I depart for a visit south."

The lad's eyes widened. "Are ye wishing to die before ye arrive?"

Ruari went into the corral. Immediately, the horse turned to watch him approach, its ears flat. "How about going for a trip with me? I'll leave the choice up to ye."

The horse didn't move, its eyes following Ruari's progress. When he reached for the strap, the animal moved backward. Ruari took his time speaking to the horse while attempting to keep the skittish animal from reacting too strongly. He'd been working with the beast for several weeks and although the horse was headstrong, it was very intelligent. Ruari had no doubt he could master the animal. However, with only three days, he'd have to work fast to gain the animal's full trust.

Leading the hesitant beast to the opposite side of the corral, he motioned to the lad to place a saddle over the fence. Once that was done, he turned to the horse. "Last time did not go well. Shall we try again?"

The horse remained still as he saddled it. Ruari ran his hand down the animal's nose and spoke to it. "No need to be angry friend. I will never mistreat ye."

It was another long while before Ruari could mount the horse and the sun was setting by the time he dismounted and brushed the animal down. Although they'd remained in the corral the entire time, he felt confident in taking the horse out for a ride the next morning.

Ruari had missed last meal, which he didn't mind. Most days when the weather was warm, he retrieved food from the kitchens and ate there or outside in the garden.

Moira, the head cook, waved him to sit upon entering the kitchen.

"I saved ye some lamb. People were asking for more, but I insisted there was none." She placed a tureen in front of him. The aroma of herbs made his stomach lurch with anticipation and he took a deep inhale.

"Ye are the best cook in the land," Ruari pronounced and tore a big hunk from the bread on the table. Ian, Moira's son, and his wife, Ceilidh, entered and joined him at the table.

The tall, blond man remained in the clan's guard force even after losing an arm in battle. Having known each other since they were lads, Ruari and Ian were as close as family.

"I hear ye may have to get married," Ceilidh said with a wide smile. "Can ye imagine it? How delightful."

He and Ian exchanged confused looks. Ruari chewed his food and swallowed. "Why would ye think it would be delightful to marry a woman I've never met?"

"Because it is the only way ye will wed. Too set in yer ways, ye are." The pretty woman motioned around the kitchen. "Have ye even noticed how pretty some of the lasses in here are?"

There were giggles from the cooks and Moira chuckled. "Aye, I do believe Ruari has noticed at least one of them."

This time, there were gasps and Ruari rolled his eyes. "I do not have a problem with marrying nor with doing my duty to the clan."

"However?" Ceilidh asked. "Ye have something to add I am sure."

"Aye. However, I will not marry when it does nothing to help our clan. The Fraser only looks to what will benefit them. Our clan is large and strong. We have no need of them as an ally."

Ceilidh huffed. Moira shook her head.

"What?" Ruari asked no one in particular.

"Listen," Moira said, tapping him on the shoulder. "The stronger a clan, the larger the responsibility to help others. It is honorable of a laird to ask for an alliance when he fears for his people."

Ruari frowned at the fact the woman had spoken a truth he'd not considered. "Ye are a wise woman."

"I know," Moira said and looked at her son. "I know everything."

This time, it was Ian who rolled his eyes.

Ruari studied the older woman. She'd always guided him well. "So ye think I should marry then?"

"I think ye should follow yer heart, lad," she replied with a warm smile and abruptly changed the subject. "I hear ye visited yer mother. How did it go?"

"Same as always. She does not wish to see me. Prefers not to be reminded of her past."

Moira grunted in disapproval. "She is a fool then. Because ye are a good man. Someone she should be very proud of."

"Thank ye." Ruari stood and stretched. "I'd best find my bed. I have much to do tomorrow."

Ian got to his feet and walked with him to the door. "After first meal, we will go out and visit the farms to the north. Hopefully, we'll be done early enough for ye to spend time with that devil of a beast ye insist on riding."

"Very well. I will ride him to do this. It will be a good test."

His friend chuckled. "I look forward to the spectacle."

CHAPTER TWO

E SME FRASER'S FEET flew across the forest ground as she raced forward, barely dodging branches, her arms pumping hard. A low branch cut across her face and Esme groaned, but continued running. Hunters had been allowed on her father's land and her pet doe had wandered out into the forest earlier.

Birds chirped around her, the small beasts enjoying the warm sun and plentitude of food from the low-growing berry bushes. Every sound they made annoyed her more and more.

Esme leaped over a fallen sapling and ran a few yards before stopping to listen. Letting out a whistle, she held her breath, hoping to hear sounds of an animal approaching. There was only silence.

She glared up at the trees when loud birdcalls alerted others of her presence. "Shush!" she called out as if the animals would understand.

Upon spying a broken branch, she let out a cry of relief and took off at a run again, sprinting between trees and jumping over rocks in the way. There was a clearing. In the distance, she heard men's voices. At once annoyed and incredulous at their lack of remaining undetected, she sprinted toward them.

"Hey, there!" she called out to ensure not to be mistaken for an animal and be shot. "I must speak to ye," Esme yelled. "Make yer presence known."

First, one young man, then another came into view. They were familiar to her, two young village boys perhaps no older than five and ten.

"Lady Fraser," one of them, a redhead, said, his eyes wide. "Whatever are ye doing out here?"

"Making sure ye do not hunt down any fawns," she informed them, her breathing hard as she'd run a long way. "I have a pet fawn, ye see, and my father informed me he may have forgotten to inform ye of it."

The other one nodded. "Indeed, he did not. We are hoping to catch rabbits or a young boar, Lady Fraser."

"Very well," she said, scanning the surroundings. Then having pity on the fact they'd catch neither as they were making too much noise, she decided to help them. "Come, I will show ye were to hunt. Do not speak." She held up two fingers and motioned for them to follow.

Once they arrived at a spot where they could see a shallow creek, she crouched low to the ground and the two young men did the same. "Animals come here often. Ensure ye only kill for yer family. Ye know the rules. And do not dare hurt a fawn, it may be mine."

"We will not hurt any wee deer," the redhead replied, his eyes scanning forward. "Thank ye."

The sense of dread did not leave even though Esme was sure the two would not kill her doe. Something felt amiss. There had been poachers about the woods regularly as of late. It had nothing to do with lack of food, but more because of the fact the larger clan whose lands bordered on theirs, regularly baited her father for a reaction. That larger clan wanted to take their land and pull them under the rule of Clan Mackenzie. For over a year now, her father had resisted. But it was proving fruitless.

The Mackenzie was powerful and unless her clan united with another of their choice, there was little that could be done to keep the much stronger clan from taking them over.

She stopped and listened. Her venturing so far into the forest, although a desperate measure to keep her wayward pet safe, had been foolish. Without guards, if she happened upon Mackenzies, it could prove very dangerous.

As the only daughter of Duncan Fraser, she was constantly followed by one or two guards. But in her haste to find little Dot, she'd slipped away alone. "Dot," she hissed at hearing a rustle, only to chuckle when the doe's head popped up with leaves hanging from its mouth.

"There ye are. Come now, we must return home." The doe came to her and nudged her hand in an obvious request to be scratched behind the ears.

"No time for it." Esme grabbed a strap she kept around the animal's neck and pulled the doe along as she gauged the best way to get back home safely. "I am going to have to keep ye in a pen. This time, ye've wandered much too far."

Dot's head popped up, the doe as still as a statue, its ears twitching. It sniffed the air and then, as quick as lightning, bolted forward, pulling the strap from a startled Esme's hand.

The undeniable sound of footfalls followed as men hurried through the woods. They must have caught sight of Dot because they rushed forward. If it was the same young men from earlier, she'd ensure her father banned them from hunting on their land ever again.

Not thinking, Esme hurried out from the foliage without saying anything. There was scuffling as if they hesitated and heard her.

"Stop at once," Esme called out, just as an arrow flew through the air and pierced her left side. Moments later, a second one hit her in the lower stomach. Too shocked to feel anything at first, she tried to see who'd shot her, but her vision blurred. There were two of them, both men. That much she could tell as they burst out from behind the trees, their voices changing from low-pitched to alarmed whispers.

She attempted to pull at the arrow in her stomach, only to be engulfed in so much pain that she stumbled backward.

"Who is she?" one of the men asked the other.

"I believe it is Laird Fraser's daughter," the other replied.

Esme attempted to ask for help but could only moan as she stumbled backward again.

There was a moment of silence as they seemed to assess her for a long moment. "She won't live." They remained blurred and she blinked to try to see them, but it was futile.

Silently communicating, they must have come to the same conclusion because they turned away and ran.

"Pl-please," Esme managed to call out just as her knees gave way. She managed to drag herself to a tree and lean back on it, her breath coming in shallow gasps.

If this was how she was going to die, Esme considered as waves of pain came and went, she could accept it. However, she wanted to live. There were so many things still to experience.

Closing her eyes, she envisioned the young men from earlier and hoped that, perhaps, they'd find her.

Despite the inability to take a full breath, she attempted to scream.

"Help me." Esme winced at the piercing ache in her lower abdomen. Her voice was barely louder than normal speak as she could barely breathe without causing the arrow in her stomach to move.

Tears trailed down her face as she struggled to stand. It would be a long trek home. She'd run for a while before arriving there. But perhaps if she started in the right direction, she'd be met by guards who'd be out searching for her.

It took several tries just to get to her knees. From there, she pulled on the tree to stand. Each movement sent pulses of pain throughout her body so that by the time Esme stood, she was shaking and wet with perspiration.

Unable to keep from it, she wept openly, unable to keep sobs from causing even more aching. This could not be happening. Why was no one coming to search for her?

One step, she willed, and took a tentative step. She held out a trembling hand to a nearby tree and took a second. Her feet felt heavy and uncooperative.

She wasn't sure how much later or how far she'd traveled, but her body refused to move another inch. Having lost count of how many dizzy spells had struck, when it happened again, Esme closed her eyes and gripped the branch she'd been using as a cane.

The sun was falling, the forest darkening as long shadows cast across the path before her.

When her vision blurred, Esme took a breath and tried her best to not fall. "No. Please," she begged herself. "Keep moving."

The trembling in her legs became worse and she looked around to find shelter. Soon, nightfall would come, and the smell of her blood would attract predators. Again, tears fell as the throbbing in her side became unbearable. For some reason, the stomach injury didn't hurt as much now.

She lowered to the ground gingerly and cried out when she accidently hit the arrow in her stomach. Gasping, she managed to move forward on her knees to a small gap between a fallen tree and a rock. After lowering to her bottom, she shuffled backward until she was inside the small space. She then managed to pull branches down to cover the opening. Once inside, she whimpered like an injured pup while waiting for the agonizing pain to stop.

As much as she wanted to break the arrows, the idea of the pain the movement would cause was enough of a deterrent to keep from doing it.

Tired, thirsty and in pain, she sat in the darkness, every sense on high alert, as the night sounds surrounded her.

A MAN'S VOICE woke Esme and she grimaced when she realized her current predicament. She could not move. Every part of her body resisted when she attempted to reach for a branch that blocked the entrance.

"Who goes there?" she called out, annoyed at how soft her voice was.

"Ye may be the devil's own son, but we are stuck together through this," the man said with an annoyed tone. "I won't stand for being thrown again."

There were sounds as if a horse pawed the ground and snorted. Then silence. "I have nothing more to do but wait," the man spoke again.

"Can ye help me?" Esme tried to speak louder. "Help."

There was silence for a long time, then the man called out, "Is someone there?"

"Yes," Esme said. This time, her voice was a whisper. She moaned when the attempt to call out again failed. Wiping a hand over her sweat-drenched face brought the realization that she was feverish. "Pl-please." As her eyes fell, she fought not to pass out. However, she couldn't keep from it. In a desperate attempt to get attention, she reached for a branch. But just as her fingers touched one, everything went black.

⇒⟫⟪⟸

RUARI WASN'T SURE if he was going mad. Although not one for fables, he'd often heard that men were caught by wood Fae and kept prisoners. The tales were often told at the tavern by men who'd drunk too much ale and from the stories, Fae were quite fetching.

He'd heard a woman's voice, clear as day, but there was no one around. He scanned the surroundings only to find nothing but trees, bushes and a large rock. Now, where exactly had men claimed to find Fae? They'd always said near water and he was not near a creek, nor a craggy hillside. He shrugged. Perhaps it had been a trick of the wind and the effect of being cross with the beast of a horse he'd made the mistake of riding.

The horse grazed now, seeming as meek as a mouse. But Ruari would not be taken in by the wily thing's ability to change from calm to furious in a matter of moments.

Just then, something caught his eyes. On the ground near a rock, there were markings of something being dragged across to it. He lowered down to his haunches and inspected the path. What he saw took his breath. A woman in bloody clothes sat between the rock and a tree, two arrows protruding from her body. She was slumped sideways and looked to be dead.

CHAPTER THREE

I T HADN'T BEEN easy to extract the woman from her hiding place. Upon finding she was breathing, Ruari carefully pulled her out and placed her on the ground in front of the rock. In his bags, there were cloths he'd planned to use for bathing, which he now tore into strips. Once that was completed, he brought them and his wineskin to where the woman was.

Thankfully, she remained unconscious, because removing the arrows would be painful. The horse neared and sniffed at the woman. Then to his surprise, it nudged her gently.

"Get back." Ruari pushed the animal's face away.

He then pulled out his dirk and tore her tunic open. She was covered in blood, which there was little he could do about at the moment. Instead, he concentrated on first the arrow in her stomach. It had gone through the right side and seemed like a clean, non-lethal pierce. With one quick push, the arrow went through to her back. The woman moaned but remained unconscious.

Thankfully, there wasn't much bleeding. He determined that she'd bled quite a bit already. If she didn't die from the wounds, the loss of blood would bring her demise. Ruari wrapped her stomach with the strips, satisfied when only a bit of blood seeped through.

For a moment, Ruari studied her face. Although dirty, it did not disguise her features. She was fair of face, not beautiful, but fetching. With long lashes and full lips, he found her to be attractive, but not in an overt way. There was a sprinkling of freckles across her nose and the tops of her cheeks that made one think of sunny days. Her long, dark hair was a tangled mess. The locks had been loosened by whatever she'd been doing.

It would be a shame for her to die in such a horrible manner.

Turning his attention to the other arrow which was lodged into the left side of her torso, he grimaced at the direction the arrow was in. It pointed inward to the center of her body. The arrow was deep, so it could not be pulled out. If he pushed it, it could cause extreme damage.

After caring for horses for so long, he'd learned to treat injuries and, therefore, had assisted the healer when treating warriors for battle wounds. This type of arrow piercing was always the most difficult to deal with.

Deciding it was best to leave the arrow in, he broke off part of it so it would not extend out so far and then bandaged around it.

He brought his tartan from the saddlebag and wrapped it around the woman. Now, he'd have to mount the unruly beast and hope for the best. With luck, he would arrive at Fraser Keep without the horse throwing him and the injured woman to both their deaths.

It took some maneuvering, but he managed to get the woman and himself atop his mount. The horse was uncharacteristically mild and allowed him to guide it through the forest, doing his best not to jostle the woman more than necessary.

It was early morning. The sun barely peeked through the trees. A pleasant day was promised as they continued forth. Strange that the woman was so close to the keep and yet had been left out without escort.

"Who are ye?"

The soft question startled Ruari. He looked down to the woman cradled across his lap and met her brown gaze. "I am Ruari Ross, taking ye to Fraser Keep, where I am headed."

"My home," she said softly and grimaced. Tears began to fall and she lifted a grimy hand to wipe them away. "I am not very well."

"No, ye are not." Ruari was not about to lie to her. If she survived through the day, it would be a miracle. "Who did it?"

She studied him for a moment as if weighing whether to tell him or not. "I wish to see my father. How much longer?" Her eyes fell closed for a moment and then she opened them.

"I can see the keep now. Only a bit more." If he urged the horse to a gallop, they would arrive sooner. But the movement could prove fatal for the woman, so he kept the reins tight on the horse that, so far, continued forward without much incident.

It seemed to take forever until they arrived at the keep gates. Althhough there were guards stationed above the open gates, he was not challenged as he rode through to the inner courtyard. It was there that four guards on horses stopped him.

"What happened?" A guard's eyes widened upon catching sight of the woman in his arms.

"I found her in the forest," Ruari replied. "Ye must fetch a healer immediately."

Two men hurried forward and he lowered the woman who cried out in pain.

He followed their progress as she was carried inside.

"We have been out looking for her all night," one of the guardsmen said. "Where was she?"

"Just north of here, in the forest. She was well hidden."

A guard looked toward the entrance to where the people had taken the injured woman. "I am sure our laird will wish to speak to ye."

"I was traveling here from Clan Ross to visit when I came upon her."

The guard motioned some lads over. "See about his horse."

Ruari dismounted but did not relinquish the reins. "I must see about my steed. He is not quite tamed yet."

"I will show ye the way then," the same guard said and dismounted.

"Oats and water would be appreciated," he said to the lad who followed close by. The lad rushed away to prepare the items and Ruari guided the horse to the stables.

They went to an empty, small corral where he guided his horse into. Then, while oats and water were brought by the lads, he unsaddled the beast. At once, it began snorting in displeasure.

Ruari studied the beast and grunted. "I can hardly wait to ride into battle. I'm not sure if the enemy will kill me or ye," he said in a flat tone.

The guard motioned to a water barrel. "Would ye like to wash up before going inside?"

"Aye, that would be good."

It was just a few moments later that he entered the Fraser great room. It was empty except for one man who stood just inside the doorway.

"Thank ye for bringing my sister," the man said, holding out a hand. "I am Keithen Fraser."

Ruari shook the man's hand. "I wasn't aware of her identity. I brought her here because it was the closest place I knew."

"Aye, she is my sister, Esme. We searched everywhere late into the night. I do not know how we did not find her."

"She hid very well between a tree and a large rock and used branches to seal herself in. If it wasn't for her calling out, I do not think I would have found her either."

It was obvious the woman's brother felt horrible about not finding his nearly dead sister by the angry expression on his face.

"How fares she?"

"I am not aware. Father wished for me to greet ye. He will come momentarily to speak to ye."

They moved to a table where a platter of bread, cheese and fruit was brought for him, along with it a tankard of ale.

Ruari was hungry. So he ate, enjoying the warm bread with freshly churned butter. He washed his food down with the cool ale and studied his surroundings. The great room was much smaller than the one at Ross Keep. But it was clean and spacious. The tapestries on the walls provided color along with the Fraser coat of arms mounted behind the high board. As per usual, the hearth was large. In front of it, two hounds lay sleeping.

"Why was yer sister in the forest unescorted?" Ruari did his best to keep annoyance from his tone. "From what I know, yer clan is not safe at the moment."

Keithen looked properly chastised. "She must have gone after that doe of hers. The animal should be freed, but she insists on keeping it until it reaches maturity. When it jumps over fences and escapes, she goes after it without regard for her own safety."

Although it was understandable that a person could care for an animal, Ruari wondered at the lack of security. He decided not to bring up the fact that their guardsmen didn't challenge him, a total stranger, upon his arrival. The same guards should have caught sight of the laird's daughter leaving the keep.

Instead, he stuffed cheese into his mouth to keep from speaking.

Just then, a slender, gray-bearded man entered the room. His worried eyes met Ruari's. "Thank ye for bringing my daughter."

Ruari stood to greet the laird. "How fares she?"

"The healer hopes she will live. She remains unconscious. The removal of the arrow was quite painful."

As much as he wanted to ask how it had been done, it wasn't his place. Instead, he focused on the laird. "She seems to have a strong will. I will venture to say it can be enough to help her recover."

The laird chuckled. "Aye. In that, ye are right. Esme can be quite willful." He looked to Keithen. "Call for the guardsmen to form at once. We must make changes."

As his son departed, the laird lowered to a seat opposite Ruari. "Unfortunately, this is partly my fault. We grow weary of the threat to our clan. I am afraid my belief that there is little we can do has bled to my men."

His keen gaze met Ruari's. "I hope ye bring hopeful news."

Ruari wasn't sure how to reply. In truth, Malcolm had left the decision up to him. He had the pretext of purchasing horses. But now, he wondered if the woman he'd save would be the one offered in marriage.

"I do bring a message from my cousin, Laird Ross. Ye have our clan's support in whatever is needed."

The laird nodded. "I need a strong alliance. Without it, more of what happened to my daughter will continue."

"Ye think it was the doing of the Mackenzie?"

"Not directly. But he sends men to hunt on our lands as a way to goad us into battle. Of course, declaring war would mean sending my men to slaughter, so I have been ignoring it. Now, after this…I cannot continue to do so."

"Did she say it was them?"

"She has not said anything yet." The laird wiped his hands down his face. "Will there be an alliance?"

If Clan Fraser was about to enter a war with the Mackenzie, Ruari could not, in good conscience, align his clan with them. He pondered the best way to reply without giving the man hope.

"Laird Ross is curious as to why ye do not align with the other Fraser Clan?"

The laird gave a weary shrug. "They fight their own battles right now. There is little my cousins can do for us. We are aligned. As yer laird may know, even united, we are not large enough to stand against the Mackenzie."

Clan Ross was almost as large at the Mackenzie Clan. And now that they were aligned with Clans Munro and Monroe, they were a force to be reckoned with.

"My laird asked me to come and speak to ye. He is not against an alliance. But he does not wish to be drawn into battle. We have just entered a time of peace after a long time of clan clashes between us and the McLeods."

The Fraser stood and paced. "If my daughter dies, I will not stand idly by and ignore it."

"Ye do not know who is responsible for it. There is little that can be done until she tells ye."

Just then, Keithen returned. "The guards are formed."

Laird Fraser motioned to Ruari to walk with him and, together, they went outside to the courtyard. Ruari noted that the men present were well armed. With grim expressions, they probably expected a call to war.

Ruari leaned into the laird's ear. "Unless ye are prepared to send them all to their deaths, I suggest a meeting between ye and the Mackenzie. I will come to show my clan's support of yers."

When Laird Fraser let out a long sigh and nodded, Ruari felt assured he had done the right thing. It could be there was a way to help the small clan without having to marry the man's daughter.

As the laird informed the guards of more stringent rules for overseeing the keep, he also chastised the men for being negligent in their duties. The men were questioned until one admitted to seeing Esme leaving that morning, but he swore he had seen a pair of guards following behind. "Who were they?" the laird asked.

"I couldn't tell from where I stood atop the keep," the guard replied. "I beg yer pardon, Laird, but the men at the gates may have seen better."

The men who'd been on guard that morning reluctantly admitted to not keeping proper watch.

"This is all for naught. Ye see what is wrong now? We are on the brink of being taken over and yet we act as if it is nothing." The laird was yelling at them now, his face reddened with anger.

While the men shifted uncomfortably, Ruari felt no pity for the lot of them.

The laird then assigned each man to a new position. They would be guarding the keep day and night. Those that were not on guard would be at sword practice.

The men were dispersed with instructions and the laird turned to Ruari. "Let us prepare to go visit the Mackenzie. I wish to speak to my daughter and find out as much as we can about who attacked her."

"May I come with ye and see how yer daughter fares?"

The man nodded. "Aye, of course."

Ruari studied the determined man beside him. "Whoever injured Esme could have mistaken her for wildlife as she'd been dressed in colors that blended with the forest."

Understandably, the man was angry and frustrated and, sometimes, emotions clouded decisions. "I do not believe it. They wished to kill her and therefore goad me into battle. If she dies, I will not hesitate."

"Have ye considered whoever caused the injury did not mean to and fled, fearful they'd killed yer daughter?"

The laird stopped in his tracks. "She left and went after two young lads from the village that I allowed to hunt." He turned on his heel, racing back outside. "This is on my shoulders to handle now."

"Lars, Gavin! Go to the forest and find the two young men I allowed to hunt yesterday. Bring them here at once," the laird called out to guards.

He then, once again, headed back inside. "Come. Let us find out what my daughter has to say."

CHAPTER FOUR

T HANKFULLY, THE PAIN had subsided, partly due to the vile liquid the healer had forced down her throat. Esme's hands shook as she lifted the light bedcover to look at her bandaged body.

Alone in the room, she struggled to remain awake. The healer had gone to make another concoction for her to take and the maid was sent to fetch water and food.

The infernal heat that took over seemed to come and go in torturous waves. Never in her life had she felt as if she were on the brink of death as she did at the moment. She moaned more out of desperation than pain.

It was terrifying to be alone. Why had her mother not come to see her yet?

The door opened and her father entered. His face was etched with worry. "The healer told me ye've been awake. Ye should sleep and rest."

She closed her eyes, not sure of her ability to speak clearly. "Mother?"

"Resting. She was too upset, and the healer thought it best for her to go to the bedchamber for a bit."

Esme didn't recall her mother being there but, then again, she'd been in and out of consciousness since arriving home.

"I need ye to concentrate," her father said, placing a hand on her shoulder. "Do ye remember who did this?"

It was then Esme notice the other man in the room. He was larger than most men, his face tanned by the sun, broad-shouldered, with a thickly muscled neck. It was the man who'd rescued her. At the moment, she could not recall his name.

"Esme?" her father prompted. "It is very important for me to know who did this."

Through the fog of her mind, she saw foliage move, arrows plunge into her body, her clothes becoming red with blood. The pain, the voices…had they said something?

"Did ye see them?" It was her rescuer who asked.

"I am not sure." She squeezed her eyes shut. "I had to have seen them. Why do I not remember?"

She met the clear hazel gaze becoming lost the depths of the man's eyes. Had she seen his eyes before? Her own eyes drooped from the effects of the tonic she'd drank.

At hearing the man's voice, she opened them.

"I found ye next to a rock. Ye'd made a shelter for yerself."

"I remember," Esme said, looking at him again. "Thank ye for tending to my injuries."

"Esme," her father said, getting her attention. "Did ye not see who injured ye?"

A vision of men running away formed. It was hard to say how many. She concentrated but a pang of pain shot through her, taking with it any other thought. "I do not think I saw their faces." She panted the words out.

"'Tis best we let her rest," the healer said, rushing in with a tray. "She is feverish and not thinking clearly. Once it lessens, it will be easier for her."

Esme wanted to protest the stranger leaving. She looked from her father to him. "Can he stay for a moment?"

Her father gave her a strange look, but then nodded. "Aye, of course. The healer will remain here as well."

Despite the pain, Esme wanted to chuckle. As if a handsome man like the one before her would find her the least bit worth of seduction in her condition. Esme was positive that she looked a fright.

Once her father left, the man lowered to a chair next to the bed. "I will venture to guess ye will recover fully."

Esme grimaced when it felt as if a part of her insides tore. "Tell that to my body. It is contradicting ye at the moment." A moan escaped when the pain increased.

"Who are ye? Why are ye here?"

"Ruari Ross. I came to speak to yer father about an alliance between our clans," the man said. "I was sent by my cousin and laird, Malcolm Ross."

His deep timbre distracted her from the pain for the moment. "Alliance?"

"Aye. Yer father sent a missive to our clan asking for it. Yer clan is being threatened by Clan Mackenzie as ye probably know."

She nodded as a wave of heat sent rivulets of perspiration down her temples. "Why can they not leave us in peace?"

He surprised her by taking her hand. "'Tis the way of mankind. The strong overtaking who they presume to be weaker and therefore growing larger and stronger."

"No!" When she cried out in pain as the healer pressed down on her wound, his hold on her hand tightened. "Stay still," Ruari instructed. "The healer is putting pressure on yer side because he is rubbing a poultice on it that will draw out any festering."

"Wh-why did yer...laird send ye?" Esme had wondered about it. If the clans were to align, lairds would usually send a party to discuss the matter, not one lone person. It had to mean Laird Ross was not seeking a strong alliance and had just sent his cousin as a show of support.

Just then, her red-faced mother hurried in. "Oh, dear," she stopped and looked at Ruari. "What is happening with my daughter?"

The healer looked up from Esme's stomach. "It is painful for the poultice to be spread on the wound."

Her mother neared and Ruari released her hand and stood. "Lady Fraser, I am Ruari Ross…"

"Ah, yes. Ye are the man who saved Esme's life." Tears spilled down her mother's cheeks as she threw her arms around the large man. "Bless ye for it. We can never repay ye."

"There is no need," Ruari replied with a soft smile. "I best go and speak to yer husband." He looked back at Esme. "Get better."

Her mother lowered to the same chair Ruari had been in and took Esme's hand in both of hers. "Ye are a strong lass. I know ye can recover."

Esme wanted to believe her. But as a new wave of pain rolled over her, she almost wished for the end to come so she'd not have to continue to suffer so.

"Look at me," her mother commanded, and she opened her eyes.

"It hurts so much," she said, fighting tears. "I cannot stand much more."

"Of course, ye can. Think about that handsome man. The way he looked at ye was endearing."

Only her mother, forever the romantic, would see this as an opportunity for matchmaking.

"Was it the feverish wet face that caught his eyes?" Esme teased. But then she sobered. "I only saw pity in his eyes, Mother."

The healer finally finished whatever he was doing and gave her a pointed look. "I have to wrap cloths around ye. It will be uncomfortable for a moment."

Despite the healer's attempts to be gentle and assisted by a maid that helped her sit up, Esme cried the entire time, her body hurting so badly that she blacked out and came to several times.

It was much later, the sky dark outside the window, when Esme woke again. The healer's last tincture had helped her sleep and the fever seemed to have lessened.

The room was cool without a fire in the hearth, which felt good to her still heated body. Next to her in the chair, her mother slept quietly, refusing to leave her side even for a moment since returning.

Outside in the corridor, there was the murmur of low voices. Whoever it was seemed to be discussing something rather ardently. Then the door opened slowly.

Someone was coming into her room and it wasn't her father or the healer. Why would someone enter so late in the night?

Slow footfalls sounded and Esme tried to see who it was, but the room was much too dark.

Just then, her mother woke and let out a scream. Whoever it was that had entered ran out and, within moments, several guards rushed in with torches in hand.

Her father hurried into the room, his eyes moving between Esme and her mother. "Are ye hurt? Why did ye scream, Meredith?"

"I thought someone was in here. Did ye see him, Esme?" She looked to her daughter and Esme nodded.

"Aye, I saw someone enter. Whoever it was, was slight of build. It could have been a woman."

"Ye may have startled a maid who came to check on Esme," her father said rather crossly. "Meredith, ye should be in our chamber, not here."

"I will not leave Esme alone," her mother insisted, arms crossed. "Whoever it was could have meant our daughter harm."

Swallowing past her parched throat, Esme reached for a glass of water. "I heard voices just before whoever it was entered. It was an argument. I swear it."

"Very well. A guard will be posted outside yer door until this is figured out." Her father gave her mother one last look and walked out.

"One of ye remain here and another at the end of the corridor. Ensure someone takes yer place in the morning." Her father gave instructions and lingered in the doorway. There was a pensive expression about him, as if realizing something. Then when he saw she was watching him, he turned away and left.

"Mother?" Esme said to her mother who'd settled once again back in the chair. "Do ye think perhaps someone in our clan wishes us harm?"

Her mother didn't look astonished, instead more pensive. "I would certainly hope not. Whoever came in earlier was not a servant. Otherwise, they'd have been carrying a lantern or such. Something is not right. I must speak to yer father directly in the morning."

"Ye should speak to him now."

As if realizing something, her mother let out a sigh, a faraway expression on her face. "I trust that he will take care of things. There is no need to worry overly."

THE NEXT DAY went by swiftly. Esme felt better, not well enough that it wasn't excruciating to move, but at least her fever seemed to have abated. When her father and brother entered her chamber, she instinctively knew they were there to ask questions again.

Her father gave her a patient look. "I spoke to the two young men who I allowed to hunt. Both admit to seeing ye, but swear ye left them unharmed."

"Is it true?" her brother asked.

She nodded. "I remember speaking to them and then heading back toward here. I realized I'd gone far and was frustrated at myself for it."

It was obvious they restrained from admonishing her by the tightness in their faces.

"What do ye remember next?" her father prompted.

"Trying to find Dot. Just after I found her, she heard men's voices and dashed away. The men Dot heard then came from behind trees and shot me. I tried to return home but, before long, I found it impossible. I hid then." Once again, a picture of foliage moving, of the arrows impaled in her body formed and she winced.

"Did ye see them?" her brother asked. "Esme, ye must have seen something."

She nodded. "Aye, I believe I did. But I do not recall their faces. Perhaps I didn't see them clearly. By the time they emerged from the thicket, they'd already shot the arrows."

"Were they shocked, surprised?" Her father moved closer leaning over her.

The men had spoken in hushed tones. "Aye, they were. I believe one wished to see about me, but the other talked him out of it. I was looking down at my body and not at them. I only saw their boots. When I looked up, they were running away."

"Esme…" her brother began, and she held a hand out to stop him.

"One had wavy hair, very light, almost blond. The other short cropped dark hair. Neither was particularly large, both slender."

"And so, it wasn't the ones I allowed to hunt?" Her father sounded relieved that he'd not made a decision that had almost cost her life.

"Nay and I did not recognize either man's voice. I am not familiar with most of the guards or village men well enough to remember voices. But I do recall neither of them sounded like someone I've spoken to before."

Keithen neared the bed and studied her face. "Ye will recover fully, I demand it."

"I shall do my best, if only to annoy ye for years to come."

"That is the spirit," her brother replied with a soft smile. From the fact neither her brother nor father relaxed fully, the healer had not pronounced that she'd recover fully. Esme shifted her legs, hips and wiggled her toes. Once she was assured all worked well, she moved her shoulders and lifted both arms slowly.

"What are ye doing?" Keithen asked with a scowl. "Ye will hurt yerself if ye keep moving about like that."

"Making sure all of my limbs work properly. Ye act as if I remain on death's door."

When Keithen and her father exchanged a strange look, Esme's injured stomach tightened. Something was wrong.

"What is it?"

Her father waved a hand dismissively. "The healer remains cautious as it is hard to tell what injury ye sustained that cannot be treated with herbs and such."

Just then, a servant entered with a tray. The girl stopped and stared at her brother and Esme bit her bottom lip to keep from giggling. Many a servant girl was enamored with her ruggedly handsome brother, who was as oblivious as a newborn.

"Did Ruari Ross leave?" Esme asked. "Did he bring good news for our clan?"

Her father's shoulders fell. "Clan Ross is supportive. I am not sure of how strong of an alliance they offer. He remains for now. He sent a message back to Laird Ross. Once a reply returns, then Ruari will inform me what Laird Ross wishes to do."

A trickle of apprehension filled her. Since she'd not seen the man since he'd come into her room, Esme expected he'd returned home. There were several reasons for him to return, but none was clearer than the fact that he was there as a token from Clan Ross. Was he to announce they'd take over her clan?

"In the end, if they become our overseers, is that not the same as being under the Mackenzie? Will we lose our freedom?" Esme grumbled.

"Tis not something for ye to worry about," her father said, with a pointed look. "What ye need to do is rest."

"What did ye propose, Father?" Esme demanded. She swallowed past the lump in her throat. It was clear that her clan was not strong enough to ever stand against someone as powerful as Clan Mackenzie. No matter how often it was whispered about, the clear and present threat never changed the fact that the possibility of becoming part of the cruel man's clan was inevitable.

"I have proposed marriage between ye and Ruari Ross."

CHAPTER FIVE

RUARI SAT IN the chamber that had been appointed to him by Lady Fraser, mentally going over ideas on how to foster a deal for several horses. What Malcolm had said was true. Laird Fraser's brother was a master breeder. The horses in the corrals were beautiful, strong beasts. Even the devil of a horse he rode wasn't as well bred. Of course, his steed was wild until captured and, therefore, his pedigree was questionable.

However, the more time he spent with the unruly animal, the better they'd understood each other. His mount would make a good warhorse. Unfortunately, only if it was him that rode the beast into battle, which he hoped would not come to be.

Any day now, the messenger would return, and he pondered what Malcolm would suggest he do next. He felt for the people at Fraser Keep who'd come into the Mackenzie's focus.

Although the Fraser Clan was small, the people respected their laird. Laird Fraser was attentive to the needs of those under his care.

Since the guards had been admonished, the change was remarkable. When the guards were not on duty, there was sword practice and regular patrols around the perimeter of the land. Several times, Ruari rode out with them to exercise his horse and get a feel for how the threat had affected the local people.

Most seemed fearful, but resilient. Several farmers had spoken up, asking the guards to take back messages of hope of remaining independent.

People deserved to belong to the clan they were born into in Ruari's opinion. A sense of responsibility made Ruari wonder how far he'd go to help them.

If Malcolm insisted that he marry, he would, of course, obey. However, he wasn't sure how to feel about it. On one hand, it would be a duty to his clan and for Clan Fraser, it meant a strong alliance that would, hopefully, keep the Mackenzie at bay.

There was, of course, the problem of what had happened with Esme. If her attackers were, in fact, Mackenzies, then Laird Fraser would be in his rights to demand reparations and that the men be turned over to him for punishment.

And knowing the Mackenzie, he would refuse. Any trouble between the clans would then, by default, drag his own into it.

The bangs at the door got his attention and he called out for whoever it was to enter. A slender man walked in. "My laird wishes to see ye. Also, this missive came for ye."

Ruari took the parchment. "I will be there in a moment."

Once the man left, he unrolled the parchment.

Just moments later, Ruari entered Laird Fraser's study. The room was reminiscent of Malcolm's with a large table, several chairs and a decanter of whisky on the side table. The laird gestured to the whisky and Ruari shook his head. "I have not eaten yet today."

"Were ye not offered to break yer fast?"

"I was out riding early this morning and it was done by the time I returned. I will seek something to eat…"

The laird stood and went to the doorway. He motioned a passing servant over. "Bring our guest meat, cheese and some bread." As the servant girl scurried away, he turned back to Ruari. "I hear ye received a missive back from Laird Ross."

Direct and to the subject at hand. Ruari preferred directness when dealing with people. He nodded. "Aye. He allows me to decide whether to accept yer offer or not. Also, he wishes to inform ye that we support ye and will ensure the Mackenzie is aware of our alliance. However, once again, he reminds ye that we will not go to battle with ye."

"An alliance by marriage is not truly one when one clan is not willing to fight alongside another." The laird went to the side table and poured himself a glass of amber liquid. "I understand that knowledge of our alliance would be a deterrent to future problems with Laird Mackenzie. However..." the man took a long swallow and then his gaze met Ruari's. "What if I discover his men tried to kill my Esme?"

"That is yer decision alone, Laird," Ruari replied. "I understand that there should be a price to pay."

Seeming tired, the laird sat and blew out a breath. "There will be a price to pay. If ye marry my daughter, it will then be yer responsibility as well."

He knew those words would be spoken and Ruari had considered how to reply. "Whoever shot Esme probably mistook her for wildlife. She herself said they were hidden at first. Once they saw what had happened, they fled. If they are guilty of anything, it is cowardice, not an attempt on her life."

The laird's face tightened, a muscle flexing on his jaw. "Then it is for two reasons that they should be punished."

The maid returned with a plate of cheese and warm bread. Not wishing to be rude, he tore a piece of the bread and chewed on it.

He understood the man's anger toward the men who had injured his daughter. The men could have owned up and brought her to seek help. If they'd mistaken her for dead, perhaps they'd been fearful of the laird's reactions. While considering his duty to his new bride, he ate a piece of cheese.

"I will stand by ye whatever ye decide. I myself will fight with ye, but I cannot bring forth my clan."

The words seemed to mollify the laird because he finally nodded. "Will ye then accept to marry Esme?"

His stomach lurched, the food instantly becoming unappetizing. He'd hoped Malcolm would have made the decision for him but, instead, his cousin had been diplomatic and left it up to him to decide. He took a breath. "Aye, I will."

The laird studied him for a moment, seeming to discern the confusion and reluctance he felt. "Yer betrothal will be announced at last meal so that news travels to the Mackenzie."

"Do ye think perhaps it would be wiser to announce it after the marriage has taken place? That way he will not try to do something to impede it?" Ruari asked him.

"I will consider it."

When Ruari reached the door, he turned to the man who held his head in both hands while looking down at the tabletop. He didn't envy him or Malcolm. The yoke of lairdship was a heavy one.

Needing better sustenance, Ruari went to the kitchen and was served once again. This time, he ate his fill.

Ruari walked up the stairs to his chamber. Upon reaching the second level, he considered whether he should speak to Esme about the possibility of them marrying. The lass would no doubt be aware, but he wished to know her thoughts on the matter.

Usually, a woman was not part of the decision. Although he considered it unfair, it was the way of the times. Personally, he hoped she was in agreement.

The guard at her door gave him a once over. "I will ensure they wish to see ye."

The guard rapped on the door and a servant opened it. Her eyes widened at seeing him. "Mistress Esme, tis the Ross visitor."

"Come in, please." She sounded better, her voice still soft, but without the hoarseness or breathlessness of being in pain.

Esme was sitting in her bed, her dark hair pulled back into a braid that had been swept forward over her left shoulder. She wore a shawl across her shoulders and was covered from the waist down with the bedding.

"I would have never imagined receiving visitors in my bedchamber while not fully dressed." She motioned to a chair. "Please, sit. I am glad ye came, I wish to speak to ye."

That it was the woman who'd initiate the conversation was interesting. Ruari found it refreshing that she, like her father, was direct.

"Ye look well."

"Thank ye." Her cheeks flushed just a bit. "I am still in pain but refuse to wallow in it. I am sure it will eventually go away."

He studied her face. Without the smudges of blood and dirt, her skin was bright and rosy. Once again, he noted the sprinkling of freckles that made her look young and alluring.

Her gaze met his and she scowled.

"Is something wrong with my face?"

Caught staring, he struggled for what to say. "Nay. It is just that I have not seen ye clearly before. When I found ye, yer face was dirty and the last time I was here, ye were feverish."

Esme let out a sigh. "Not the most appealing look for a woman." Her lips curved. "I wish to thank ye for saving my life. I know that my parents have both spoken to ye. In truth, I had given up hope when ye found me. Truly, it was fate that ye saw where I was hidden."

He was taken aback when her shiny eyes looked to him. "I thought for certain I'd die there, hidden by the rock. I hadn't the energy to move, much less travel any further. Thank ye, Ruari Ross."

Pride at his actions made Ruari's chest expand. "I am glad that I did see ye. Once I got ye here, it was the healer who saved ye."

"He tells me ye cleaned one wound out and tended to both."

"I have worked with horses all my life and have taken care of their wounds, especially after a long time of battles that my clan has recently emerged from."

She thought for a moment, her eyes downcast. "Did many die?"

"Aye, on both sides. Not just warriors, but innocents who lost their lives and homes to fires set by the warring clans. Battles are never fair. That so many pay with their lives over land and power is part of it."

"My father informed me of his offer. Is yer laird willing to help us?"

Ruari waited, unsure if she meant their marriage or not. Lady Fraser entered the room and looked to her daughter. "Esme, it is not right for ye to discuss such matters that have yet to be resolved between Mister Ross and yer father."

"I have a right to know. This is my life that is affected."

"I do not mind telling her," Ruari interrupted. He looked to Esme. "I have agreed to marriage, however, my clan will not go to war against the Mackenzie."

For a moment, Esme looked taken aback. Her eyes widened as they moved from him to her mother.

"I see." Esme looked to her mother and then back to him again. "Ye do not have to do this. No one should marry out of duty or by force."

Ruari felt a kinship with her in that moment. Although without any real say in the matter, she was trying to help him.

"I agreed to it. Now, I await yer father's decision on other matters." He knew it was not customary to involve a woman in the matters regarding talks of clan alliances and such. But in Ruari's opinion, if Esme was to be his wife, he wished her to be informed.

For a long moment, she studied his face. Something about the open curiosity was charming. When her gaze moved down his body, something new stirred within. He was attracted to the lass and, although not knowing her well, something told him they would be a good match.

Esme dragged her gaze away from him to her mother. "I do not wish for father to take our clan to war because of what happened to me. I do believe it was not intentional."

Lady Fraser's eyebrows lowered. "Must I repeat? It is not our place to decide or speak on these matters." She looked to Ruari. "Would ye please allow me to speak to my daughter in private?"

Ruari stood, feeling Esme's gaze upon him. He nodded first to Lady Fraser and then looked to Esme. "Be with care."

CHAPTER SIX

C ALUM ROBERTSON SAT back in his chair and considered the
information the Fraser had imparted to the council. It was a
small group of only four men. In addition to Laird Fraser and Keithen,
there was the laird's brother and him, the village constable. The men
mulled over the information Laird Fraser had imparted, each deep in
thought.

"I do think an alliance with them is futile. They are too far away to
be of any assistance if we come under attack. By the time a messenger
is sent, and help arrives, it will prove too late," Calum said.

Keithen, ever so aggravating, gave him a narrowed look. "The
Mackenzie wishes to take us over, and if we do not comply soon, he
will attack. Father and I believe he will turn his attention elsewhere
rather than earn the ire of Clan Ross if he learns of an alliance."

"Ross warriors are a ruthless bunch from what is said," the laird's
brother interjected. "Malcolm Ross is said to have a heart of stone."

If there was to be some sort of alliance, it would have a horrible
effect on Calum. Already, he'd made headway with the Mackenzie and
now it was all crumbling around him. "I suggest we send a party. I am
more than happy to go and meet with Laird Mackenzie. Perhaps
joining with him would prove well. I do believe he would leave our

people be."

"How is that?" Keithen snapped. "Care to elaborate? In the past, there has only been oppression in the small clans he's absorbed."

In truth, their small village had recently grown by several families displaced when Laird Mackenzie took their land for lack of tax payments. None of that mattered to Calum as he'd been promised a handsome amount; land and power if he brought the Fraser to his doorstep.

"What is wrong with negotiation? It is how things are accomplished," Calum said, unable to keep the annoyance from his tone.

Laird Fraser studied him for a moment. "Perhaps ye are correct. I do plan to speak to the Mackenzie. However, without anything to offer in exchange for him standing down, I do not see how it will do much more than give us more time."

Calum fought not to smile. "I will be honored to travel with ye."

Just then, a guard entered. "Laird, ye wish to speak to Ruari Ross?"

"Show him in."

"He is not one of us and should not be included," Calum protested as the interloper entered.

The imbecile, Laird Fraser, shook his head. "On the contrary. I wish for him to tell ye personally what Laird Ross proposes."

Ruari Ross was a formidable man. Young, handsome and muscular. From what he'd learned, the man trained horses admirably. Cousin to Laird Ross, no doubt he enjoyed many benefits from it. There was a menacing presence about him, probably a family trait.

When the hazel, flat gaze met his for a moment, Calum felt a trickle of apprehension. It was as if the man could see through his façade. That he was there to impede Clans Ross and Fraser from an alliance.

Although as village constable, he did have certain privileges in exchange for his duties, it was a pittance compared to what Calum felt he deserved.

He was afforded a large cottage, free grain from the mill and other conveniences and was exempt from paying taxes. On top of that, when collecting from the villagers, he kept a tidy sum for himself.

However, the Mackenzie's offer was truly generous. A large home, a wife and a large sum that would ensure he lived comfortably for the rest of his life.

A wife added to the offer proved most enticing. His wife had died just the year before during childbirth. Now the bairn was being raised by a village woman, not that he ever saw it or wished to.

"My laird sends his regards," Ruari started, bringing Calum out of his musings.

Everyone, including him, waited for what the man would say next.

"He has agreed to an alliance by marriage between our clans. I, myself, will be who will marry. However, he stipulates and wishes ye to understand that we will not go to battle against the Mackenzie but will send a large contingency as a show of force and alliance with yer clan."

"What good is this joining of our clans then?" Calum spat. "Tis only ye taking the lass away that will happen."

When his laird gave him a pointed look, Calum quieted. But he was satisfied to have planted the seed of doubt.

Ruari nodded. "He's decreed that I, along with a small force of men, will come here to live."

This was a development he was not prepared for. Calum looked to the other men who listened intently, waiting to see what else Ruari would say.

"Our clan will be asking for volunteers who wish to come here. We are hoping for a group of at least fifty."

Calum waved his hand dismissively. "What good are fifty against five hundred?"

"True," Ruari said. "As I said, we are not to go to battle, but to be here to help defend and to show a willingness to protect. The Mackenzie has no way of knowing what is said in this room, correct?"

Once again, the hazel gaze drilled his and Calum narrowed his gaze. "Of course not. It is only that our clan is entrusting a great deal to show and not action."

"What do ye propose then, Calum?" Keithen asked with uplifted brows. "Other than going and speaking to the Mackenzie, which we plan to do, is there another alternative ye wish to enlighten us with?"

He got to his feet. "I am not the enemy here. I have lived here most of my life and worked tirelessly to ensure yer interests are protected. Tis only that I have seen what happens to small clans when they oppose the Mackenzie. Even now, there are several new families newly arrived in the village because their clan refused…"

"That is precisely why we are not bending," Laird Fraser said. "I refuse to fall under a man I do not respect." The laird looked to him for a moment. "Yer concerns are understandable, and I thank ye for feeling free with yer opinion. There is still much to consider. We must come to a decision as I cannot ask Ruari to remain here indefinitely if we decide against allying with Clan Ross."

The entire structure of what he'd been building was crumbling under his feet. If only the damned lass had died.

As soon as the laird called their conversation over, he'd have to find a way to meet with the Mackenzie. The man had forbidden him from traveling there, but there were ways for Calum to get the laird's ear.

He scanned the faces of those present as they discussed how to proceed. It seemed they were all in favor of the marriage. He was not family, not a Fraser, and therefore felt left out, especially when they sought Ruari's opinion on several things.

What did the newcomer know about life there? He'd not been around through the years and stood alongside the clan's people year after year.

Just because the interloper came from a larger, more powerful clan did not mean he had any wisdom to impart.

"Tell me," Calum started, getting Ruari's attention. "What exactly is it that ye do for yer laird?"

"I serve as the horse handler, stable master and…"

"So ye are not normally part of any negotiations, nor have ye done this before?"

Ruari Ross' lips pressed together in obvious displeasure. Laird Fraser gave Calum a direct look, no doubt displeased at his lack of manners.

Calum attempted a nonchalant expression but was sure he failed. "I am curious as ye seem to expect him to have answers for things most horsemen would not have experience in."

"I am included in every council meeting at Ross Keep," Ruari began. "I am a warrior as well as care for the warhorses. I am practiced in healing, farming, sword fighting and have traveled to meet with lairds with my cousins and sat in negotiations. This is, by far, not the first time I have experienced something like this and not my first time dealing with either of the two Laird Mackenzies. I can say I know this Mackenzie well enough."

A cold shiver of apprehension traveled down Calum's spine. If anything, he'd just handed the Frasers a stronger reason to marry Esme with the man.

Clamping his jaw tight, he gave the man a firm nod, hoping that it conveyed agreement. However, he could not bring himself to say anything in reply. Fury raced through him until an idea struck.

At one point, he was sure to have gained Esme's admiration. What if he tried to seduce the lass?

"How does yer daughter fare, Laird?" Calum asked.

A concerned expression crossed over the laird's features. "Esme will live. We have a remarkable healer. I can never repay him or ye," he looked to Ruari, "for what ye've done for my precious daughter."

"Will she recover soon then?" Calum inquired. "I certainly hope so."

"The healer expects that she'll be out of bed at least by week's end. Perhaps, she'll be able to walk unaided soon."

BY THE TIME the sun fell, Calum had come up with a plan. It would take some work, but first he'd ensure to remain at the keep.

After last meal, he waited for Laird and Lady Fraser to be alone and walked up to the high board. "My laird, is it possible for me to remain here at the keep? I would like to be available to ye at short notice in case my presence is required."

There was a short hesitation, perhaps not normally noticeable, but Calum was quite astute and noted it. "Aye, of course. I will order a room prepared."

"I must travel to the village to retrieve clothing and see that things are taken care of, but I will return in the morning." He bowed slightly, ensuring to meet Lady Fraser's gaze. "I am glad to hear that Lady Esme will recover fully."

Lady Fraser smiled. "Thank ye, Calum. Ye are kind."

When he turned to walk away, he couldn't help the curve to his lips. It would be easier to ensure the plan for Esme and Ruari not to marry by being inside the home.

Calum hurried outside to find his mount, only to stop at seeing Ruari Ross standing next to a huge, black horse. The man's calm demeanor contradicted the beast's. It pawed the ground and huffed with agitation. The entire time, Ruari ran a hand down the animal's back and spoke to it softly.

"A beautiful beast ye have there. Seems a bit untamed," Calum said, making sure to keep his distance.

Ruari slid him a look but, instantly, returned his attention to the horse. "He is not quite domesticated. Are ye leaving?" the man asked.

With a chuckle, Calum shook his head. "For tonight, yes. I will return early in the morning as Laird Fraser asked me to remain for a few days. Ye see, he has come to rely on my counsel for important matters."

"And ye give it freely?"

Whatever the question meant, Calum had to take a deep breath to keep from telling the man it was none of his concern. How dare the imbecile ask such a question?

"Of course. I am but a humble servant."

The large Scot looked directly at him then. "As town constable, do ye consider it the right kind of experience that ye should travel to see the Mackenzie?"

It was hard not to react. Instead, Calum smiled. "One would think not, however, after attending so many negotiations with my laird, I am as well versed as any nobleman. As ye observed, I am also a member of the council."

Although he did not have to explain himself, he knew there was nothing the interloper could say once he was informed of his standing.

"We have a large council," Ruari started. "They keep my cousin well informed and give good council. I've never heard one of them trying to convince us to allow being overtaken."

At the comment, words left him. Calum looked to the horse, giving himself time to think. "Not every circumstance is as simple as it seems on the surface. Perhaps ye do not understand that, at times, many things are at play. We are a much smaller clan than yers."

Once again, the hazel gaze seemed to pierce through his. "That is when things become dangerous."

Calum could not stop the narrowing of his eyes. In that instant, he hated the man. "It can be. Especially for those who are not familiar with a particular situation."

"Sometimes, seeing things as an outsider means my view is clearer."

At the comment, Calum's stomach clenched. He would have to proceed with caution. The man saw through him and that could prove deadly.

Thankfully, his horse was brought, and he turned away, purposefully dismissing the Ross idiot.

CHAPTER SEVEN

WHILE THE MAID tossed the dirty water out of the window, Esme stood nude before the looking glass and studied her body. It felt refreshing for the cool air to fan across her moist skin. Although purple bruising and scratches were still bright, the swelling had receded. It was strange how small the wounds left from the arrows were in contrast to all the pain she still felt when moving.

"Yer mother said to wrap yer middle and stomach," the maid said, nearing with a roll of cloths.

"That will be fine," Esme replied, unsure what good it would do as they no longer bled. However, it was best to keep her mother happy as she'd finally spent the night in her own bed instead of a cot that had been moved into Esme's bedchamber.

Although it was painful, Esme was determined to go out that day. She'd lost count of how many days had passed since returning home. Spending another stuck inside the four walls would surely drive her mad.

To keep her from lifting her arms, her ever creative mother had slit several of her chemises and gowns down the center and sewn in strips so that they could be tied down the front.

"I will wear the green dress," she instructed, knowing the color was flattering. It was still a bit of struggle to get dressed. But it was no longer the agony it had been before.

Finally, after asking for a simple braid down her back, Esme accepted the maid's assistance and carefully went down the stairs to the main floor of her home.

The only people about in the great room were two women, one was scrubbing the tabletops while the other swept up dirty rushes.

The one scrubbing the tables smiled at her. "Nice to see ye up, Lady Esme."

"Thank ye." She slowly made her way to the front doorway. "Is my father outside?"

"Aye. He is receiving the clanspeople in the courtyard as yer mother requested the great room be cleaned thoroughly."

She wanted to ask about Ruari since she'd not seen him in two days. No one had informed her of what would happen as far as the wedding. Her mother had refused to speak on most things, saying once final decisions were made, they'd both be informed.

The sunny courtyard beckoned, and she turned to her maid. "Can ye ask one of the lads to send a message to Catriona? She has not come to visit me in days. Ask that she come. Send him in a wagon."

More than ever, Esme needed a confidant. Her friend, a village woman named Catriona, and she often spent hours at each other's homes sharing stories while sewing or completing other tasks. It struck her as strange that her friend had not come to see her. Surely, Catriona knew of what had happened to her.

Just then, her brother appeared. He seemed in a hurry as he headed toward the gates. But upon seeing her, he turned in her direction.

"Should ye be about unaided?" He took her elbow. "Where are ye going?"

"I wish to sit in the garden for a bit. I need fresh air and sunshine. My bedchamber is to be cleaned. Mother is ordering the entire house to be cleaned and pushing everyone outside."

"Aye, I know." Keithen looked toward the house as water was tossed from a second-story window. "It will be quite pleasant once we are allowed back inside."

They walked to the garden, her brother forcing her to keep a slow pace.

"I sent for Catriona." Esme said. "I am confused as to why she'd not been to visit me. Surely she is aware of my injury."

Keithen scowled. "We've kept yer injuries a secret. Father did not wish for the clanspeople to become alarmed. Especially as we do not know who did it."

"I am sorry that I do not remember. I have tried over and over to recall exactly what they looked like."

A wagon with a lad and a maid exited through the gates and headed toward the village. Esme followed their progress for a long moment. "It still does not explain why Catriona has been gone for so many days. Normally, we see each other frequently." Esme narrowed her eyes at her brother. "Did ye do something to hurt her feelings?"

"I have not seen, nor spoken to the lass."

Catriona had been in love with Keithen since she was very young. It was often the topic of discussions between Esme and her friend. Catriona's feelings were unrequited as Keithen seemed to barely notice her beautiful friend.

Once, during a celebration when Catriona had been about ten and two, Keithen had danced with her and, after the dance, he'd kissed her on the lips. It had been a friendly sign of affection. But since then, Catriona had sworn to have fallen in love.

If Esme was to be honest, she would love for her brother to take more notice of Catriona. One day, Keithen would be laird and, in her opinion, Catriona would be a fine Lady of the Keep.

"There must be a reason for her not to have come."

"I suppose ye will find out when they return with her." Keithen waited until she sat down on a bench where she could see the courtyard and out toward the fields, past the gate. "If there is nothing else ye require, I will return and check on ye later."

As he walked off, Esme pressed her lips together and scanned the courtyard. Her father stood behind a table that had been set up on the far side of the courtyard. Next to him sat a scribe with an open ledger and quill.

People milled about, waiting for their turn to speak to him. Most huddled in groups, watching those who approached or holding private conversations.

A couple was brought up to the front. The woman began talking loudly, gesturing with both arms, while the man looked up at the sky as if he were bored. Moments later, the man was taken to the center of the courtyard. He was bound to a pole by guardsmen. The woman walked up and kicked him in the lower leg.

"That is what ye get for beating me, ye brute." She stormed off with a young child running after her.

The man hung his head, accepting his fate. No doubt, he'd remain tied to the pole for three or four days. A light punishment, Esme considered. No man should beat the mother of his children.

She admired her father for the way he handled situations. Although she couldn't hear what was said, most seemed to bring their grievances and were promptly sent off with whatever solution was given.

"It is nice to see ye out." The deep voice caught her unaware. She'd been so focused on what her father was doing that Esme did not notice Ruari had neared.

She cleared her suddenly dry throat and her breath caught. It was embarrassing to have such a reaction to him.

"Yes...well..." Esme tried to come up with a suitable reply but failed. Annoying as her lack of speech was, it was nice when he lowered to sit next to her.

"I hear yer mother has banished all from the keep," he went on to say, not seeming to notice her lack of words.

"Does yer mother do the same?"

"I rarely see her, so I do not know."

It occurred to Esme that she knew very little about the man she might marry. "Do she and ye not live at Ross Keep?"

He looked away for a moment, seeming to mull over what to say. "Only I do. When my da disappeared, I was very young. Mother could not get over it. At the time, we lived at Dun Airgid, Ross Keep, with our clan. But soon thereafter, she left. It was decided best that I remain there, with my aunt and uncle."

"Did ye ever find out what happened to yer father?"

Ruari shook his head. "No. I barely remember him, but I am told I look a lot like him."

Her chest tightened. It was sad to hear of a young boy losing both parents. "Did ye have a good life then with yer aunt and uncle?"

His lips curved. "Very much so. I was raised as if I were one of four brothers. I was treated the same. For that, I am thankful."

She knew that his uncle, Laird of Clan Ross, had recently been killed, but she refrained from mentioning it. "What do ye think will happen?"

At the abrupt change of subject, his hazel gaze snapped to her. "In regards to yer clan?"

"Yes...no. Between us. Has father agreed to our marriage?"

"He has." Ruari studied her face for a reaction. Esme couldn't figure out how, exactly, she felt. On one hand, he was attractive and seemed a fair man. On the other, she was to marry a complete and total stranger and, in all probability, be taken to live far away from her family and friends.

"When will it happen?"

His gaze softened. "The details have not been discussed. I imagine he wishes to wait until ye recover."

At his regard, her breathing quickened. "Do ye wish to marry me?"

"It is a duty to my laird and clan that I accept without hesitation. My cousin left the decision to me. I could have said no."

What kind of a reply was that? The reply made little sense to her. She wanted to know if he found her attractive, did this "duty" mean that, to him, it was more of a chore?

Of course, she could not ask without seeming like a whimpering simpleton. Esme looked toward the gates. If only Catriona was there, she'd know exactly how to word the question without sounding like a ninny.

"So ye chose to do as asked, or did ye choose to marry because it would benefit ye in some way?"

Ruari chuckled. "Ye are inquisitive."

When she gave him a pointed look, he met her gaze. "It is my duty to obey my laird and yer da wishes for a strong alliance. Marriage is the strongest way for it to come about."

So it had nothing to do with her. "I see…"

"How nice to see ye about." Calum Robertson approached and looked to Ruari and then to her. "I was hoping to have a word with ye."

Ruari stood and gave her a light nod before walking away.

The constable could not have had worse timing. However, Esme strived to keep from glaring at him as he settled on the bench.

"What do ye wish to speak about?" Esme asked, noticing that he'd slid closer.

Esme didn't care for the man. He'd always been dismissive and arrogant toward women. There was the death of his wife, which had been a sad occurrence, and she'd felt badly for him then. The feelings had been dashed when she'd gone to the burial and found out he'd given his child away. Several times, he'd been inappropriate toward her, often touching her in what could be construed as an accidental gesture. However, she knew better and often kept her distance when he was about.

Calum's gaze locked on her lips. "I hear alarming rumors that ye may be forced to marry and be sent far away."

"I cannot answer yer question as ye interrupted me from asking." She knew it was a rude reply but, at the moment, there were pressing matters. The sooner she understood what would happen, the sooner she could prepare.

A child ran across the courtyard, tripped and fell. The poor thing began crying and was quickly picked up by a woman who then inspected the squalling child for any scrapes.

"If ye agree to marry me instead, ye can remain here. My home is not so far way."

What he said was true and she did know Calum better. Although not a love match, he was pleasant of face and it would mean her remaining there.

Esme sighed. "Ye are kind to offer, Calum. But what would it accomplish? We'd still be under threat by the Mackenzie."

"I do not believe becoming allied to Clan Mackenzie is as bad as people make it out to be," Calum said, his face suddenly much too close. "Say yes, Esme. Ye know I have harbored feelings for ye for a long time. Tis enough of playing coy."

If only her injuries wouldn't cause extraordinary pain, Esme would have stood and stalked away. Instead, she slid sideways to put distance between them. "I am not playing coy. Ye have never declared yerself. Ye come here often. This is the first time ye've sought me out."

She held up a hand when he started to speak. "I am sorry, Calum, I do not wish to marry ye. I must do what is best for my clan. If my father wishes that I marry Ruari Ross, I will do it. As much as I appreciate yer offer, I do not share yer feelings about us joining Clan Mackenzie."

Calum's face hardened. "It is a great mistake. An error of judgment." With those cryptic words, he stood and looked down at her with an expression that gave her shivers of apprehension. Then he stalked away.

"That was not an agreeable conversation," Esme mumbled to herself.

When Keithen and Ruari walked by, her brother looked to her. "Do ye need assistance going inside?"

Esme nodded. "Ruari, do ye mind helping me."

"Of course." Ruari came to her while her brother continued on his way.

Upon him taking her elbow, the touch brought tingles of awareness. She took a breath and lifted her free hand to him. "This is going to smart."

Using her legs, she pushed up to stand, grimacing at the pull in her midsection. "That was not too horrible," she said in a strained voice.

"Ye're a brave lass," Ruari said, waiting for her to take a first step.

Esme decided it was best to speak to him before they were interrupted again. "How long after we marry would ye wish for us to leave?"

"I plan to remain here, lass, for the time being. Yer father agreed it would be for the best. I, along with fifty guardsmen, will come to live here at Fraser Keep."

"Truly?" She smiled up at him, enjoying the nearness.

For a moment, they remained quiet, both looking at each other. Esme, of course, could not remain silent. "I am pleased for us to marry then."

He looked away for a moment. "What about Robertson? He seemed like he was trying to persuade ye away."

So, he'd been watching. Esme was secretly pleased. "He did offer marriage in an effort to help me from having to leave."

When he looked away in the direction Calum had gone, Esme almost told him about her apprehension.

Once inside, she motioned to a table. "Will ye join me for a small repast? I am a bit hungry."

Ruari gave her a quizzical look. "I can for a moment. Yer uncle waits for me to discuss purchasing horses. I am going to acquire some for my cousin."

"What will happen back at Ross Keep? Is there someone there to take yer post?"

With a pensive nod, he helped her to sit and then sat across the table from her. "I am not sure yet about it. I plan to travel there once we are married to discuss such things. I have an apprentice that is almost ready, so I am not overly worried."

"Yer clan is at peace at the moment, is it not?"

"Aye. After a long time, we finally have had a period of no battles."

Esme looked about the great room. Her clan had not fought in many years. They'd relied on the alliance with the larger Clan Fraser, which deterred most would-be encroachers. Until they'd caught the eyes of the Mackenzie, there had been little threat to their borders.

Now, guards patrolled the borders, often returning injured or not at all after a clash with Mackenzie warriors.

"I do not understand why he will not let us be. Our lands and people would be of little gain to him."

Ruari studied her for a long moment. "If he overtakes yer clan, then it would force the larger Fraser Clan to defend ye. Ultimately, Clan Mackenzie could very possibly defeat them, and it would make him the most powerful laird in the region. Once that is done, only Clan Campbell would be able to go against him."

That he took the time to explain such things to her was extremely rare and pleasant. Ruari did not insist that she, as a woman, should not be concerned with such things. In her mind, it was important for the women of a clan to be knowledgeable in order to stand next to their husbands and provide proper counsel.

When a servant brought warm bread and cuts of meat, Esme ate and washed it down with cider.

Ruari bit from the bread and studied her for a moment. "It is best that I go speak to yer uncle. Do ye require help with anything?"

Without thinking, she reached for his hand and he allowed it. Long, callused fingers wrapped around hers and it felt natural. Esme looked up into his eyes. "I owe ye so much already. How can ye ask that? Not only did ye rescue me from death, but now ye will save my clan from a powerful man. Thank ye."

When he bent over their joined hands and pressed a kiss to hers, her breath caught at the intimate gesture. No, it wasn't so much the kiss to the hand that was sensual in nature, it was the way his gaze never left hers and the lingering of his lips on her skin.

"Ye need to go rest." Her mother approached, breaking the spell.

The corners of Ruari's lips twitched and he winked at her before turning to her mother. "Lady Fraser, I assisted Esme inside and now I must go speak to yer husband's brother." He gave a soft nod and walked out of the room.

Her mother's gaze followed his movements. "He is much too handsome."

When Esme giggled, her mother gave her a pointed look. "Men like him can cause women not to think clearly and give them too many liberties."

So her mother had seen what had transpired between them. Esme smiled, looking in the direction Ruari had gone. "Is that so, Mother?"

"I must speak to the healer and ask that he come and ensure yer injuries were not made worse with all this moving about," her mother said, changing the subject.

"I will not remain in bed every day," Esme replied, placing a piece of meat on bread and lifted it to her lips. "It is time for my recovery as there is much to do. We must discuss my wedding."

At the mention of the wedding, her mother's eyes lighted up and her worries seemed to evaporate. "Oh, goodness, ye are right. There is much preparation to be done."

"Esme!" Catriona burst into the room and raced to her. "I did not know. Forgive me." Her friend neared and fell to her knees so to inspect her face. "What happened to ye?"

"I am recovering from injuries that occurred in the forest. It was mostly my fault for chasing after Dot." She looked to her mother. "Where is Dot?"

"She is in the corral, tied with a long rope to ensure she doesn't escape again," her mother replied with obvious disapproval. "Yer brother had men go to the forest to find her. They returned with three other fawns before Dot was identified by yer father."

Esme giggled at the picture of the men returning with random deer.

"It is not in the least bit a reason to laugh," her mother chided. "If anything, the animal should be let free."

"I am aware, Mother. However, Dot has been around humans for far too long. She is much too trusting of people. Otherwise, how were the men able to catch her?"

"They caught three others I remind ye."

"With snares no doubt," Esme insisted. "I am willing to bet Dot was the easiest catch of all."

By her mother's expression, what she said was true. However, she did not press the subject. Instead, she turned to Catriona and hugged her friend, careful not to hurt herself. "Why did ye stay away so long?"

"My grandmother was horribly ill. She died." Catriona squeezed her eyes shut as pain rolled over her.

"I am so very sorry," Esme said, hugging her friend again. "I wasn't aware."

Catriona shook her head. "I can only be grateful that ye were not taken away from me as well."

Her mother huffed. "She is recovering well. As long as we can keep her from moving about so much, I do believe ye will have a quick time of it."

"I was just telling Mother there is much planning to do. I have something exciting to tell ye," Esme said, motioning for Catriona to sit.

Her mother stopped Catriona. "Do not sit. First, let us get Esme to her chamber. Ye must rest." Her mother took one arm and motioned to Catriona to take the other. "Up we go."

The entire keep was clean and refreshed as her mother had instructed that every inch be scrubbed and mopped.

Upon entering her bedchamber, Esme was pleased to note the same went for the now pleasant and airy space. The bedlinens had been changed, flowers placed on a table by the window and the curtains had been exchanged for a lighter fabric.

Used to their close relationship, her mother made excuses and left Esme alone to speak to Catriona.

"Tell me what is happening, I am most curious," Catriona said as soon as Esme's mother left.

"My father sent a missive to Laird Ross. He asked for an alliance by marriage."

Catriona's eyes widened. "Did he reply?"

"Yes. He did so by sending his cousin here to speak for him. His name is Ruari Ross."

"What did he say?"

"That he agrees to the alliance...through marriage." Esme gave her friend a tentative wry smile. "I am to marry him once I recover."

Both hands over her mouth, Catriona's wide eyes met hers. "Ye are to marry a total stranger? Does this mean ye will be leaving?"

Esme shook her head. "Nay. He has decided to remain here. Actually, there are fifty men traveling here from Clan Ross in a show of support."

Catriona's wide eyes met hers again. "It must be the tall, handsome man I saw just before entering. He is most bonnie."

Esme could not help the curve of her lips. "Aye, he is. But that is not what is most important. It means we will be allied with Clan Ross.

They are as powerful at Clan Mackenzie."

Her friend let out a sigh. "That is very good news."

Catriona let out another long sigh. "Ye must spend time with him. Get to know more about him."

"Aye, I know," Esme frowned. "What if he is not as he seems? I have no way of knowing."

"What do ye know?"

She considered the short conversations they'd had. "When he was young, he was left by his parents to live with his uncle, Laird Ross." Then something sprang to the forefront. "When I asked, he did inform me of his interactions with father, which I find quite different."

"That is different." Catriona bit her bottom lip in thought. "Does he seem glad for yer marriage?"

It was not like bedtime stories in faraway lands where a princess and a prince fall in love. Instead, the reality of marriage for most people was a means to an end. "When I asked why he agreed to the marriage, he replied it was his duty."

"Duty?" Catriona blew out a breath, looking quite annoyed.

"Aye, then I asked him if he chose to do as asked by his laird or because he would gain from it. He replied that he did what was best for both clans. Or something to that effect."

"Certainly a loyal man, is he not?" Catriona's disapproving tone made Esme glad to have her to speak to.

"That is certainly a good quality, but not what I wished to hear." Esme shrugged. "I suppose I do value his honesty."

"Not one mention of finding ye attractive?" Catriona tried again.

Esme shook her head. "Not at all." She leaned closer to whisper. "He did kiss my hand. His lips lingered longer than necessary. Mother was not at all pleased."

"That is something then," Catriona replied, seeming a bit mollified.

Through the window, the sounds of nature intermingled with

guards' swords clashing, bringing to the forefront the reminder of what her clan was facing.

"I have to marry him, Catriona. The sooner our clans are allied the better."

If things were switched, Esme would have the same concerns as her friend. The fact that she had always known her marriage would be arranged did not mean it was easier to accept and go into without some kind of trepidation.

"Tell me about his clan," Catriona interrupted her musings. "What do ye know about it?"

"His cousin is Laird Malcolm Ross. Ruari says he was raised like brothers with him and the other two brothers." Esme paused in an effort to remember anything else. "He works with horses. He's spending time with my uncle to acquire some for Clan Ross."

Esme sighed. "How strange that a total stranger, someone I do not know well at all, will be my husband for the rest of my life."

Catriona gave her hand a squeeze. "I am hopeful all will be well."

⇒⇒⇒✦⇐⇐⇐

TIRED OF ROLLING from one side to the other, Esme sat up in bed. It was dark, much too late not to be sleeping. Her mind kept returning to Catriona's comments. Was she, indeed, to marry a stranger? What did she know about Ruari other than speaking to him but a few times?

Her chest tightened. There was so much at stake and she had little choice. There were others making sacrifices much greater than her. Even Ruari, who was leaving his home to come and live there.

What of the fifty men coming to Fraser lands? They were leaving all they knew. Families would be displaced. All because of one overbearing and cruel man.

In that moment, she hated the Mackenzie and hoped to never have to see his face again.

Sliding to the edge of the bed, she sat with her legs hanging over the edge and allowed her mind to wander. What would it be like to marry Ruari Ross? Although he seemed like an even-tempered and fair man, only time would tell.

His chamber was only two doors down. A thought came to her and, before she could ponder overmuch, Esme crept to the door and out into the corridor.

The guard sat on the floor, wrapped in a tartan. He started and looked up at her. Esme put a finger to her lips. Then she whispered, "I am going just two doors down."

Although he frowned, he didn't speak, but got to his feet.

A bit mortified at the man following her, she would rather that than be killed in her sleep. "I will not be but a moment," she whispered to the guard who didn't reply but, instead, put his back to the wall and stared straight ahead.

She pushed the door open and peered in.

Moonlight shined in through the window, landing on Ruari who slept soundly. With one arm up over his head and under the pillow, the other was across his midsection. She gazed at him from the doorway, unable to keep from scanning his unclothed chest.

He was formidable. Even while asleep, he exuded raw masculinity.

Emboldened by his light snore, she walked in, pushed the door to almost closed and took several steps closer to the bed. As crazy as it was to be in his bedchamber, she could not turn away.

Slowly, she reached to touch his shoulder. Quick as lightning, Esme was yanked forward and flipped flat onto her back. Ruari's body crushed hers and he held a dagger at her throat.

A whimper escaped despite her inability to breathe. Surprisingly, she was not in a lot of pain, but he was much too heavy, and her breathing was constricted by his weight on her chest.

He blinked several times before rolling off of her but kept the dagger at her throat.

"What the hell are ye doing here?"

Esme swallowed while he groaned and moved the dagger away. "I w-wanted to talk."

Before she could see anything, he pulled the bedding up to his waist. The look he gave her was a mixture of disbelief and curiosity. "Now?"

She remained silent as he shoved the dagger back under the pillow and yawned loudly.

When he gave her a questioning look, Esme shrugged. "I suppose it could have waited until morning. But, ye see, I cannot sleep and I thought it would be a perfect time to speak without interruptions." She gave him what was, hopefully, a friendly smile.

Ruari shook his head and raked his right hand through tussled hair. "I suppose ye are right. What do ye wish to speak about?"

Caught by surprise at his patience, she scrambled to sit and lean back on the headboard. Her injuries smarted, and she grimaced at the reminder that much healing still had to happen.

"First of all, what do ye expect from me once we are married? Am I to submit to yer every whim?"

"Whim?" He remained on his back, but now both arms were under his head. She couldn't help but wonder if he was completely nude.

"Aye. Husbands can make a woman's life miserable."

"Esme," he started and stopped. "What is really bothering ye?"

She sighed. "I do not know ye. We are to marry and spend our lives together. What if ye do not care for me?" She hesitated. "I know it is not a high price to pay, not compared to keeping my clan safe."

He rolled to his side, the bedding slipping from his waist to his unclothed hip. The man's body was distracting her from why she was there. Esme curled the hand closest to him to keep from reaching out to touch him.

CHAPTER EIGHT

R UARI WASN'T SURE why the beauty was truly there, in his bed, but he thanked the gods for it. If they were to be married, he preferred a woman who was bold and confronted situations.

The lovely woman had more freedom than he did at the moment being that he was totally naked. Upon further consideration, perhaps he was not at a disadvantage upon noting the way Esme's gaze kept moving over his body when she thought he didn't notice.

After allowing the bedding to slip precariously low, he met her gaze. "I would not ask ye to do anything that ye would find distasteful. I look to my uncle, Robert, for the way he treated his wife. Always with respect and mindful of the position he placed her in. Although as yer husband, I would have final authority over ye, I do believe ye should have a say in matters that are important to the marriage."

For a long moment, she studied him as if assessing the truth of his words. "What if I defied ye?"

"I would hope ye would not without a strong reason. Do not mistake my being fair to mean I would allow ye to walk over me."

Esme looked to the doorway. The door had swung almost closed and he wondered what she would do next. "Do ye think ye and I will be compatible?" When she turned back to him, her gaze roamed down from his chest. "I-I do not know much when it comes to what occurs between a man and a woman. My maid tells me sometimes couples are not compatible in bedsport."

His cock stirred at her perusal and he fought not to slip a hand under the bedding. "There is only one way to find out." Ruari allowed his gaze to touch on her lips before traveling down to her breasts. The flimsy chemise did a poor job of hiding the firm mounds beneath.

Esme inhaled sharply. "Will ye kiss me?"

It was a mistake. There was nothing to stop them from taking it too far. It had been an entire season since he'd last laid with a woman so, at the moment, he was not strong enough to keep from taking her fully.

"Aye, I will." Ruari reached for her, sliding a hand around her neck and pulling her down to him. Upon their lips touching, his entire body came to life, but he refrained from drawing Esme against him.

At first, she did nothing. But soon, Esme responded to his kiss. Ruari deepened the kiss, pushing his tongue past her lips and she reacted by opening for him. When her hands slid from his shoulders to embrace him, he fortified himself. However, moments later, at the feel of her plush breasts against his chest, he could not stop from wrapping an arm around her waist and pulling her close.

Being she was injured, Ruari was gentle when he rolled her over him and then ran his hands down her body. Esme had the most delightful figure; a small waist, wide hips and long legs. While their tongues twisted around the other, each of them took turns suckling.

She was passionate. Possibly, it was that he knew it would be best not to take things too far, but the tryst was proving to be the most enjoyment he'd ever had with a woman.

"Teach me what to do," Esme said breathlessly into his hear. "I feel as if my center is aflame."

He was harder than a rock and considered if he should show her how to pleasure him.

"Lay on yer side," he instructed, careful to turn to his. She complied and did not move away from him, but lay closely, her hand on his waist. Like her, he did not want to stop touching.

With slow and deliberate movements, he pushed the strap of her camisole off her shoulder and exposed her breasts. "Close yer eyes and allow yerself to feel."

He took the tip of her left breast into his mouth and drew on it, enjoying the taste of her skin.

"Oh," she responded and arched her back, pushing the breast against his mouth. Ruari could barely keep from rolling over her and taking her then and there. Instead, he continued sucking at the tender tip, enjoying the sounds she made.

He lifted up and once again took her mouth while guiding her hand to his throbbing cock. Esme instinctively knew to wrap her fingers around it. He wrapped his own over hers and guided her to slide it up and down his shaft.

The feeling was like no other and he groaned at the pleasure of it.

"That's it," he gritted out, taking breaths as a climax threatened to hit.

When Esme took control, her hand moving with precise strokes, Ruari thrust his hips forward to match her rhythm. Within moments, he shuddered in release.

Before she realized what had happened, he slid a hand under her chemise and in between her legs.

She was hot and wet, aroused by what she'd done. With his index finger, he caressed the very center of her, and she gasped. "What are ye doing? It feels...oh."

Esme clenched his shoulders, her head falling back when he flicked the tiny nub between her nether lips. He did his best to keep her steady so as not to cause pain to her injuries, but when he slipped a finger into her, she began to shake uncontrollably.

"Ahhh," Esme cried out. Immediately, he covered her mouth with his. It wouldn't do for the guard to overhear and burst into the room. Although he imagined the man knew she was there, it was better not to take a chance.

Placing his thumb over her nub, he slid his finger in and out of her steadily, trying to match her movements that, within moments, became erratic.

As he watched, his cock reacted, hardening at the beautiful spectacle before him.

When Esme's mouth fell open and her entire body shook, once again he covered her mouth and swallowed her screams of release.

"I feel light as a feather," Esme said, her head on his chest. "That was wonderful. Although we did not join, did we?"

"No," Ruari replied, tracing a finger over the soft skin of her shoulder. "That will wait for the marriage bed."

She looked up at him. "I wish I could remain here tonight."

A chuckle escaped and Ruari pressed a kiss to the tip of her nose. "It would be dangerous. It would be impossible for me to keep from taking ye fully."

"Hmm," was her only reply. "Ruari?"

"Aye?"

"Why have ye not married before?"

"Because I had not met ye yet."

⤜⤜⤜✦⤛⤛⤛

HE'D HAD A successful meeting with the laird's brother and would be purchasing several horses. Clan Ross would probably purchase more since, according to the older man, he was not as interested in continuing to breed horses as he preferred to spend his days with his hunting dogs now.

The Fraser's brother had offered Ruari to take over the breeding and his stables once he married. It was an incredibly generous offer that Ruari promised to consider.

Returning to the keep from the laird's brother's home, Ruari had a good view of the area surrounding Fraser Keep. It was useful to have a good understanding of the lay of the land where he would be living. Although hilly, it was lush, with farmlands to the left of the keep and a rather large village south of it. A bit further south ran a river that divided the Fraser clans.

Atop a hill was a large keep, which he guessed belonged to Laird Chisholm, who had always managed to remain neutral despite his lands lying between the Fraser's and the Mackenzie's.

Ruari guessed the man's alliances, whoever they were, were strong. Although he wasn't sure who they'd allied with.

The way of men, to form alliances and fight for power, was interesting to Ruari. At times, it was wearying to worry about such things when there were people to help and stronger causes than battles between clans. There were always the threats of the Norse or the English to contend with.

Deciding to ride to the village on Fraser lands, Ruari urged his horse forward. The beast had seemed less temperamental that day. In a way, it was a bit alarming being the animal did not enjoy the saddle or being ridden.

Deciding not to worry overmuch, Ruari allowed the horse to set the pace. When crossing the field and into a small portion of wooded area, something caught Ruari's attention. Broken green branches signaled that someone had ridden past recently.

Normally, it would not worry him to be on the same path as someone else. But being that he'd been warned that the Mackenzies often trespassed, he ensured to keep on guard.

The unmistakable sound of movement made his steed jerk, its ears moving toward the noise.

Ruari drew his sword.

"Do not move," a voice from atop a tree called out and he looked up. On tree branches over him were four archers with arrows pointed at him.

Horsemen appeared from behind the trees and he recognized the colors of their plaids.

Just a few moments later, Ruari fell from the horse and onto the ground. Someone had thrown a rope around him and yanked him off the horse.

He struggled to pull free, but the rope held his arms tight against his sides. Before he could do more than kick, they dragged him backward to the bushes.

Ruari caught sight of the men on the ground. There were three of them. The men on horseback joined them as he fought the trio who tried to bind his hands.

"Whoever ordered this will pay," Ruari gritted out and then let out an "ooof" as someone kicked him in the stomach.

At the painful strike to his head, he fought not to lose consciousness. Ruari grunted and kicked at one man so hard that the aggressor stumbled backward and fell to the ground. Taking advantage of the momentum, he struggled to stand, but the other men were able to shove him back to the ground.

Finally, they managed to tie his hands and legs and blindfold him.

"Let me go at once," Ruari hissed, annoyed at the situation. Obviously, they did not mean to kill him, else they'd not bother with the blindfold.

"Bring the wagon," a man said, barely able to speak. He was too winded from the struggle.

Moments later, despite his struggles, Ruari was loaded onto a wagon.

"What about his mount?" someone said. "It acts as if it's wild. I cannot get it."

"Leave it then."

⇥⇥⇥⇤⇤⇤

IT WAS A long time later, perhaps an entire day's length, that he was pulled from the back of the wagon and half-dragged into a building. Upon being placed in a chair and the blindfold removed, Ruari glared at the Mackenzie.

The man sat in his study, a tankard next to his right hand.

"I apologize for the manner in which ye were brought here. I did not expect them to mistreat ye. But when laymen do the work of warriors, one cannot know what will happen."

"Ye could have sent a messenger. I would have come willingly," Ruari replied through clenched teeth. His head throbbed and throat was dry from a dirty cloth being shoved into his mouth.

The man's shrewd gaze met his. "I could have, I suppose." He looked to a guard and motioned to Ruari impatiently. "What are ye waiting for? Untie his hands and legs. Ruari Ross is not our prisoner."

A servant neared and held out a tankard. The woman's hand shook as she took in his bruised face. "Tis ale," she said in a soft voice.

Furious but at the same time needing to know what the imbecile would say, Ruari shook his head and glared at Laird Mackenzie. "What do ye wish to speak about? Surely ye do not wish to gain the ire of my cousin. Although I am sure ye could have me killed and none would be the wiser. However, ye would be the first he comes to for answers."

The Mackenzie didn't seem fazed. "Yer cousin is tired of battles."

What the comment was meant to do, perhaps scare him, Ruari wasn't sure. All it did was annoy him more. "Speak. My head hurts and I must find my mount."

Clearly the Mackenzie was not pleased at his lack of appropriate reaction because his nostrils flared. "Drink the damned ale. I know ye must thirst."

The Mackenzie lifted a tankard and took a long draw.

Ruari did the same, drinking while keeping his eyes on the man.

It was at that precise moment that he realized how precarious the situation was. Depending on how things went, it could mean war for his clan or the absorption of Clan Fraser into the Mackenzie's.

On this day, Ruari carried a burden like none he ever thought to bear.

Ruari met the laird's gaze. "What do ye wish to speak about?"

"Is it true yer clan plans to unite with Clan Fraser through marriage?"

His blood ran ice cold but, somehow, he managed to keep his demeanor unchanged. He gave the laird his best confused look. "Nothing has been agreed upon."

Laird Mackenzie was older, perhaps almost sixty. At his age, the strength of character was evidently larger than the physical. "I do not wish to have any conflicts with yer clan. It is best that ye leave and return to Ross lands. What happens between Laird Fraser and me should not be interfered with."

"I went to see the laird's brother about purchasing horses. Why did ye instruct that I be brought here in such a manner?" Now that he was untied, Ruari stood to his full height and towered over the man.

Two muscular warriors moved forward. One of them held up a sword and pointed it to the center of Ruari's chest. "Move away from the laird."

It would take three days to ride to Dun Airgid, the Ross keep, from the Mackenzie keep, another two from Ross lands to the Fraser keep. At that point, Ruari wasn't at all sure which direction he'd ride in upon being let go. If it happened.

The Mackenzie could have him killed and his body left out in a field. No one would be able to prove who'd murdered him.

Ruari mentally calculated what would happen once he left. Did the Mackenzie plan to immediately overtake Fraser and his lands?

He fought to come up with something to do or say that would appease the power-hungry man who mulled over a reply.

"I have ears everywhere. I am told ye and Laird Fraser were discussing marriage between ye and his only daughter. Interesting that ye tell a different story."

Ruari shrugged. "I do not have a stake in this. I am a Ross and we have nothing to gain from an alliance with a small clan like Fraser's."

"We shall wait, Ruari Ross. The truth of who is telling the truth will come out." Laird Mackenzie waved a maid closer. "Bring ale and food. We shall share a meal with our guest."

CHAPTER NINE

"I AM SO happy ye will stay here for a few days," Esme told Catriona as they slowly made their way down for the evening meal. Her maid walked alongside her to ensure she did not stumble. As much as Esme appreciated the effort, being treated like an invalid was becoming annoying. She was steady and able to walk without much discomfort.

The great room was not full on that day. There were only her family and several guards at the tables. She noted that Calum had returned. He sat at a table with other council members who'd come from the village and farms to meet.

Her mother motioned for Esme and Catriona to join her, her father and brother at the high board.

"Everyone seems in good humor," Catriona remarked sarcastically, her gaze directly at Keithen.

"I suppose ye're right. The idea of the marriage celebration and not having to worry overmuch does have everyone in good spirits."

"Not yer brother," Catriona said with a light shrug.

Esme studied Keithen. "My brother takes matters much too seriously. I worry about him at times."

They sat and were immediately served. Esme searched for Ruari.

Neither he nor her uncle were present. Perhaps Ruari had stayed over there for last meal. It was customary, after all, to invite guests to eat with the family.

A guard hurried in from the courtyard. He rounded the table and spoke in soft tones to her father and Keithen.

The men stood and hurried out of the room toward the courtyard.

At noticing what was happening, Calum also got to his feet and went out after them.

"What happened?" Esme asked her mother. "Did ye hear?"

Her mother frowned. "Something about a horse. I did not hear more than that."

Esme shrugged. "Perhaps one of father's horses has been injured."

Moments later, the same guard entered and went to the table where guards and archers were eating. "Ye must all come to the courtyard at once."

Without hesitation, the men got to their feet and hurried out.

"Come," Esme called to the man who'd brought the message. The guard looked to the departing men, seeming to consider if he should respond. Finally, he hurried up to the high board.

"Yes, Lady Esme?"

"What is happening?"

"Leave it be, it is not our concern," her mother said with annoyance.

Esme ignored her. "Why is everyone being summoned?"

"The man who is visiting, Ross, his horse returned without him. We think that perhaps he was injured or attacked while riding back from the other keep."

Esme gasped and got to her feet. The quick action caused pain, but she ignored it.

"Where are ye going?" Her mother grabbed her wrist. "This is not a matter for women to become involved in."

Unable to keep from it, she snatched her hand away. "Mother, will ye please stop repeating that? I do not care what my place is at the moment. The man I am betrothed to may be hurt. I must know what is going on."

There was chaos in the courtyard. Men were mounting horses and joining into teams as her brother shouted out orders. Her father stood with the stablemaster, their heads together as they looked over Ruari's unruly horse who fought against four men that attempted to pull it into a corral.

The animal rose to its hind legs, the giant hooves kicking in the air.

"Let him go!" Esme screamed. "Release him."

The startled men did as she asked and the horsed bolted toward the gate. Keithen gave her a puzzled look and then turned to his men. "Follow the horse."

Half of the men galloped after the animal, while the other half waited for instructions from her father.

"Take my message to the Mackenzie," he called out.

Twelve men rode out.

Her father, with Calum alongside, walked to a side doorway that would lead down a corridor that went directly to his study.

Just before going in, Calum looked to her. Something about his expression, almost gleeful, made a shiver of apprehension travel through her.

"I am famished." Her mother returned inside and everyone else in the courtyard returned to their duties. Within moments, it was as if nothing of importance had occurred.

"What is it?" Catriona asked, studying Esme.

With a shudder, Esme fought not to allow tears of fear to fall. "I am afraid of what happened to him. What if the Mackenzie is responsible?"

"Do ye think? It is possible he fell off his horse. There are many possibilities." Catriona placed a comforting arm around her shoulders.

She could not shed the feeling that something horrible had happened. Somehow, the Mackenzie must have learned of a Ross being there. There were always spies who worked for an opponent in exchange for coin. If someone had informed the Mackenzie, it meant the man would do what was necessary to stop them from uniting with a larger clan.

"If only that dreadful man would just let us be. I will never forgive myself if something horrible has happened to Ruari. He came only to help us."

Catriona walked alongside her to the garden where they settled onto a bench. "Ye care for him already."

At the statement, Esme huffed. "I do not know him enough to care for him strongly, but I do care what happens to him. Ruari should not have to pay for this."

A tear trickled down her cheek and she brushed it away. "I am so tired of having to constantly worry. Do we have any chance to beat the inevitable?"

Catriona shrugged. "I do not know."

"Come with me." Esme got up and hurried to the center of the courtyard where guards were gathered. She ignored the twinges of pain when her injuries protested the fast movements.

She walked to a guardsman she'd known her entire life. "Timothy, may I have a word?"

The guard nodded and walked to where she and Catriona stood next to a well. "What can I do for ye, Lady Esme?"

"Oh, stop that," Esme said, waving away his words. "Ye know I do not require formalities. Did anyone who lives here travel away from here in the last few days?"

The gate guard was used to her being overly curious, so he wasn't surprised by her question. Timothy's eyebrows moved low as he considered her question. "Several. Two guardsmen went to help at the Munro farm. One went north to visit his ailing mother."

"Who was that?" Esme asked, the skin on the back of her neck prickling.

"Edgar."

Esme had never cared for the man, but she did not know him well since he'd only joined the guard late the prior year. "Anyone else?"

"Nay. I do not believe so."

"Thank ye."

Catriona studied Timothy and then Esme. She looked to the gates as if pondering movements people made throughout the day.

Catriona was curious by nature and quite intelligent as well. The daughter of the village miller, she had taught herself to read and write. "People can leave without it seeming odd. Many live outside the keep. Tracking where they go upon crossing the gates is impossible."

"Very true, but I have to know who almost succeeded in killing me," Esme said.

"What are ye thinking?"

"I have more questions to ask. If my suspicions are right, we have a spy in our midst." Once inside the keep, Esme went to the kitchens. The head housekeeper, Eileen, looked up from a pot she was stirring. "Do ye wish to finish eating, Lady Esme?"

Esme motioned for the woman to come out to the corridor.

"What is it?"

"Eileen, do ye know the guard, Edgar? Is he from north of here?"

The housekeeper was known for her keen memory. The woman gave Esme a questioning look, but then replied, "He comes from a fishing village south of here. He came with two men, do ye not remember? The trio showed up in the dead of winter."

Esme shook her head. "I do not recall."

"He and two others said they had come from a village where everyone was slain by the marauders."

Esme and Catriona exchanged looks.

"Did something happen?" Eileen asked.

Catriona replied, "If someone's village in the south is overtaken, then one would suppose his mother would be included in those slain. Why would Edgar say that he would have to travel north to visit his mother?"

Eileen shook her head. "Men tell lies for all sorts of reasons. If we try to figure out why, we'd go mad."

Back in the great room, her mother sat alone at the high board. She had a full plate of food which she picked at. Her eyes brightened at seeing them. "Esme, ye should not be traipsing about. It has not been long enough that ye will not injure yerself again."

Esme hurried to the high board. "Mother, I am worried about Ruari Ross. I think he may have been taken by the Mackenzies."

"Sit down. There is little we can do by worrying. I am sure yer brother and father have the matter well in hand."

"I have learned something interesting about one of the guards. Perhaps he is a spy."

Lady Fraser looked up to the ceiling as if tempering her patience. "Have ye given thought to what kind of flowers ye would like on the tables for yer wedding?" her mother asked. As always, she was unwilling to speak on subjects she considered not her place.

"If he is not found, there will not be a wedding," Esme snapped. "Honestly, this is not the time to be thinking about flowers."

Her mother let out a suffering sigh. "Too many freedoms. I have told yer father he allowed ye to get away with speaking freely for far too long. Now, ye try to think like a man."

Esme looked toward the study. Once her father emerged, she'd try to get him alone and tell him of her discovery.

It was of no use to attempt to make her mother see the urgency in her discovery. Esme looked to Catriona. "Let us go up to my chamber. From the balcony, we can see when the men return."

This time, her mother gave her an exhausted look. "I will ask a servant to bring ye both something to eat and honeyed mead. Ye need to rest."

Inside her chamber, Esme hurried to the balcony. From her vantage point, the sun was low in the sky. Soon, it would set and darkness would fall. Her brother and his men would return then, hopefully with Ruari and the wild horse.

"He is very handsome, yer betrothed." Catriona came and stood beside her but looked out to the horizon. "It would be a shame for anything to happen to him."

"Aye, he is." Esme thought back to the night before and how they'd pleasured one another. It had been so intimate and, at the same time, beautiful in a way.

The view from her balcony was perfect. Her chamber was close to the front corner of the house where she could see both out toward the forest and part of the courtyard. Keithen had the chamber next to hers. From his balcony, he had a clearer view of the front gates and courtyard.

"My brother will listen to reason. Perhaps I should speak to him upon his return. Wait up with me."

Catriona nodded, a light flush coloring her cheeks.

"Is he the real reason ye stayed away for so long?"

The wind blew tendrils of hair across Esme's face. She pushed it back and studied her friend who seemed to consider how much to share.

Finally, she nodded. "Aye. I saw him…with a woman. They were having an…intimate moment."

"Oh, no. I am so sorry," Esme touched her friend's arm. "I know it must have been painful for ye."

"It was. However, I am glad for it because, although I was heartbroken, I now see he will never care for me the way I wish it." Catriona's bottom lip quivered as she tried to smile. "I am foolish. I feel horrible for not coming to visit while ye were so ill."

Her brother was a fool. Esme wanted to say something that would give Catriona hope. But at the same time, it was hard to tell what

Keithen thought at any given point. He was so stern, rarely showed emotions.

"I remember once, he was upset over the death of his favorite hound," Esme started and let out a long sigh. "I believe he was seven at the time. It was the only time I've seen Keithen cry. He is only two years older than I, but has always been so emotionally stable."

Catriona shook her head. "I wonder."

KEITHEN AND HIS men returned late that night. With them was Ruari's horse. The animal seemed tamer as they took him to the corral.

At the keep doorway, Esme waited for her brother to speak to several men before they all disbanded and headed to find a place to sleep. She was surprised when her father emerged and came to stand next to her.

He gave her a puzzled look. "Why are ye up, Daughter? It is late."

"I have to know what he found."

Her brother came up to them and, together, they went into the great room. There were smudges of dirt across her brother's face, his hair disheveled by the wind. "The horse stopped just inside the woods. There were signs of a struggle and we found a piece of cloth and some leather straps, which I assume were used to bind him. There was nothing else."

"So he was taken prisoner then?" Laird Fraser asked, an angry frown marring his features.

"We can assume so," her brother replied.

Calum hurried into the room, his gaze scanning each face. "I take it Ross was not found? It could be he decided the stakes were too high for his clan and left."

"Without his horse?" Keithen shot Calum an annoyed look. "For whatever reason, ye do not like him, but we have evidence that he did not go of his own accord."

"We will wait. If he was indeed taken, I am sure either us or Laird

Ross will be notified shortly," Calum explained unnecessarily.

"What did yer uncle say?" her father asked Keithen.

"Ross did not remain for dinner, but left shortly after promising to purchase horses. He should have returned in time for last meal."

Her father motioned a guard to come closer and considered what to say. Finally, he said, "Go to Laird Ross. Inform him that his cousin was abducted from the forest between our keep and my brother's home. Also tell him that we are doing everything in our power to find him."

"Aye, my laird. Is there anything else?"

"Tell him, I would welcome the fifty men he planned to send."

Calum coughed. "Surely ye cannot be planning to go to war over a man who is not part of our clan."

If it were not for the fact the men had not seemed to notice she remained among them, Esme would have kicked the fool for his callousness. Thankfully, her father was able to formulate the words that she could not speak.

"If anything happens to Ruari Ross, it will be me who is responsible. He was on my lands, invited by us, and betrothed to my daughter. Our enemy is who, in all probability, is responsible for his absence." Her father glared at Calum. "I think ye should seek yer bed."

Thankfully, Calum remained silent. The idiot was smart enough to know when he'd pushed things too far with her father.

"There is something else we should consider," Keithen said with a pensive expression.

"What?" Forgetting her vow to remain silent, Esme spoke in a louder than needed tone.

Keithen looked to her. Then seeming to dismiss her, he said, "There is the idea that perhaps he has enemies we do not know about or Ruari was mistaken for someone else and taken by said persons."

As everyone disbanded to head to bed, her father took Esme's elbow. "Ye should rest, Daughter."

"I am scared of what could have happened to him," Esme said, feeling free to speak to her father about anything. He'd always listened to her and, for it, she was grateful.

"Do not be afraid. Ye will always be protected."

Esme sighed. "I am worried for our clan and for Ruari. I pray he is not harmed."

In silence, her father walked her to her bedchamber door. "Sleep, Esme. For now, we wait."

"Father, do ye know the guard, Edgar? He left the day I was injured, traveling north."

Her father gave her a patient, but tired look. "I do know of him."

"Eileen says that upon his arrival, he'd claimed to be from a decimated village to the south. Yet he claimed to go visit his mother and traveled north."

"I will ensure Keithen sees to questioning him." At his pensive expression, Esme couldn't help but hug her father. "I wish we had peace and ye could rest."

His soft chuckle made her heart melt. "As do I, dear one."

CHAPTER TEN

IT WAS AFTER two entire days in the back of a wagon that Ruari was finally released.

"Ride without looking back," someone barked at his ear.

"I know ye are Mackenzies. Why would I look?" Ruari asked in a bored voice. "Ye are a red-haired guard with a twisted nose."

He was dragged off the wagon, yanked down by his feet and then roughly shoved forward. Perhaps it was a bad idea to have angered the guard.

Two men held him while a third untied his hands. "Go on with ye."

Ruari tore off his blindfold as a wagon flanked by two men on horseback rode away. On the side of the trail was a mare. The animal had been tethered to a small tree.

The mare was skittish, seeming not used to allowing a rider. "If they took my horse, I will return to retrieve it. Thieving bastards," he muttered under his breath.

It took several hours before Ruari realized he was near Ross lands.

No matter how much coaxing he did, the mare refused to go faster than a slow walk. When he slapped and kicked the animal's sides, it would take several steps backward or become still, seeming terrified to move.

Ruari dismounted and ran his hands up and down the beast's snout. "Ye have had a terrible time of it. I recognize what ye are doing. How about we come to an understanding? Ye get me home and I ensure that ye are treated well henceforth"

Previous owners had obviously treated the poor animal horribly to the point that it no longer seemed to understand normal commands. The sad creature froze upon feeling threatened.

Despite being in a hurry to arrive home, for a long time, he pulled the animal along, coaxing it gently and then guided it to a creek. The horse became animated at the sight of water and, for the first time, showed signs of life. At the water's edge, it hesitated until Ruari kneeled down to drink and then the horse took water for itself.

While the animal drank, Ruari ran his hands down its sides ensuring that there were no injuries. Then he inspected each of its legs and hooves. There were old scars, but it seemed that in the recent past, it had been groomed and fed well. Perhaps a Mackenzie had rescued the animal but given up on it being useful since it remained fearful.

Once again, he mounted and was satisfied when the horse went a bit faster, still not at a run, but at least it trotted.

By the time he was sighted by Ross guards, Ruari was exhausted. It had been three days since he'd been taken and released by the Mackenzie and he wondered if, in that time, they'd attacked Clan Fraser.

He immediately recognized three of the riders who approached. Along with guardsmen were his cousins, Tristan, Kieran and Ewan. Each of their gazes roamed over him searching for any injury.

"What happened to yer horse?" Kieran asked with a scowl, his hazel gaze inspecting the mare who shuffled sideways in fear of the warhorses they rode upon.

"Tis a long story. It is best I tell ye at the same time as Malcolm." The men nodded.

Ewan guided his horse alongside Ruari's. "Are ye hurt? It looks like ye've been in a fight."

"I was in a fight," Ruari said with a huff. "With a bunch of idiots."

The men managed not to ask any further questions. Thankfully, the mare kept up with their horses, seeming to sense she was safe.

Once inside the courtyard, Ruari did not release the mare's reins until one of the lads he'd trained came to get it. "Treat her gently. Give her a stall in a corner to ensure she feels safe."

The lad studied the horse, his face softening. "Had a hard time of it, have ye?" He ran a hand down the horse's face and it settled. "I will take care of her," he said, looking to Ruari.

"Thank ye."

Along with his cousins, he made his way inside. Although Ruari's stomach grumbled at the aroma of food, he pushed hunger away and hurried to find the laird.

Malcolm met his gaze and once Ruari neared, his cousin embraced him. "Welcome home. I am glad to see ye are not too badly hurt."

As a group, they made their way to Malcolm's study. Immediately, his cousin poured him a glass of whisky. "Sit down. Tell us what happened. I received a missive from Laird Fraser that ye went missing."

"The Mackenzie. He sent men to get me. They were not guardsmen or warriors, probably to not arouse suspicion in case they were seen by villagers."

"His ambition knows no bounds," Malcolm said, his face hard. "What did he want?"

Ruari drank down the amber liquid, the warm trail traveling down his center. "For us to not involve ourselves with what happens between him and the Fraser. He wishes to take over the clan but not have any confrontations with us."

"How did he know ye were there?" Tristan asked.

"A spy," Ewan remarked. "Do ye have any idea who it is?"

"Aye," Ruari said. "I think it's the town constable. The man is transparent in his insistence they unite with Clan Mackenzie. Already, the village has taken people in who were forced to flee when Mackenzies razed their homes and killed their livestock."

Malcolm was pensive. "The man must have been promised something. I do not understand why the Mackenzie would provoke Clan Fraser. They are a small clan alone. But if they are joined by the other Frasers, they can be a challenge."

Tristan huffed. "Until now, the other Frasers have watched quietly, but I will not be surprised if the other Frasers decide to come to their rescue if the Mackenzie tries to overtake them."

"I am going back as soon as I eat and get a fresh horse," Ruari announced.

His cousins were struck silent. Finally, Tristan, the diplomatic one, nodded. "Ye should sleep and get rest first. We will send a messenger to let the Fraser know ye are well." Muscular and as tall as him, Tristan had a fierce appearance. "I will go with ye."

Ruari shook his head. "This is not yer fight."

"That is not true," Kieran said. "The Mackenzie has made it our fight when he dared to take ye as prisoner."

"Ye will remain here and rest. Once the sun rises, ye will return to Fraser lands with fifty warriors. I will send the other Fraser a missive asking that he join with us to keep the smaller clan from being overtaken."

Malcolm was fair but firm, always a good leader. Nonetheless, Ruari considered disobeying him.

"They could be under attack. A few hours could make the difference between…"

"Ye cannot expect to beat the Mackenzie even with fifty men." Malcolm crossed his arms, his keen gaze narrowing.

His cousin understood there was more at stake for him. He was thinking about Esme and what would become of her if the Mackenzie had his way. However, Malcolm was right. No matter when he arrived, with only fifty, there was little he could do to save them.

In the kitchen, Ruari ate and drank his fill. Ewan sat at the table keeping an eye on him, while a couple lads prepared a hot bath.

"What do ye suppose yer betrothed thinks of yer disappearance?"

He considered it for a long moment. "Esme is intelligent. She will know I did not leave of my own accord."

"Ye care for her already." It was a statement more than a question.

True, he found her alluring and attractive, but they'd not known each other long enough for feeling to have emerged. Every night, he'd thought back to the night she'd come to his bed and how very passionate the interlude had been.

He'd been looking forward to bedding the lass and now he wasn't at all sure the marriage would ever take place.

"I do care about what happens to her."

Ewan met his gaze. "I am one of the fifty that volunteered to go to Fraser lands. I will come and live there with ye."

Despite the situation, Ruari smiled. "If it comes to be, I am glad for it. Nothing is better than family. Having ye there will mean a great deal to me."

"If ye plan to leave first thing in the morning," Tristan announced, entering the space, "get some rest, Cousin."

Ruari nodded. Although he looked forward to forging a future, he'd miss his family. "I will."

⇿⟩⟩⟩⟨⟨⟨⇷

Laird Mackenzie's mount pawed the ground, the beast seeming much too large for the man astride who'd arrived at the appointed place with a great show of banners and warriors.

Despite her brother and father not wishing her to be present, Esme had ridden with the archers. Lined with the archers meant she was behind the warriors and away from where her father, brother and Calum spoke to the man.

Thankfully, the Mackenzie spoke quite loudly. "I imagine ye have conferred with yer clan and are aware ye do not have a chance if ye stand against me."

The Mackenzie's gaze moved past her father and brother before looking in her direction with curiosity.

"Where is Ruari Ross?" her father asked. "He was our guest and any harm that comes to him will fall on my shoulders."

The Mackenzie's expression was flat, as if he were bored. "Ross came to me of his own accord. He informed me that ye had asked for help from Clan Ross. After that, he left, I assume back to his family lands."

It was a lie. His father and brother knew it. By the straightening of Keithen's shoulders, Esme recognized her brother was on guard.

"Ye have a sennight to declare yerself to be in alliance with me." The Mackenzie once again looked to the guards. "It will be that or I will consider ye my enemy."

Hatred like she'd never felt before filled her. Esme wanted to grab the bow strapped to the side of her steed, set an arrow and shoot it directly in the man's black heart.

The archer next to her must have noticed that her hand inched to the bow because he reached over and grabbed her wrist.

"An alliance with ye means falling under yer rule," her father pronounced. "I have an alliance with the other Clans Fraser. I have no need for more. I ask ye one last time. Leave us in peace. There is no need for strife."

The Mackenzie did not look away from her father, sending a trickle of fear through Esme. Keithen angled his horse to move in front of his father, protecting him from the guards who flanked the other laird.

The Mackenzie threw his head back and laughed. It was without mirth, more maniacal than joyful. "Everyone needs allies. Ye more than anyone who is surrounded by my allies must realize it. What of yer people? Do ye not care they are in constant danger?"

They'd met on semi-neutral territory, on lands between the two clans. Laird Fraser arrived with a guard contingency of fifty. And as if showcasing how much larger and stronger he was, the Mackenzie had traveled with at least a hundred men.

Her father was first to turn away, guiding his horse back toward their home. Esme itched to ride alongside him. She threw glances toward him and her brother as they spoke. It was then she caught a strange interchange between Laird Mackenzie and Calum. The laird nodded at Calum, who glanced first toward where her father was and then returned the gesture.

It was also noticeable that the constable did not hurry to ride alongside Keithen or her father as he always managed to do.

She waited for him to catch up and gave Calum a worried look. "I fear we will all be killed. Father would rather go to war than fall under Mackenzie rule."

"There is no need for ye to be fearful. I will see that nothing happens."

Esme shook her head. "There is nothing ye or any of us can do. My uncle will send his men, so will the Frasers of the south, but still it will be a slaughter if they do not arrive in time."

"Certainly, battles will not begin so quickly. Ye do not know the ways of negotiations." Calum became impatient with her and craned his neck to search out her father.

Not wanting to lose his attention, she sniffed loudly. "Reassure me. How would ye keep our clan safe?"

For a moment, he seemed to ponder how to reply. Finally, he shrugged. "I am a man who is always prepared. A smart person ensures to have good plans set in case things go badly."

"So ye have a way to escape or avoid battle? Perhaps ye can share with father."

His gaze narrowed and his lips curved with distaste. "I doubt yer father or brother would do anything that I suggest. They would prefer to lead men to certain death than to do what is best for the clan."

Despite bile in her throat, Esme forced a look of sadness. "We Frasers are a stubborn but brave people. Ye should know that by now. I cannot agree with ye. We have lived in peace, with no conflicts with our neighbors. The Mackenzie's only interest is growing more powerful at the expense of people like us."

"Remain close to me. Ensure that I know where ye are at all times. I will keep ye from harm." Without another word, he kicked the sides of his horse to get away from her and toward where her father and brother rode.

Esme did the same but remained just a few feet behind. Once they returned to the keep, she'd speak to her father. Something was not right. If the constable was Laird Mackenzie's spy, there was little anyone could do to save him from her father's ire. The only time Laird Fraser didn't touch his heart was when punishing a traitor.

CHAPTER ELEVEN

EVEN BEFORE ARRIVING at the top of a ridge, Ruari knew the Fraser keep was under attack. Archers atop the ramparts shot flaming arrows down at the approaching warriors. There were so very many. It was hard to count as the columns of men stretched quite far.

"What is happening?" Ewan asked, coming up to stand beside him. He peered across the field to where the Fraser keep was. "I will say that we may have a hard time getting inside."

"Aye, I am sure it is surrounded on all sides. Although it seems to be early in the battle, so there may be a chance they have not discovered the back entrance as of yet."

He motioned the men ahead. They were a small group of only fifty, twenty-five of them archers. They rode fast and hard, rounding the ridge, having to travel farther than necessary to avoid being seen.

Ruari's heart pounded, the air rasped in an out of his lungs. His entire body was tense with anticipation. Each time he went to battle, it was the same. The sounds of nature disappeared and were replaced by a keener sense of smell and the only things he heard were the pounds of the hooves on the ground and the harsh breathing of the men astride.

When they arrived at the rear of the keep, the opposition had not yet reached it. Since the Mackenzies traveled from the opposite direction, they would have had to ride in plain sight of Fraser archers to get to where Ruari and his men were.

"I am sure they will be coming soon," Ewan said, seeming to read his thoughts. "I pray the Fraser's men recognize ye and allow us in."

The Ross banner was lifted and, moments later, a man with torches signaled for them to come forward. They had to ride in a single file to reach the rear gates. Guards hurried to open the narrow opening to allow them in.

"Ye returned?" Laird Fraser hurried over to where Ruari was and he dismounted. Together, they watched as the Ross warriors rode in.

"Of course, I did not leave of my own accord."

"I know." The Fraser looked to the front of the keep where archers continued releasing arrows and guards atop the keep gates struck at opposers attempting to climb ladders and scale the tall walls.

"We will not be able to hold them off much longer." The laird looked to the Ross warriors. "I am indebted to yer cousin. Will yer men fight for us?"

Ruari nodded. "We will not sit back and allow yer men to fight alone while we do nothing."

"Come. Let us see what is happening." Just then, someone fell into the courtyard from atop the gate, arrows embedded in his body.

"Their archers have advanced."

Ewan, who remained astride, motioned the archers forward. "Assume secondary positions at the east wall."

The men hurried to the wall that was not being defended.

Fury filled Ruari. There was no need for this to happen. "How many men did he send?"

"I estimate at least five hundred," Laird Fraser replied as they rushed toward the main house. "I only have three hundred here, another fifty are defending the village."

Ruari looked over his shoulder to the warriors who began climbing ladders to the top of the rear gate preparing to defend when the enemy made it there.

"How long ago was a missive sent to yer brother?"

"As soon as my talk with the Mackenzie ended two days ago. They should be headed here. I am just not sure how long it will take. They must cross a river to come."

A boom was followed by the sound of cracking wood. The Mackenzies were using a catapult or large battering ram in an attempt to break in the gates. Screams filled the air as the archers continued their assault on both sides. More men fell into the courtyard as a second boom sounded.

When Ruari and the laird entered the great room, a group of women rushed to them. Lady Fraser stood tall, Esme by her side, their terror-filled gazes flew to him.

"Did ye bring men?" Esme asked. "We are not going to be able to keep them at bay for long."

Ruari went to her and, without thinking, brought her against his side. "Aye, I did, but only a few. I did not expect to arrive to a battle."

The laird motioned to two young guards to come closer. "Take the women. Ye must all escape. Get away through the passageway into the woods. There is a wagon there, I will see that a horse is brought. Head north and to the east."

The two young men did their best to look brave as they began herding the servant women and Lady Fraser away.

"Come, Esme, hurry!" Lady Fraser screamed. But Esme shook her head. "I will not leave father here alone. I will remain."

"Ye should go," both Ruari and the laird said.

Esme pushed away from Ruari and went to her father. "I am good with the bow, allow me to fight. We need every able body to do so."

"Go!" Laird Fraser motioned to the young men and women. "I will keep her safe," he said to his wife and then rushed to the stairs. "I must see what is going on."

A hysterical Lady Fraser was dragged away and, soon, only Ruari and Esme remained, alone.

Esme studied his face and took in the bruising. "I knew ye would never leave of yer own accord. I would like hear what happened, but first I must fetch my bow and arrows."

"Go up with yer father. Ye will have clean shots from there and remain out of danger. I must see what my men are doing."

Ruari brought her against him for a short moment and covered her mouth with his. Ignoring the demand from his mind and body to keep her close, he pushed away. "Go."

The ringing of metal against metal alerted Ruari that the gate had been breached. Fraser warriors, even with the help of his fifty men would not last long. There were too many streaming in through the gates.

Fraser guards remained atop the walls, every single one drawing out bow and arrows. The Ross archers joined the attack.

It was a good tactic for the outnumbered clan. It was impressive to see how many invaders were sliced down immediately by arrows even when holding up their shields.

Ruari looked up to the top of the keep and there were rows of archers that included Esme and her father. Arrows flew with deadly precision, like he'd never seen.

From the second-story windows, more men appeared, also with bow and arrows and began shooting into the courtyard. Ruari walked close to the building and then climbed to the rear wall.

Sword drawn, Ruari entered the fight. It was well known that Mackenzies relied on their numbers and were not expert swordsmen. It was evident by how quickly he was able to cut a path toward his men.

A large warrior appeared in his path and he recognized the red-haired male from when he'd been dragged to the Mackenzie. Ruari charged, the swords colliding with so much force that his arm shook.

Taking one step back, he swung a second time and, once again, the guard blocked effectively. When the warrior held his weapon with both hands and sliced across, Ruari jumped back to avoid being cut.

The man was a better swordsman then most of his clan. Ruari growled and charged, sweeping across with his blade. Each swing was blocked and then he, in turn, did the same to blows from the man.

He managed to cut the man's upper arm, but it was not a deep wound. When he charged again, the red-haired fighter pulled one of his own men to use as a shield. Ruari's sword sunk into the hapless man's stomach and he withdrew it just as the red-haired man dropped the dying man.

A scream from behind caught his attention and he turned just in time to block the downfall of a strike. It was a quick moment before he downed the man and turned to face his earlier opponent.

The red-haired warrior had gone.

Ruari reached the rear wall and scaled up to the top where Ross guards shot arrows down at the courtyard.

In the distance, a large contingency of riders appeared. At seeing the number, his heart sank. He turned to look into the courtyard. Even though Clan Fraser was holding its own, it would not be for long. Eventually, they would run out of arrows.

There was one evening he'd been up late, unable to sleep and he'd stood at his balcony and watched as basket after basket was lifted up to the gates. He'd wondered what they were storing in them and now he knew. Clan Fraser had been preparing for this.

A new group of Mackenzie warriors entered the gates. They grouped together using their shields as a barrier.

He exchanged looks with the guards on the wall. "We wait until those arrive and try to hold them off as long as possible. I do not expect ye to fight to the death. We must just try to keep them at bay until the rest of Clan Fraser arrives."

With hard expressions that would make most men's blood run

cold, the warriors nodded. His clan had been at war for a long time. These men were not strangers to conflict.

Below, Fraser guards fought valiantly against their enemy. Thankfully, the rumor about Mackenzie leaning too heavily on numbers seemed to be true as the Fraser warriors were much better at hand-to-hand battle.

Although there was no doubt that they knew they were outnumbered, there was bravery in fighting to keep one's home and defend what rightfully belongs to the people of the clan.

The fighters were almost even in number now proving what amazing shots the archers were. The Mackenzie would not have an easy time conquering Clan Fraser.

Until the other warriors, who rode at full speed, arrived, the Frasers stood a chance to win.

Ruari looked to his men. "When the reinforcements arrive, head out the same way we came. Return to Ross lands immediately and ensure the archers do the same."

He climbed down from the wall and upon hitting the ground, once again, he drew out his sword.

Slicing a path through to the front entrance of the keep, he had but one goal in mind. Not to let Esme die. He had to save her from what was sure to be a slaughter.

He raced through the great room, his heart thundering in his chest and raced up the stairs to the top of the keep.

Once atop the keep, arrows whizzed by and several men lay on the floor with arrows impaled in their bodies. No one was dead. Not yet.

"Esme!" he called out. He spotted her as she loosed an arrow.

Her hair flew around her head like flames as she concentrated on the scene below. Her gaze did not waver to him when he came to her side, holding up a discarded shield in front of them.

"We must go, more come."

"They will fall, too, then." She loosed another arrow and it hit her target, the man falling with it impaled in his neck.

"Ye should go with him." Her father neared and Ruari noted he'd broken an arrow off that had hit him in the upper left arm.

The man had continued to fight despite it, which didn't surprise Ruari. A true laird fought alongside his men to the death.

The three of them rushed to the other side of the building to see the huge army headed their way.

"Why would he do this?" Esme exclaimed. "If he kills us all, what will he gain?"

Ruari took her arm and led her away from the edge. "We must go. I did not bring my men here to die."

She smiled up at him, her brown eyes full of tenderness when meeting his. "I agree, ye and yer men should go. This is not yer fight."

It would be useless to try to convince her to leave with him. It was obvious she would die alongside her father. Ruari cupped her jaw. "Ye are extraordinary."

Esme shrugged. "What I am is determined to take down as many of those bastards as I can. Please move aside. I do not have time to watch ye leave." Although her words were said with impatience, her eyes became shiny with tears.

Of course, he would not leave. Esme was the woman meant for him and if fate decided they'd die together, then so be it.

Ruari grabbed a bow and arrows from one of the downed men and stood next to her. Although a good marksman, he preferred hand-to-hand fighting. However, it was best to do what he could from up there and not waste more time.

Without knowing who the local people were and who was the enemy, Ruari had to pay extra attention before shooting, which meant he was a lot slower than the other archers.

It was a short while later that battle cries sounded. "Buaidh no Bàs!" At first, he wasn't sure of what he heard. Then again, the arrivals cried out, "Victory or death!"

"Do not attack those who arrive," Ruari called out and hurried back to the opposite side just in time to see the red banner with three lions upon it. His heart squeezed at the sight of his cousins, Tristan and Kieran, leading hundreds of Ross warriors at full speed.

"Retreat!" the Mackenzie lead guards called out. The ones that were left began rushing to their horses, many riding off without waiting for their comrades.

Esme rushed to his side. "Who are they?"

"My clan," Ruari replied, his voice hoarse with pride. "My family."

Together with Laird Fraser, they hurried inside and down to the great room. There was chaos as men who'd been dragged in were being cared for by the healer and his helpers.

Outside, the clanging of weapons still sounded as some of the Mackenzie warriors had not been able to get away.

The laird went to the doorway, Ruari and several other guards with him. "Cease at once!" the man called out. "Take those that remain prisoners."

Several Mackenzies immediately put down their weapons, but two of the Mackenzie men refused to stop fighting. Blood-soaked, they fought on and Ruari understood. They would rather die than accept defeat.

Finally, one fell, too injured to continue. The other was cut through with a sword and fell next.

"Bring the one who is alive inside," Laird Fraser instructed. "Ensure the healer sees to his wounds."

A brave warrior was respected and, as such, the man would be allowed to live. A code of battle that baffled Ruari at times.

Moments later, Mackenzie warriors that had been captured were bound and lined up on their knees and his cousins, along with a small group of Ross warriors, entered through the gates.

Kieran dismounted and headed to him. "Where's Ewan?"

"Ye missed all the fun!" Ewan approached, his tunic bloodied. He took two more steps and fell forward like a plank.

Both Kieran and Ruari stared at their cousin for a moment before reacting and picking him up and carrying him into the keep.

"Are ye injured?" Tristan, his other cousin, asked Ruari, the hazel gaze roaming over his body. "The men here put up a good fight."

Ruari shook his head. "Nothing of note." Together, they walked after his cousins to see about Ewan.

"I do not need to be sewn up," Ewan protested as a healer held up a needle and thread.

Ruari stepped closer to where the injured cousin lay atop a table, his tunic torn open to show a gash across his left rib cage. "I will hold him down," he told the woman who looked to Ewan with a worried expression.

Ruari chuckled when Ewan glowered, but lowered his head back to the table. "I will kick ye if ye stick me too deep."

"I will stick it deeper if ye do," the feisty woman replied.

CHAPTER TWELVE

E SME WASHED OUT her father's wound, inspecting it to ensure there was no part of the arrow left.

"Go see about the others, I am able to take care of this myself," he protested once again and looked around her to a guard. "Has my wife and the other women been found yet?"

The guard hurried off to find out.

"Keithen and his men will bring them back safely."

In truth, she wasn't sure. Both her mother and Catriona were among the women who'd been sent off.

"Yer brother's men have arrived," a guard announced.

Her father none-so-gently pushed her aside and stood. "Ah, very well. With the number of the men here, the Mackenzie will know we are a force to be reckoned with. Alone without reinforcements, we were winning even outnumbered."

The look of pride on her father's face was reflected on the other men in the room. This would be a day which would be told about for many years to come. Esme was proud not only of her clan, but of herself. She'd not cowered or left but fought alongside her father.

She beamed at the guard. "We are Frasers. We are strong."

"Ye are a brave lass, tis true," Ruari said, his gaze clashing with hers. There was a definite connection with him that she could no longer deny. Something about Ruari Ross made her soft inside.

BY THE END of the day, a mixture of happiness and sadness hung in the air. The dead were taken to be buried by their families. The great room would be used for the many injured to be cared for. And as a sign of compassion, the Mackenzie prisoners were released and sent on their way on foot without shoes or weapons.

Several tables had been set up in the courtyard.

Cows had been slaughtered to feed the many people who'd gathered. Out in the fields, campsites were set up and scattered among them were fires with cauldrons of stew being cooked for the warriors.

The bakers from the village arrived with carts heaped with loaves of bread to feed the men as well.

"Keithen should have returned by now," her father said to them as they sat at a long table to eat.

Esme had been thinking the same. They'd not had time to get far. Why had her brother not returned yet?

"Someone comes," a guard announced, and they rushed out.

A lone rider entered through the gate and upon recognizing him as one of Keithen's men, Esme jumped to her feet and ran toward him.

"What happened?"

The man dismounted and stalked toward her father with purposeful strides. "Laird."

Her father was on his feet. "Where is my son? My wife?"

"We found the group. The servants are all alive and well. The young men who escorted them are dead. Lady Fraser as well as Miss Catriona were taken."

Color left her father's face. "Was it the Mackenzie?"

"They believe so. They left behind a message with the servants."

"What is it?" Her father's voice shook with fury. They were surrounded now by her uncles, Ruari, his cousins and two lead guards.

"That Lady Esme be sent to marry a man of the Mackenzie's choice. Upon the marriage, yer wife and Miss Catriona will be released."

Her father's shoulders fell. "And we will then be in alliance with the Mackenzie by marriage."

It was all for naught. In the end, the Mackenzie would win. Esme looked to Ruari who studied her face without expression.

Her father's decision would be to sacrifice his wife and Catriona in exchange for the clan. Everyone there knew it.

"I will go, Father. I will do as they ask until my mother returns. Then I will murder the man he marries me to."

"I forbid it," her father barked.

Esme would not be put off. "Father, think on it. This way, we have a chance of not losing Mother."

"They will be suspicious. Especially if ye go right away," her father said. "I doubt the bastard will let either woman live."

Turning to her uncle, she hoped for him to see that what she proposed would be the best way to handle the situation. "Uncle, do ye not agree with me that this is the only way to save Mother's life?" Her voice caught at not mentioning Catriona. What would happen to her dear friend?

"Please." Tears trickled down her cheeks, and she wiped them away with her sleeve. This was not a time for weakness.

Silence hung in the air like a storm cloud. Finally, her uncle shook his head. "I agree with yer father. We cannot sacrifice the lives of many for two."

Esme dashed around them, planning to go to the corrals. But Ruari caught up to her and wrapped his arms around her. "Do not go against yer father's wishes."

"They will kill my mother. I know the bastard will not touch his heart. He is ruthless and unwavering. There is nothing that can be done to stop him."

Tears of fury flowed forcefully now. There had to be something she could do to stop them from killing her mother. "Help me, Ruari, please."

"Take her to her chamber. Make sure she remains there." Her father's voice was tinged with anger. She knew he hated the decision he was forced to make. Perhaps she was not helping at the moment, but Esme could not bring herself to care. Sacrificing herself for her mother was an easy decision. Even if she died in the process of killing whoever the Mackenzie forced on her, it was worth it.

"Come," Ruari said in a soft voice, half-dragging her back inside. "Let us talk about this. Maybe there is another way."

The thought mollified her somewhat. "Do ye have an idea?"

"No, but I think we should all sit down and discuss alternatives."

"What if the entire army that is here goes to rescue her?" Esme said, pushing away from Ruari and turning back to her father.

The sight of him with his head hung and the other men circling him made her stop. Of course, he was considering other ways. The decision would not be made lightly.

"As soon as the army is spotted, the Mackenzie will have yer mother killed." Ruari's words seeped through her skin like red hot pokers.

Esme closed her eyes and, like her father, hung her head. "There is no other way. I have to go, Ruari. I must go and do what I plan. Ye know it would be the only way."

"If ye fail, then ye will be the cause of yer people coming under his rule. Think about it."

Because the servants were busy with the injured, Esme went to the doorway just outside the kitchen and lowered a bucket into one of the rain collection barrels. She then hauled the water inside to pour into a large cauldron that hung over a bright fire.

Once the water was warmed, she filled a basin and hurried behind a screen set up on the opposite side of the room. Esme quickly washed away the grime and blood from her body.

She'd promised Ruari to go to her chamber after she cleansed herself, but he obviously did not believe her because he stood just outside the kitchen doorway waiting for her.

"There is more heated water if ye wish to wash up as well," she offered.

Eyes narrowed, he kept his attention on her as he removed his tunic. Unlike her, he was beside the screen. Then, he, too, removed the evidence of battle. The beauty of his body distracted her away from thoughts of what had happened. The light from the fireplace glistened off his wet skin, making every muscle more pronounced.

When he hooked his thumbs on the top of his breeches and lifted a brow in question, she realized he'd caught her staring. Esme turned her back to give him privacy to finish.

Splashes made her wonder where he was washing. She fought not to turn and look. Although she'd touched the most intimate part of him, she'd not been able to see much of his body.

"Come, it's best I get ye upstairs before yer father thinks I disobeyed him." Ruari took her elbow and guided her through the great room and up the stairs.

She shivered and wasn't sure if it was from the dampness of her skin, or the ending of a horrible day. "Come inside with me," she said to Ruari upon arriving at her doorway. "Please."

The room was dark with no fire in the hearth. Every servant was put to use downstairs caring for the injured or cooking for the hundreds of warriors.

Ruari placed several logs into the hearth and used kindling to start a fire that soon grew to life, sending warmth into the space.

"Be truthful," Esme said to him. "What would ye do in my place? Would ye not go?"

He studied her for a long moment, the darkness emphasizing the chiseled features of his face. "I do not have a relationship with my mother, so I cannot, in truth, say what I would do if it was she. If it was my aunt, who raised me, then I would grieve and try to come up with a way to save her."

"Do ye think yer cousins would not go after her?"

He shook his head. "Esme, ye know that in most cases, the person held is killed. I am sorry to say it, but tis the truth. We would do exactly what yer father is doing. Weigh the options and do what is best for the clan."

"If he will keep her alive while waiting our reply, then it makes my plan the best." Esme wanted to stomp her foot but, instead, moved closer to Ruari. "Why does it always come to him winning over others? Why doesn't he leave us alone?"

"The Mackenzie has set his mind to winning. It has more to do with showing his strength and power over others than actually acquiring yer clan's lands."

When she went limp, Ruari pulled her against him. "Do not give up. There may still be something to be done. In the morning…"

"I cannot." She tried to push away, but he held her still. When she looked up at him, it was obvious he was as torn as she about the situation. Esme wrapped her arms around his waist and pulled him into an embrace.

"Help me to forget. Do not let me continue from this day without knowing what it will be like to lay with ye. I want to be touched by ye again, to be claimed by yer body. I give myself to ye freely, Ruari. Take me to bed."

Upon entering her chamber, he took her mouth, running his hands down her back and pulling Esme tightly against him.

Urgency intermingled with need. Esme didn't wish to think about anything but how his solid muscular body felt under her palms. Their bodies aligned perfectly, the hardness of his sex pressing to her lower abdomen.

They made quick work of undressing, each taking in the other in the moonlight that streamed through the windows. Her breath caught at seeing him completely bereft of clothing, every muscle toned, his legs well formed. His arousal caught her by surprise.

She knew the mechanics of joining with a man, of course. But wondered how, exactly, it would feel.

There was something mesmerizing about the way his gaze moved over her. Every inch of her skin came to life where his darkened eyes landed.

"Come to me." Ruari held out a hand and she moved to him, taking it.

"I am nervous," she admitted.

"I know." He lifted her up easily and laid her upon the bed. "There is nothing to be anxious about. We will take it slowly. If ye wish to stop at any moment, just say it."

Esme couldn't believe the words. He was like no man she'd ever met. Caring, patient and respectful. Her lips curved. "At any time?" She lifted a brow. "I may have to test ye."

Ruari chuckled. "Do not be cruel."

When he climbed onto the bed and pulled her closer, she melted against him. The moment their skin touched, her entire body came to life. Unsure of what exactly she felt, Esme lifted her face to him. "Kiss me, Scot."

There was a soft demand in the way his mouth took hers. At the prodding of his tongue, she opened gladly, allowing him to tease at hers.

Her skin tingled as his hands traveled down from her waist to caress her thighs. Esme let out a soft moan.

Raking her fingers through his hair, she kissed him back hard, her mouth showing him what her body needed.

Rolling Esme to her back, Ruari trailed kisses from her mouth to her breasts, taking a taut point into his mouth and sucking it gently at first, then harder. Esme arched up, silently demanding he do more.

Ever so slowly, his fingers traveled the path from her thigh to between her legs, sending her to whimper with anticipation.

Ruari slipped his hand between her thighs, urging them apart and then began stroking gently down the center of her nether lips. "Take me in hand," he demanded, his voice breathless and hoarse.

Obediently, she wrapped her fingers around his engorged manhood, marveling at the velvety skin.

His deep moan gave her a sensation of power over him that sent her mind reeling. How was it possible that she could affect the strong man in such a way?

"Ah!" Esme exclaimed at the invasion of his finger into her sex and her eyes flew open. There was something different about the way he took her this time.

First it was one finger, then two sliding in and out of her, while his thumb stroked up and down her center. Something akin to fire began to develop and she tightened the walls of her sex around his hand.

Esme grabbed at the bedding with both hands and bit her bottom lip to not cry out as her body came to life.

When Ruari climbed over her and cupped her bottom, lifting it and pressed his hardness against her sex, she was somewhat relieved. He took her mouth and she returned his kisses ardently while caressing his wide back.

Settled between her legs, he whispered in her ear. "Wrap yer legs about my hips."

She did as instructed. Her senses were on high alert as he reached down between them.

The prodding of the thick head at her entrance was exciting. Esme held on to his shoulders and pressed her lips on the side of Ruari's throat. His breathing was harsh as he held back, allowing her sex to adjust to his girth.

It was hard to hold still. She wanted him to enter her fully. Esme raked her nails down his back and cupped his bottom to urge him forward.

With one strong thrust, he took her fully and she cried out, unable to stop from it as the pain of being torn was piercing.

"Shhh," Ruari whispered and kissed her. He lifted his face and looked at her. "It will become enjoyable again, I promise."

Esme nodded, somewhat embarrassed at the tears that trickled down the sides of her face to plop on the pillow. She believed him but wondered how it would be so.

When he began moving, his sex slipping out and back in, Esme soon found the movements soothing. The more he moved, the further away any pain was from her mind.

Soon, she was urging him to move faster, her entire being overtaken by need.

"Oh. Oh. Oh," Esme repeated as the surroundings evaporated and all that remained was her and Ruari and the exquisite sensations.

Suddenly, she floated, the sounds of Ruari's grunts like music as Esme's body exploded into a million pieces. While drifting into a wonderful abyss, Ruari joined her, his strong body shuddering as he, too, found release.

ESME SNUGGLED AGAINST Ruari, her head on his shoulder. She kissed his jawline as he made lazy circles on the arm she tossed across his stomach. "I wish everything would stop and this moment would last for a long time."

"Me, too." Ruari pressed his lips on her hair. "In time, everything will settle."

"I cannot help thinking of Mother and what she must be going through and my dearest friend, Catriona. The poor dear."

He remained quiet, most likely because there was little he could say that would make her feel better.

In all probability, this would be their one and only time together and Esme wanted to take his scent and possession of her body with her. Nothing would stop her from going. It was up to her to save not only her mother, but the clan as well.

Esme trailed the tips of her fingers from Ruari's stomach down. They skittered through the trail of hair that directed to his, once again, hardened shaft.

Boldly wrapping her fingers around his sex, Esme pressed kisses to his chest, circling the small nipple with her tongue.

By the deep grunting sounds, he enjoyed her attentions and it sent powerful surges of heat through her as well. Although she wasn't quite sure how to proceed, instinctively she slid her hand up and down his hardness and licked from his nipple up to his throat.

"Ye are so enticing," Ruari pulled her over him. "Take me as ye wish."

He took her waist and lifted her to straddle him and then took himself in hand. "Lift up and lower onto me."

Arousal sent her mind reeling as Esme did as he instructed. The head of his sex prodded at hers and she took a deep breath and lowered slowly, allowing herself time to expand around him.

The power of controlling the joining was intoxicating and her mind swam as she flattened her hands onto his chest and began to lift and lower, taking him deep inside.

Ruari threw his head back, showcasing his powerful neck and wide shoulders as he allowed her freedom over his body.

"Faster," he grunted out, and took her hips to help her move. A trickle of fire traveled to where they joined and Esme lost control, lifting and lowering faster. Still, her body demanded more and her movements became erratic.

Ruari rolled her over and took control. Within moments, she flew into an abyss of lights as she shattered with a powerful release.

CHAPTER THIRTEEN

ALARMED CRIES WOKE Ruari and he jumped from the bed. He was still in Esme's bedchamber. After grabbing his breeches and yanking them on, he rushed to the balcony. From there, he spotted guards rushing to horses and he turned away, pulled on his boots and tunic and raced from the room.

Laird Fraser rushed to one of the lead guards and grabbed him by the tunic with fisted hands. "How can our guards be so incompetent? Was it not enough that my wife was taken?"

Ruari went to where his cousins stood and watched with blank expressions. "What happened?"

Ewan gave him a puzzled look. "Yer betrothed is missing. Gone."

Despite his attempt to hide any emotion, a low guttural sound came from him. "When? I was just…" he let the sentence hang.

By the look of the room, first meal had been eaten. How late was it? Then it occurred to him.

The drink. Esme had insisted he share a drink with her late the night before. It must have been laced with herbs that he'd slept so late."

"When was it discovered?" he finally asked, meeting his cousin's gaze.

"Just a few moments ago. A servant went to her bedchamber and discovered that she was not in the bed." Tristan gave him a pointed look. "She did say ye were there."

Ruari knew his eyes widened. "I think she gave me something so that I would not hear her depart."

The laird stalked to him. "Did she tell ye of her plans?"

"Nay. Although she kept insisting it was best to go and do as she proposed to marry whomever the Mackenzie decided so that he would release yer wife. She then plans to kill the man she is forced to marry."

"And ye allowed her to leave?" The laird's face was red with fury. "Why?"

"I was asleep. She gave me a drink." Ruari stopped talking. "I will go after her."

Laird Fraser looked to Tristan. "Will yer army go with us?"

"We will accompany ye but will not engage in battle. My brother sent us as a show of force and support. That is all."

After directing a glare at Ruari, the laird stalked away. Ruari let out a frustrated breath. "How did she manage to slip away? Did she take a horse?"

"I heard she left through a secret passage," Ewan said, following him to his chamber. "Where are ye going?"

"To fetch my sword," he replied, rushing up the stairs. "I will go after her. Ye and my cousins can come, but I do not expect any of ye to put yer lives in danger."

Ruari rode with the first contingent of warriors, led by Keithen, toward Mackenzie lands. He could not shake the feeling of responsibility. How had he not seen what Esme plotted? When she'd given him the drink, he was intoxicated with the aftereffects of their lovemaking.

Now, as he rode with the sun already high in the sky, he tried to remember how late it had been when they'd fallen asleep.

A rider came toward them from the west. "A horse is missing from a farm not too far from the keep."

Ruari nodded at the man. "How long ago did they discover it?"

"Early morning. The farmer went to feed it."

They'd lost almost a third of the day. Hopefully, as they rode warhorses at a gallop, they'd be able to catch up to a farm horse.

Behind them, five hundred men would follow, most from Clan Fraser. At the end of the day, blood would soak the ground and it was very possible the Mackenzie would lose. However, breaching the keep would be difficult for the Fraser Clan.

The keep came into view. The field was bare of any people, no riders or wagons in sight. To the right of the keep, the large village was quiet. The streets were empty as people had either gone into hiding at the keep or were locked indoors.

The Mackenzie expected a war.

They brought the horses to a stop. If Esme had come to the keep, she was inside now. There was nothing they could do but await the arrival of the Fraser, who would request a visit with the Mackenzie to negotiate.

It was either that or attack. If they attacked, the women inside would die.

Ruari's chest constricted and he fought not to growl in frustration.

Why had Esme not listened to him? The stubborn woman had forced her clan into action before they'd had time to discuss and decide a course of action.

"We will wait for the rest to come," Keithen said. Esme's brother looked to Ruari who kept his gaze on the keep. "I appreciate ye coming with me, but it is not necessary that ye fight."

"She is my betrothed. I will do what I can to save her." His stomach clenched at the words.

Keithen studied him for a moment. "It is up to ye."

"I will ride around the other side. Hopefully, there is a way for me to get in and search for her." Not waiting for Esme's brother to reply, he urged the horse forward.

The beast was glad to be out from the corral and was easily encouraged to a gallop. Ruari kept his eyes forward, scanning the surroundings for anyone that might spy him. He rode toward trees, from where it would be easier to approach without being sighted.

He slowed the horse and searched for any person patrolling the area. Finally, when he was almost too close to the keep not to be seen, he dismounted.

The vibrations from horses' hooves on the ground told Ruari that the warriors from Fraser lands neared. He let out a long breath. What could he possibly do to help?

There was no way to get inside the keep. The walls were high and, atop, guards stood with bows and arrows.

"Why did I end up with a stubborn betrothed?" he grumbled under his breath.

"I am not stubborn. I would describe it more as determined." Esme emerged from behind a tree. "I thought ye were a Mackenzie."

Her face was smudged, her dress torn and her hair askew, but a more beautiful sight he'd never seen. Ruari rushed to her and pulled her against him. "What are ye doing here?"

"I thought to approach the front gates but got scared they'd shoot me with an arrow. It is still fresh in my memory how that feels. So I came here to search for a side entrance." She pushed away from him.

He pushed hair away from her face. "And?"

"There is one door that can be reached, but it is locked." She gave him a defeated look. "Probably a secret escape that most wouldn't find, but I crawled under a bush to hide and found it."

"Yer father comes to speak to the Mackenzie. It would be for the best if he finds ye not to be inside."

Esme tugged at his hand. "Please come with me, help me get inside. I must do what I can to save Mother."

Branches breaking and horses' nickers were the unmistakable sounds of men approaching on horseback.

Ruari grabbed Esme around the waist and lifted her atop his horse, he then mounted and guided the beast away from where they were and deeper into the forest.

"Be quiet," he whispered to Esme.

They waited for a long while, listening intently. "Yer father and an army arrive. We will ride to them."

"No." Esme turned and looked up at him. "Please, I have to save Mother. If they come, the Mackenzie will kill her."

Although his heart broke, Ruari met her gaze and forced the words out. "Esme, listen to me. If ye go in there, ye along with yer mother and friend will die together. The Mackenzie is a heartless man. Stay with me, do not do this to yer father."

When she sagged and began weeping, he guided the horse back to where he'd separated from the others. They cleared out of the forest just as warriors exited the keep and lined up, the warhorses close together.

From a nearby ridge, the huge army of men approached from the south. They rode at a steady pace to ensure the horses were not overly tired.

When he joined the men he'd arrived with, Keithen gave his sister a warm look. She turned away, too angry to understand it was for the best that she be kept from inside the keep.

"What happens now?" she asked him. "We go to war against them? No doubt he has sent for the surrounding clans to fight alongside him. There is no winning for us. We will all die."

Her words were somewhat true. However, the Mackenzie was, in all probability, too proud to ask for help. Ruari prayed that was the situation in that moment.

"Come, we will go to yer father. He must know ye are not inside."

Moments later, along with her uncle and brother, the three sat atop horses. Esme had insisted she go with them to speak to the Mackenzie and, surprisingly, her father had agreed.

Ruari tried to argue against it, but the laird shook his head. "I wish to have her with me." When Keithen protested remaining behind, the laird held up a hand to quiet him. "Ye are to take over as laird if I die. Do not go to battle first. Obey me in this."

A sense of helplessness enveloped Ruari as he watched them ride toward the gates. The laird, Esme to his right and a warrior to his left. He and ten guardsmen rode just behind them. Would he be able to stand idly by if the lairds agreed that Esme would marry a Mackenzie?

The gates of the keep opened and a line of about twenty horsemen rode out. Then a second line joined.

The flanks of Mackenzie warriors parted to reveal Laird Mackenzie with two men. One of them was Calum Robertson.

Chapter Fourteen

Esme's heart thundered in her chest at seeing Calum on a horse beside the Mackenzie. The traitor had the nerve to meet her gaze and lower his eyes to her mouth. She snarled in return.

"I demand ye release my wife and the other woman." Her father's loud words seemed to bounce from the keep walls.

The Mackenzie gave them a droll look. "If ye concede and join my clan by marriage, I will. After all, she will be the future grandmother to Mackenzie bairns."

"There will be no concession. Ye have broken yer word too many times for me to trust anything ye say." Her father's voice trembled with fury. "Let us avoid bloodshed, Mackenzie."

The man looked past them to the huge assembly. He seemed taken aback, his sharp eyes narrowing. "Ye bring Ross warriors with ye? So ye have allied with them then?"

"I am married to a Ross now," Esme said, the words spilling out of her mouth before she could stop them. "Last night, our union was consummated." She met the laird's gaze, not wavering.

Esme fought not to look over her shoulder to Ruari.

When she slid a look to Calum, he'd paled. "I am Ruari Ross' wife now."

"Is that true?" the Mackenzie snapped, looking to her father who'd remained without expression.

"Aye, they came together last night, as husband and wife. We have witnesses."

Esme didn't dare look at her father. Was he aware that, indeed, Ruari had spent the night in her bedchamber? Certainly, Ruari had left her chamber upon awakening.

"Is that why he is here then?" The Mackenzie's shrewd eyes moved past her to Ruari.

The Mackenzie looked to Calum who swallowed visibly. "Why were ye not informed of this?"

"I left before it happened."

"Was a clergyman inside the keep when ye left?"

Calum nodded. "Aye." He lifted his gaze to Esme and then to her father. With a guttural cry, he pulled out a dagger and attempted to stab Mackenzie but was cut through by a warrior swiftly. With a shocked expression, Calum fell from his horse.

The Mackenzie looked down at the dying man and chuckled. "It seems I've been bested by a strong-willed lass. This time." He looked to the men behind him. "Bring the women."

"I hear ye are a brave young woman," the Mackenzie said, meeting Esme's eyes. "I would have been glad to have ye as part of my family."

He then looked to her father. "There will not be bloodshed today, Fraser. However, ye will soon see that an alliance would have been in yer favor."

When her mother and Catriona appeared, they were escorted by warriors who released them to run toward them. Catriona stumbled the entire time, seeming disoriented and unstable on her feet. Esme held her breath, expecting at any moment for an arrow to fly through the air and strike them. Only when both were lifted to horses by guardsmen did she let out a relieved breath.

Her father kept eye contact with the Mackenzie. "I would like to return to my clan and guarantee them peace, but I know ye will not cede this easily."

Laird Mackenzie shrugged. "I am not one to give up, however, I am also not foolish enough to fight a clan with a strong army behind it unless provoked."

"Is this a truce then?" her father asked. Esme held her breath.

Finally, the Mackenzie replied, "Aye." When his gaze moved to her, Esme knew he lied. The man was formulating what to do next as the word left his mouth. She looked to her father who seemed satisfied and wondered if she'd imagined the look. Surely the man would not speak the agreement in front of so many and then go back on his word?

As they turned away, she turned and glanced at the man again. The corners of his lips lifted. Her skin crawled.

Things were not over. Not by a long shot.

Halfway between Mackenzie Keep and hers, the Ross warriors split off and headed north. The Frasers from across the river continued forth. They'd remain for another few days before returning.

"Ye and I do not have to marry," Esme told Ruari. "I do not trust this will ever end. There is no need for ye to remain."

When his gaze met hers, there was uncertainty. "Is that what ye wish?"

"Does it matter anymore what anyone wants? There is no need for our clans to unite. The Ross has shown his support of my clan and that is ultimately all we can ask for."

"I gave my word," Ruari replied. Interestingly, he did not say anything else which made her wonder if he was glad for the reprieve.

"However?"

"There is no however," he replied and looked straight ahead. "Everything has already been decided. I see no reason not to go ahead and marry." Although he smiled at her, it did not reach his eyes.

"Ruari?" Esme reached over and touched his arm. "Once I see

about my mother and friend, I hope that ye and I can spend time alone to talk."

He nodded and met her eyes for a moment. He was so extraordinarily handsome, her heart constricted at the perusal. When she looked to his wide shoulders, all she could think of was how enticing his body was.

"Something does bother me," Esme told him. "The Mackenzie. He had this strange look when we left."

"He will move to another target. Someone else will raise his ire," Ruari said. "Do not worry overmuch."

Upon arriving at the keep, Esme hurried to her mother who, other than disheveled, looked to be unharmed.

Catriona, on the other hand, had obviously been beaten. Keithen had her upon his horse and lowered her gently to waiting men who then quickly took her into the house.

She raced after them. "What happened to her?"

No one answered. She directed them to take Catriona to a bedchamber just past the great room.

"Catriona?" She hovered over her friend as the healer came in.

"I did not think I'd ever return here." Catriona's voice was weak. Blood trickled from her split lip when she spoke. "I wish to die..." she swallowed.

"Water, please." Esme held a hand out to a maid who gave her a filled cup. She lifted Catriona's head to press the cup to her lips.

Esme moved away from the bed to allow the healer and his helper to see to her friend. Unable to keep from it, she let out a shaky breath to keep from crying out loud.

It was obvious what had happened. Catriona's dress was torn, her breasts exposed, her neck purpled with toothmarks.

"How could that man have allowed this?" she said to Keithen when he entered and stood as still as a statue.

Catriona let out a scream when her arm was straightened so that it could be splinted.

The rage in her brother's expression startled Esme. She'd never seen him so angry. "Whoever did this will pay with his life." He stared at Catriona's contorted, bloodied face and then stalked away.

Catriona's midsection was wrapped as one of her ribs was fractured and so was her right arm. There were cuts and bruises all over the poor woman's body. Dark purpling bite marks on her neck and shoulder told a horrible truth about how much had been done to Catriona.

The healer moved back and motioned to maids who waited with a basin of water and cloths. "Ye may clean her now. Ensure not to jostle her arm overly."

Esme returned to Catriona's bedside. Her friend whimpered, tears mixing with the dirt on her cheeks. The maids neared with warm water and cloths and they began to clean Catriona, who seemed to hurt with each jostle.

"There, there." Esme did her best to console Catriona and took a wet cloth to wash away blood and dirt from her face. "Ye will feel much better once the herbs take effect." Esme looked to a maid who tossed dirty water out of the window. "Bring more water and some whisky."

The young woman hurried off and Esme returned her attention to Catriona. "Ye are alive and safe now."

"Wh-where is my mother?"

"She was quite upset at seeing ye. I will send someone to fetch her once ye are cleaned up." By the shocking swelling of Catriona's face and so many injuries, she wondered if her friend's mother would pass out at the sight.

"Is there something ye wish to say?" Esme said to a guard who stood at the doorway.

"The laird wishes a word with ye."

"Go fetch her mother," Esme said to another servant and then turned her attention back to the guard. "Tell my father I will be there as soon as Catriona's mother is here."

The guard hesitated, his gaze going to Catriona and widening, his face became like stone.

ESME WALKED PAST a great room filled with villagers and straight into her father's study and stopped upon seeing her mother, who'd washed up, Ruari, Keithen and the local vicar. "What is happening?" She was tired and hungry and wanted to sleep. But she'd already planned to remain with Catriona. Now something else was afoot and Esme was not sure she could handle another problem.

HER FATHER MOTIONED her forward. "Ye and Ruari Ross will marry immediately. Upon the marriage taken place, ye will go with him to Ross lands."

Her legs wobbled and she reached out to grasp the back of a chair. "What? We'd agreed that I would remain here. Fifty warriors..." She stopped talking.

Of course. Her father, like her, had realized the Mackenzie had no plans to abide by the agreement. He would target both her and Keithen next.

"What about Keithen. How will he be kept safe?"

Her brother huffed. "I can take care of myself."

"I do not wish to leave. I will not leave. I can and will fight alongside ye both to defend our clan, our people."

She looked to Ruari, expecting that he'd support her. It had been his idea, after all, to move there and be with her clan.

Whatever he thought was hidden in the hazel gaze that met hers.

"Do ye not think it matters where I am? The Mackenzie can still send men after me."

Ruari shook his head. "Ross Keep is unbreachable. No one has ever been able to enter during an attack. Ye will be very safe there."

"This is not just about me," Esme cried out, too angry to keep from stomping her foot. "This is about what is right. How can ye allow that man to intimidate us?"

Her father slammed his fist on the table, making Esme jump.

"Enough. Ye will do as I say and hold yer tongue. Ye take too much liberty, Esme."

She didn't want to marry Ruari in that moment. Did not wish to be treated like an object and marry who was chosen for her, sent to live where they decided. No questions or regards for her opinion.

"We will go out there," her father said, pointing toward the great room. "A marriage ceremony will be held." He gave her a pointed look. "A ceremony without incident."

Esme clenched her teeth. "Do sheep protest going to slaughter?"

"Esme!" Her mother came to her side and grabbed her upper arm. "Cease at once. Ye cannot possibly compare what ye are about to do to what others have suffered in the last days."

There was pain in her mother's gaze and Esme realized something horrible had, indeed, happened to both her and Catriona.

"I am sorry, Mother."

"Shall we proceed?" the vicar asked, motioning to the doorway. First her father, followed by Keithen and Ruari walked out. She and her mother followed.

Murmuring began at their presence. Esme clutched her hands together to keep her trembling from showing. She kept her chin lifted, her gaze straight ahead, refusing to look anyone in the face.

It was a solemn night, after all. No one would celebrate. Injured men recovered in the adjoining halls, others were recently buried. Her dear friend lay upstairs battered and bruised, her own mother recently suffered a traumatizing event.

The vicar held his hands up to quiet those gathered and motioned for Esme and Ruari to come before him.

Never before had she felt small next to Ruari as she did in that moment. It wasn't so much his physical size as it was the entire situation.

Yes, she cared for him and was very attracted to Ruari, but they'd made a decision for her to leave and go away without ever asking her opinion. Her father was trying to protect her, that was true, but he knew she would rather die there fighting than to hide far away.

Ruari's hand enveloped hers and a ribbon was wrapped around them by the vicar. The warmth of his callused hand seeped up her arm and she let out a long breath.

They repeated the vows after the vicar, their gazes on one another, never wavering.

"I, Ruari Lachlan Ross, take thee, Esme Lenora Fraser, to be my wedded wife, to have and to hold from this day forward, for better for worse, for richer, for poorer, for fairer or fouler, in sickness and in health, to love and to cherish, till death us do part, according to God's holy ordinance; and thereunto I plight thee my troth." His voice remained strong and clear.

Even before speaking, Esme could barely keep from crying. This day, she knew, would come eventually. However, in that moment, every dream of how her wedding would be was dashed. She felt foolish that, as a grown woman, the thought of how ugly she looked would be the way she'd remember her wedding day. In a soiled gown, face etched with dirt from travel, hair askew, she was standing before her clan getting married.

In a quiet voice, she repeated the vows, each word like a needle scratching into her skin. "I, Esme Lenora Fraser, take thee, Ruari Lachlan Ross, to be my wedded husband, to have and to hold from this day forward, for better, for worse, for richer or poorer, in sickness and in health, to love and to cherish, till death us do part, according to God's holy ordinance; and thereunto I plight thee my troth."

The vicar gave her a warm look and blessed their union.

When Ruari leaned in and pressed his lips to hers, it shook Esme out of feeling sorry for herself and she looked into his eyes. "When must we leave?"

"At daybreak," he replied and squeezed her hand. There was no warmth in his gaze, nor did he linger at her side. Instead, he went to speak to the Ross men, probably instructing them to prepare for the departure.

Her mother neared and placed her arm around Esme's waist. "We must go and prepare yer belongings. I am told a cart will follow the party in the morning so ye can take as much as ye want."

"Mother, I am not prepared to leave. Catriona is still very ill and what about ye? I cannot bear to leave ye right now."

Her mother, as usual, had little opinion other than to cede to her husband's wishes. "It is not our place to deem what shall be done. We are to obey. Did ye not just recite vows? Ye are now beholden to yer husband and must do as he says."

"He's barely said a word to me." Esme blew out a breath. "I must go see about Catriona."

CHAPTER FIFTEEN

R UARI LEANED ON the corral fence. People were leaving the keep, heading to the villages before darkness caught them along the road. Horses were hitched to wagons and families loaded. Chatter was gleeful despite the lack of festivities. Each family had been given smoked boar and tarts that had been quickly cooked in the kitchens, which made everyone happy.

There was no light from Esme's window and he instinctively knew she was seeing to her friend. She would probably spend the night there.

The poor lass' injuries were extensive, and he understood that if it were his close friend, he, too, would prefer to be bedside than anywhere else.

Now that Esme would return to Ross Keep, there was much to consider. He did not possess a home. He'd spent his entire life inside the keep. First inside the home and then upon his thirtieth birthday, he'd decided to live in the two rooms behind the stables. Always a loner, he'd preferred the quieter space to that of the crowded keep.

The rooms were not a place for his wife to live in. Other arrangements had to be made.

"The men wish to speak to ye," his cousin said, motioning to the warriors and archers who stood huddled together.

"Very well." Ruari walked to the men. "I wish to thank ye for yer willingness to come with me here. For now, we will return to Ross lands, whether permanently or for a certain amount of time, I do not know for sure."

"We have something for ye," Ewan said and held up a sword that gleamed in the last of the sunlight. "Upon hearing of an expert swordmaker in the nearby village, several men went to fetch ye a wedding gift."

The weapon was astonishingly beautiful. Ruari reached for it, his hand trembling.

"Stunning," he said, holding it up. The men looked on with pride that echoed his own. His men, clan and family accepted him fully. No matter what happened to his parents, Ruari understood, in that moment, how lucky he was.

Once again, he looked up to Esme's window. Although she was a strong lass, she would be forced to leave her people and it would be hard on her.

"Thank ye all for this. I will treasure it always. She feels good in my hand."

There were crude remarks that made him chuckle. Men always found a way to turn every comment into a sexual reference.

Ewan remained behind after the guards all went in search of a place to sleep. His cousin studied the sky for a few moments. "Do ye wish to return?"

"No. I would prefer to remain here. However, I must keep my wife safe."

They stood together for a few moments, neither speaking. "Ye should stay." Ewan looked at him. "The Mackenzie will do the same whether ye are here or not."

"Yes, but Esme will be away from danger." Ruari shook his head. "Why are ye against departing? What does it matter?"

Both turned to watch the keep gates close for the night. After a moment, Ewan let out a breath. "It feels as if we're abandoning them."

Ruari considered his cousin's words. Is that what they were doing? The clans who'd come to show their support would also be departing. If the Mackenzie decided to attack again, this time, they'd all perish. Although fifty men did not represent a huge number, it was enough to help them hold their own until reinforcements arrived.

"I do not know what to do," Ruari admitted. "Without our men, they are vulnerable. I should go and speak to the laird. Perhaps it is best for us to remain."

"Do ye wish me to accompany ye?"

Ruari shook his head. "Thank ye, but it's best that I do this alone."

Upon entering the keep, only a few people remained in the great room. Off-duty guards settled onto pallets near the hearth and some servants scurried about doing last chores for the day.

"Where is the laird?" Ruari asked a lad who pointed toward the stairs. "He just went up."

Hoping to catch Keithen, he went to the laird's study and found the man standing next to a side table holding a glass of whisky. Upon seeing him, Keithen motioned to the decanter. "Help yerself."

"Am I to presume there will not be a wedding night for ye?" Keithen asked without expression.

"Yer sister is with her friend. I understand."

Keithen frowned into his glass. "Catriona seemed broken. The ride back here was the longest of my life."

"Ye have known her a long time then?"

After letting out a breath, Keithen nodded. "Since we were young. She and Esme have been friends since childhood."

"I am sorry."

"So am I."

Ruari poured whisky into a glass, lifted it to his mouth and drank. "I must speak to ye about our departure. I have decided it would be best if my men and I remain. By departing so soon after everyone else, it will leave the clan vulnerable to attack."

"Our main concern is keeping Esme safe. The Mackenzie is intent on her for whatever reason. Father could not bear losing her."

"I understand. I, too, wish to keep her safe. However, to what price? Repeating yer father's words. We cannot sacrifice the clan for one."

When Keithen didn't argue the point, Ruari knew the man agreed. There was no choice in the matter. If no one else could send their loved ones away to be safe, the laird shouldn't either.

Ruari went back out to find the guards. They would not be leaving in the morning.

⟫⟫⟫⟪⟪⟪

IT WAS LATE that night when Esme finally came to the bedchamber. She hesitated at the doorway upon spotting her husband. "Ye are still awake." She came to him and placed her head on his chest. "Catriona is sleeping. I came up to get a bit of rest."

It felt good to put his arms around her. Already, she felt familiar and comforting. "Ye must be very tired."

Esme peered up at him. "Aye. I will sleep for a bit and then get up and pack."

"We will not be leaving in the morning."

Searching his eyes, she frowned up at him. "When then?"

"Yer father is looking after yer mother in their bedchamber. I have not discussed it with yer father as yet, but I am considering not leaving at all."

Her arms went around his midsection and she held him tightly. "Thank ye. Oh, Ruari, thank ye so much."

Ruari chuckled and held her for a few moments longer. "Go to sleep. We will speak in the morning and then go to yer father together first thing."

Before he finished speaking, Esme rushed to the corner of the room and behind a screen to undress. She emerged in a nightshift and splashed water onto her face.

Turning to him, she motioned to his body, sweeping her right hand in the air in his direction. "I suppose we should consummate the marriage." The sentence was punctuated with a wide yawn. "At once."

"We can wait."

Esme closed the distance between them. "Please take yer clothes off, Ruari. I am so very tired and do not wish to argue about it."

"More romantic words I have never heard." Ruari undressed and then joined her in bed. He pulled her against his side. "If I were given the choice of wife and had to describe her, I am sure ye would be it."

"Mmm." Esme kissed his throat and then yawned into his ear. "Ye have never felt strongly about a woman then?"

"I remember as a lad, I fancied myself in love with a village girl. I think her name was Genevieve or was it Giselle? She was not very pretty. Actually, she was a bit of a cranky sort. But she shared her mother's sweet tarts with me…"

A soft snore made Ruari press his lips together to keep from chuckling. "No, perhaps her name was Lilibeth. I wonder what happened to her. Probably married with twelve bairns by now…" He let out a long sigh and wondered how many children he and Esme would be blessed with.

"SHHH." THE WHISPER so close to his ear woke Ruari. A moan escaped at the stroking of his rock-hard arousal.

"Esme…what are ye doing?" He grunted out the words while fighting not to release his seed. "Stop."

It was still dark outside and, yet, he had no idea how long it had been since he had fallen asleep. Reaching down, he removed her hand from his erection. "Ye should rest."

She rose and straddled him. "We will consummate our union tonight. It must be done." Her face was almost angelic as she peered down at him. "Are ye not willing? I will not take ye by force, if ye prefer I do not."

A bark of laughter erupted, and he pulled her mouth down to his. Only a hairsbreadth separating their lips, he whispered, "I am more than willing. It is just that I was about to find my release much too soon."

"Oh." She frowned and lowered her lips to his.

It was no use to attempt to wait. He was painfully hard and the need to plunge fully into Esme's delicious heat was desperate.

Rolling Esme to her back, Ruari pushed her legs apart and guided himself to her center. "I will do my best to be gentle." The stilted words were not in the least convincing.

***

HEADS TURNED TO them as Ruari and Esme walked into the great room. The gazes that followed their progress varied. Some with admiration, some with obvious contempt. The news of their departure must have spread already.

Guiding Esme to the head table, he lowered to an empty seat next to the laird, who gave him a quizzical look. "I must speak to ye," Ruari said in a low voice. "Can we speak in private?"

The laird shook his head. "This is nothing to discuss. Whatever ye have to say can wait now that I see ye did not depart as we had agreed. What are ye doing here?"

"Esme and I have decided to remain."

"I gave ye an order," the laird replied, his face tense. "Ye must take her…"

"What I must do is keep her safe. What about everyone else?" Ruari directed his gaze to the others in the room who were watching them. "Who is going to keep all the other women safe?"

It was a rebuke that could earn him punishment, he was aware. And although he doubted anyone could hear their conversation, he'd disrespected Laird Fraser in public.

"Are ye questioning my ability to keep my clan from harm?" the laird gritted out.

"I do not question yer loyalty to yer people. But I do think yer daughter should remain here to show that ye mean to keep everyone safe."

The laird turned to Keithen, who'd approached and stood between them and others in the room. "Both of ye, to my study at once." He stood and stalked away.

"I should come with ye," Esme said.

Ruari met his wife's gaze. "No. Remain here. Eat and then go see about Catriona."

After a moment's hesitation, she nodded.

He followed Keithen into the laird's study to find two head guards were in the room with a very angry Laird Fraser.

"How dare ye question my decision," the laird barked. "Ye were ordered to leave at daybreak, not to remain here and then make an entrance."

Ruari straightened and met the man's gaze. "I did not mean disrespect. But ye know I am right. Sending yer daughter away is not fair to yer people."

"Will losing her be fair? The Mackenzie will attack again. I have little doubt."

"Then why do ye not ask the other Clan Fraser to remain?" Ruari asked.

The laird blew out an impatient breath. "Because Mackenzie will take his time. He'll wait for us to become complacent. He assumes I believed him when he agreed to a truce."

"I have given my word to come live here, to bring fifty warriors to live here and support yer clan. Both of us know it is what is best."

When the laird began to argue, Keithen interrupted. "Father, we should wait. As ye said, the Mackenzie will not attack right away. Let us give people time to get over what just happened. If ye still wish for Ruari to take Esme away, then I will stand with ye."

Anger rose, but Ruari tapped it down. It was best to accept a small victory and, hopefully, have time to convince the laird to allow them to stay.

"Very well," the laird replied. "For now, ye can remain. However, I repeat, do not ever confront or question me in my own home."

Ruari wanted to remind the man he'd asked to leave the great room but, instead, he bowed his head. "I apologize. It will not happen again."

Keithen then spoke to the guards in the room. "Keep the conversation that was held in here private. A word of this comes to my ears and ye will be punished without question."

The men nodded, seeming annoyed that their loyalty was questioned.

The laird cleared his throat. By his expression, he remained annoyed. "Ensure the Ross men are given proper housing for now." He then met his son's gaze. "Send word to the village that we require builders to come and build a new guardhouse."

Finally, he directed his gaze to Ruari. "Once ye break yer fast, see that yer men are aware that they will come under my lead guards' command." He motioned to the first guard, a tall, lithe man. "Fergus is head archer." Then he nodded to the other man, a muscled, rugged man with a crooked nose. "Ivan is head guard."

The men met Ruari's eyes with challenging expressions, as if expecting him to argue the point. Instead, he looked to one and then the other. "I've already told them to expect a Fraser to be over them and that they are to obey without question."

The guards exchanged surprised expressions, came forward and shook his hand. The laird dismissed the guards and they left.

"Ye are part of my family and I do not wish to have any animosity between us," the laird began. "I am hopeful ye will be a good husband to Esme."

"I will do all I can to ensure she is safe and well treated," Ruari replied, unsure of where the conversation was headed.

The laird frowned. "I expect ye wish to work with horses."

Ruari nodded. "Aye, that is where my knowledge lays. If ye allow it, I would like to continue my work there."

"That is fine."

Keithen and his father exchanged looks and Esme's brother spoke next. "Will ye be participating in sword practice? I hear ye are quite accomplished in hand-to-hand battle."

"Aye, of course. I pride myself in my skills and swordsmanship and plan to continue to remain prepared."

"Good," Keithen said. "We shall run practice with the men after eating."

Together, the three men went back to the great room while speaking of what kinds of drills the men did at Ross Keep. There were puzzled looks from the people who'd obviously remained to see what would happen. Upon seeing that the three were amicable, most lost interest.

Esme was gone, so Ruari sat next to Keithen to eat. The air was heavy, death and destruction still very present. The familiar feeling of anger and hopelessness coated every surface. Just like at his own clan after so many battles with the McLeods.

The only thing that would transform things back was time. That knowledge reinforced his decision.

CHAPTER SIXTEEN

E SME PEERED THROUGH the window to note men lined up receiving sword fighting demonstrations. Keithen and Ruari stood before them, each taking turns sharing different techniques. Her chest expanded at seeing the two admirable men working side-by-side.

"What are you watching?" Catriona asked in a soft voice.

Rushing back to the bed, Esme's took her friend's hand. "It is the guardsmen, both Fraser and Ross practicing. Nothing to worry about."

Although they were still horribly swollen, Catriona was able to open both eyes. "I feel much better at the moment. Ye do not have to remain here all day."

"Yer mother had to go rest. She and I will take turns to ensure ye are not left alone for an instant. I cannot have ye needing anything."

A tear spilled down Catriona's cheek. "I do not know why I am here. Death would be preferable to living with what happened to me."

Her imagination had already filled Esme's mind with all sorts of horrible images. She did not dare ask Catriona to speak what happened out loud. Surely her friend was already silently constantly reliving it.

"Ye will not only live, but ye will be happy once again. I swear it."

Catriona's eyes closed and she let out a long breath. "It does not feel possible."

"Of course, it does not. Not now. I will be strong for ye, remain with ye always."

At this, Catriona opened her eyes and met Esme's gaze. What should have been white was blood red from being beaten. The sight made Esme want to look away in horror, to cry out in fury. Instead, she smiled at her friend. "What is it?"

"Shouldn't ye be gone by now? I thought ye said goodbye. Or did I imagine it?"

Esme shrugged. "Ruari saw reason. We are to remain here." She left off the part that they were not sure for how long. It was possible her father would change his mind and ask them to leave. "I am happy because I cannot fathom being away from ye."

At her friend's shaky breath, Esme's heart broke. If only there was some way to ensure those that hurt Catriona would pay.

"Perhaps I shall go to the village today. I can bring ye back something."

She continued when Catriona listened. "'Tis important for me to be among the people right now. Let them know I remain here."

Thankfully, during the last attack, the Mackenzie had spared the village, which was rare. More than anything, it made her more nervous. What if next time he wasn't as kind?

When Catriona's mother entered a bit later, Esme hurried out. Each day, she spent the morning with Catriona and the afternoon with her mother. As she neared the end of the corridor, Esme heard men speaking in low voices.

"Ye must find a way. I do not care how," a man said.

Although it felt wrong to eavesdrop, she stopped walking to listen.

"There are too many eyes. Someone will see me," another man replied.

Goosebumps formed on her arms. Were the men planning something horrible?

"Lady Esme, is there something I can get for ye?" A maid walked up to her and Esme shook her head. She hurried forward in an effort to get a glimpse of who had been talking. But upon reaching where the voices had come from, the corner behind the stairs was empty.

What had the men been referring to? Because of the hushed tones, she'd not been able to decipher who it was. She went to a guard who stood by the doorway. "Did ye see who was there a moment ago?"

The guard looked past her to the corner she pointed at. "No, Lady Esme. I only just walked up."

"Did ye replace someone? See two men walking out?" Esme was becoming frustrated.

The guard nodded. "A group of men walked out just now." He moved to look out and she did the same. "Them." The guard pointed out the men to her.

Esme studied the group. All were elderly. The group usually came to the keep for first meal. Then they'd meander about and return to the village. She was quite familiar with the men and was sure they were not the ones who she heard speaking. Knowing they'd remain for a bit longer, she hurried back inside to see who remained in the great room.

There were a few people milling about. Only one man stood out and she looked at him for only a moment so as not to rouse suspicion. The man was slender and looked travel-worn. He was speaking to a council member.

She then joined her mother and aunt who sat at a table with several village women.

"Good morning, ladies," Esme addressed the group. "Thank ye for seeing that Mother remains indoors for now."

Her mother waved her concerns away, although by the warmth in her eyes, she enjoyed the attention. "I am fine. Tis poor Catriona we should worry about." She held up her bandaged hand. "My wrist is already feeling healed."

The man she'd noticed walked to the front door. She followed his movements. "Who is he?" she asked her aunt who looked to see who Esme was watching. "He does not look familiar to me."

Her aunt shook her head. "So much despair. He comes representing several families who seek asylum."

"Do they run from the Mackenzie?" Esme asked.

One of the village women shook her head. "Nay. From another clan south of here."

Why was this turning out to be so frustrating? Esme hurried out to the courtyard and wandered to where the elderly group still remained. Listening intently, she pretended interest in the water well. None of their voices were like the ones she'd heard. The men she'd overheard had been younger.

Frustrated, she gave up and went in search of her father to inform him of what she heard. Esme hesitated. Or should she speak to Ruari? Being newly married, she wasn't sure what was the best course of action.

Her father and Ruari were cordial, but she knew there was an underlying tension between them since her husband had refused to leave. Although she understood her father's point of view, in this instance, Esme was glad Ruari had not yielded.

Lifting her skirts, she walked to the side of the keep where the men were practicing. Ruari stood with several men around him demonstrating a side slice. His muscular arms flexed as he swung.

At noticing his wife, he said something and walked to her. When their eyes met, she felt a rush. Her body's response was a bit alarming. There was fluttering in her stomach and Esme let out a breath that she wasn't aware she'd been holding and looked up at him.

"I must speak to ye about something."

His hazel gaze studied her. "I need a drink of water." They walked to a water-filled jar. Ruari dipped a cup into it and drank from it.

When he finished, Esme took his wrist and tugged. "In private."

Her husband allowed her to pull him away from everyone and out of earshot. Still, she looked around to ensure no one was near. "I overheard something troubling just now."

His brows creased. "Where?"

"I was coming from seeing to Catriona and, just before approaching the stairs, I heard men speaking in hushed tones. I heard one say to the other to 'Find a way, it has to be done'. The other then replied with fear about being caught."

"Do ye know who it was?"

"I did not recognize the voices. I would have been able to see them, but a maid called to me and they stopped talking and left."

Ruari's broad shoulders lifted and lowered. "It could have been a discussion about anything."

As much as she wanted to shake him, it would have been comical being he was so much larger than she. "It sounded ominous to me. What if they mean someone harm?"

"Guards are posted at the end of the corridor and at every entrance. If, for some reason, someone who means harm makes it past the gates, they will not reach any of the bedchambers."

What he said was true. However, the men were already inside. Whoever they meant to harm only had the guard at the end of the corridor for protection.

When Ruari cupped her face and lifted it, Esme was jarred out of her musings. "What do ye think we should do?"

"I am not sure. Will ye walk with me this evening? I wish to search the entire keep and know who is here for the night."

"Of course. It is a good idea. Not only to put yer mind at rest, but to be sure the only people here are trusted." He looked over his shoulder toward where the men who'd been practicing remained. "I will see ye at last meal." He caressed her face and went back to the practice field.

"Ye are proud of yer husband I see." A village woman whom Esme had never cared for sauntered closer. "Ye should be." The woman looked appreciatively to where Ruari was.

The woman, Alondra, had always been loose with her affections. Married to a guard for a short time, she and he now lived apart. Rumors swirled about the reason, which Esme ignored.

"Why are ye over here?" Esme asked. Usually only the guard came and went from that side of the keep. The area was used for practice and, many times, because the edge of creek ran close by, guards bathed in the open afterward.

"I bring soap and drying cloths for them. Yer brother hired me to do so. Ask him if ye do not believe me." With a basket on her arm, the woman continued past.

Esme rolled her eyes and walked back to the courtyard. Women like Alondra annoyed her. There were more important things to do than work so hard to catch glimpses of naked men.

Just then, she caught sight of Dot. The deer easily jumped over the corral fence and dashed to her. "Oh, dear Dot. I have been neglecting ye as of late, haven't I?"

Esme ran her hands down the animal's back, and it preened at her attention. Dot would never be free. It was much too trusting of humans. Although the young deer was skittish with others, it often followed Keithen about like a hound.

"'Tis a shame that we will not get to eat that one." The cook stood just outside the kitchen, a basket of vegetables from the garden at her feet.

When Dot hurried over and picked a carrot from the basket, Esme laughed. "Not only will we not eat her, but she will eat our food."

Eileen, the cook and head housekeeper, made shooing motions. "Away with ye, beastie. This is not for ye."

Unbothered, Dot wandered to the garden and sniffed at the plants. A maid screamed and shooed Dot away. The deer grabbed a leafy plant and slowly walked back out, which made both Eileen and Esme chuckle.

"I need to figure out how to keep her penned," Esme said. "She is unruly."

Just then, two guards appeared. They studied her for a moment before one of them spoke. "We heard a scream."

"My deer startled her." Esme motioned to the maid in the garden. "Everything is well."

Most of the guards were familiar with Dot's escapades. The same one looked to where Dot now grazed on green grasses. "Perhaps a pen can be built for her near the stables."

"That may not be a bad idea," Esme replied. As much as she hated the idea of Dot being penned, it was preferable to the animal roaming free and ending up in someone's pot.

As she walked away, the other guard spoke to his companion. "I wouldn't mind eating it."

It was the voice she'd heard earlier. A familiar voice that had sent chills down her spine. But why?

Walking slowly, she turned to look at the guards. They were somewhat familiar, one of them was a farmer's son that had been hired as guard recently. Going to fetch the deer, she considered what Ruari had said. The conversation could have been about anything.

"Miss Esme." The unfamiliar of the two guards caught up with her. "I can build the pen. Show me where ye would like it."

Esme let out a breath and relaxed. Everything that had happened lately caused her imagination to go too far. "I have a perfect place that Dot will enjoy. She can have the security of a pen, plus freedom to get out and graze. The corner behind the stables."

They proceeded forward, pausing only for a moment to discuss plans for sewing together later with a guard's wife.

Once they reached the appointed spot, Esme walked from a specific point to the back wall to show the men where she wished the pen to be.

One guard shook his head. "It will not do, Miss Esme. The deer can escape in this direction. What if we build it closer to there?" He pointed to an area further away.

Esme shook her head. "There is barely any sun in that area." She released Dot. "Pick a place ye'd like."

The deer wandered a few feet, leaped over the corral fence and began to graze. Esme chuckled. "I think it's best not to worry about it for now. She remains inside the keep and is safe here."

When she was snatched backward, Esme gasped. Had she about to be bitten by something?

"Do not make one noise," a harsh voice said, and she felt the prick of a knife's blade at her neck. The other man quickly gagged her and, together, they lifted her and tossed her over the wall.

Upon landing on the opposite side, all air left her lungs and Esme struggled to breathe. The men were already scrambling over the fence, but there was little she could do. It was impossible to move, her body reacting to the fall.

"Bring horses," one of them ordered, and began dragging her to low growing bushes. "I'll keep her here. Hurry."

The voice. She knew where she'd heard them before. It was clear now. They'd been the ones who'd shot her in the forest. All this time, they'd been there in the keep. Informing the Mackenzie of everything that occurred. Calum Robertson had not been the only traitor amongst them.

Esme's scream was muffled by her gag but she tried again and again. She rolled to her stomach and the guard lost his grip on her right wrist. Finally, she managed to get to all fours, but he was too strong for her and yanked her around the waist.

Esme reached above her head and scratched her assailant's face while, at the same time, kicking with all her might. Her struggles had some effect, but not enough. When he threw her to the ground on her stomach and placed his foot on the center of her back, it was hard to move.

Despite the situation, her mind remained clear. At the moment, Esme was breathless and unable to move, but she'd find a chance. Somehow, she'd wait to catch him unaware and fight more. The man was winded and breathed heavily. At least for now, he'd not been able to drag her farther away.

Hopefully, the other guard would be stopped and questioned when attempting to leave with more than one horse. She prayed one of the lead guards or Keithen saw him.

Ruari came to mind. Would he notice her absence? How long would it be before he started searching for her? Since she'd been spending so much time with her mother or Catriona, he'd not miss her absence. It was still hours until last meal and the men could have her far away by then. If they had planned to kill her, they would have done so by now. Obviously, they were taking her to the Mackenzie. But what if this had nothing to do with the feud?

What if they were taking her somewhere to kill her so that she'd not identify them as the ones who'd almost caused her death?

Her mind whirled and she did her best not to give up hope. When the other guard returned, it would be harder to escape. There had to be a way to distract the guard who held her hands fast. He'd not tied them, knowing she'd fight and could possibly get free.

It was just moments later that hope evaporated when the other guard appeared on horseback, pulling a second horse behind. The man looked around. "They will see her if ye put her on the horse. We have to get her away for a bit before ye can mount."

"It will look strange for ye to ride away with the other horse," the man who held her protested.

"We can cover her up."

They continued back and forth. The entire time, she looked to the wall. There were no guards atop the wall there because there was no way to get away except in one direction. They would have to pass where guards patrolled.

There was only one way out from that area because, on the opposite side, there was a steep hill that was almost impossible to climb on foot and horses could not traverse.

Esme wanted to smile at their predicament. However, a desperate person was also a dangerous one and she could only pray they did not decide to kill her then and there.

"We cannot leave her now. If we kill her, they will remember me coming out and heading here," the guard on horseback said, sounding distressed.

The one who held her grunted out in annoyance. "Help me bind her. I have an idea."

Esme fought but, in the end, could not win against two men. They wrapped straps around her, binding her arms to her sides. Then they collected thin branches and neatly placed them around her body until she was fully hidden. The two idiots grunted with the heavy load but, finally, she was atop one of the horses.

They spoke in whispers and she could not hear past the thundering of her heart. Soon, she was moving as the horse was guided out.

CHAPTER SEVENTEEN

R UARI WATCHED AS a guard walked in through the gates. He looked as if he'd just been in a fight. It struck him as odd when the man scanned the surrounding before rushing to the stables.

"Did ye see that?" he asked Keithen with whom he'd just been discussing the sword practice.

When Keithen shook his head, Ruari began walking toward the center of the courtyard. "The guard who just walked through the gates. He looked scratched up and seemed very nervous."

"Which one?" Keithen asked.

After Ruari motioned to the man who was now saddling a horse, Keithen frowned. "He is not married. He may have had an encounter with an angry woman."

Something about the man's actions seemed strange. From his stilted moves to the way he kept looking around and up at the guards on the wall. He then looked toward where Ruari stood, but then quickly looked away as if afraid of being caught. There was something definitely wrong with the guard.

"He is acting somewhat odd," Keithen admitted, his gaze pinned to the guard who tied the straps to the saddle. "I should speak to him just to ensure he is not in trouble." Ruari agreed, walking with Keithen to the man who jerked, startled upon their approach.

Keithen placed a hand on the horse's rump. "Where is yer horse?"

The man looked from Keithen to Ruari and then back. "John took it. We killed a deer and are taking it to his father's farm to slaughter."

Ruari recalled that, indeed, a guard had left with two horses earlier.

"Why did ye not build a stretcher for the deer and drag it there?"

"Very far," the man replied, his eyes narrowing. "Is something amiss? I am hurrying to complete this task so that I can return promptly to be atop the gate this night."

Keithen shrugged. "I suppose not. See that ye are back on time."

When the man rode out through the gates, the tightness in Ruari's gut did not leave. Warnings of something wrong would not leave him.

Unsure of what exactly to do, he rushed into the keep. After scanning the great room, he went down the corridor to Catriona's chamber. He peered in to find the injured woman and her mother both sleeping.

Then he ran up the stairs to his and Esme's bedchamber. It was empty. Finally, he went to the laird's bedchamber. The door was open to show no one was there.

In the sitting room across the corridor was Esme's mother and several other women sewing. "Have ye seen Esme?"

Lady Fraser shook her head. "When ye find her, tell her we are waiting. She promised to join us." The woman waved him off.

The more he searched, the stronger the urge to follow the guard who'd left. Where was his wife? He asked several maids, and none had seen Esme. After searching the kitchen and side garden, he raced back to Esme's brother who gave him a questioning look.

"Esme is missing."

No other words were necessary. Keithen let out a loud whistle and several guards came running. "Search the entire grounds. Find my sister."

More guards joined them as they rushed to the stables. Ruari called out to a head guardsman. "We need ten men to come with us. Close the gates and secure every entrance. Be vigilant in case this is a tactic by the Mackenzie to distract us so they can attack."

The guards dispersed to their posts with practiced precision.

Quickly mounted, Ruari and Keithen's horses galloped through the gates which were immediately closed behind them.

People raced away toward the village, some jumping on wagons after being warned to find shelter.

An overwhelming fear consumed him. Picturing how broken and near death she'd been just short weeks ago fueled fury like he'd never known. His wife was in danger, her life threatened, and he would never forgive himself if something happened to her.

In that moment, he became consumed with urgency that he had to catch the men because if they dared to hurt Esme, he would not rest until every single person responsible lay dead.

In the distance, the guard appeared. He turned upon hearing them and urged his mount to go faster.

"He is guilty of something," Keithen said as they gave chase.

By the way the guard guided his horse to run faster, he was an accomplished horseman. However, desperation would lead him to make a mistake.

When Keithen slowed, Ruari turned to look at him then noticed the man had pulled a bow from across his back. With precision, Keithen loosed the arrow that flew directly into the fugitive's side. The man fell to the ground, the horse continuing on without a rider.

They caught up to find the guard moaning and writhing on the ground.

Ruari barely set feet on the ground when he rushed to the man and yanked him up off the ground. "Where is she?"

The red-faced man winced and attempted to reach for the arrow. "Help me."

Instead of letting him go, Ruari shook him violently making his victim cry out in pain. "Where is my wife?"

When the man screamed, he realized Keithen had pushed the arrow through. "Ye best speak. I doubt Ruari will let ye live otherwise."

Young and barely able to withstand pain, Ruari realized the man was not an experienced warrior. He narrowed his gaze and pinned the now whimpering idiot. "I will run ye through with my sword over and again. I know exactly where to do it that will cause the most pain and not kill ye." He loosened his grip and the man fell to the ground. Then pulling his sword, he held it to the guard's throat. "I will only ask once more."

"Murray's farm. We did not mean to harm her. It was an unintentional..." he continued babbling, but Ruari didn't care to hear any excuses.

He stood over the hapless man and glared down at him. "If something happened to my wife, ye will die."

They had no choice but to leave the injured idiot there. Ruari considered killing him but did not wish to lose another second, which could mean Esme's demise.

Leaving the man on the ground, they rode off toward where he'd indicated.

It had seemed like many hours had passed but was probably only one as they neared the farm. In the distance, they spotted the horses that had been tied to a fence. One of the horses had a large bundle of branches on its back.

They urged the mounts to go faster than the already fast speed until arriving there. A farmer, who stood in the field, waved at them in a friendly manner.

Obviously, the man was unaware of what had happened. He headed closer to welcome them.

"Interesting day it is turning out to be," he said by way of greeting.

"First my son and then the laird's."

They dismounted and Ruari raced to the horse with the bundle, Keithen and the farmer at his heels. With his sharp dagger, he cut at the straps and, moments later, barely caught Esme from falling to the ground.

Pale and limp, she seemed to have fainted. Both he and Keithen quickly untied the restraints around her arms and legs.

"Esme?" Ruari tapped her face. As quick as a rabbit, she punched him in the center of his face.

"Esme, it is me." He barely got the words out when she hit him again. Her eyes widened. Finally seeing who she'd hit, she yanked the gag from her mouth.

"Where are they?" she said with a snarl and coughed.

Upon noting his sister was well enough to hit Ruari, Keithen sped off to find the other guard.

"I-I am not sure what is happening," the farmer sputtered. "I will get ye water." He then yelled to a woman who'd emerged from the house. "Get water, cloths." Worry was etched on his face, the poor man confused and obviously fearful.

Ruari pulled Esme against his chest. "I thought I had lost ye."

His feisty wife pushed away. "Ye should be going after them, not coddling me."

"I will watch after her." The farmer lowered to Esme just as the woman arrived with a pitcher of water. Her hands trembled so badly that water sloshed over the sides.

"Lady Esme. I cannot fathom what to say," she said in a trembling voice. "Ye poor dear," she continued while pouring water into a cup.

Feeling assured, Ruari ran to find Keithen. Around the back of the cottage, Keithen had the man pinned to the ground, sword to his throat. They'd obviously fought by the guard's bloodied face.

"Tell him," Keithen order. "Admit what ye did, ye coward."

The man swallowed visibly and looked to Ruari. "We were the

ones who almost killed yer wife. She was badly injured, and we thought she'd die. So we shot a second arrow into her so that she wouldn't suffer..." he stopped talking when Keithen pushed the blade deeper into his neck. A trickle of blood dribbled from the spot.

"Then ye ran away like cowards, leaving a defenseless woman to die and letting the clan think it was the Mackenzies."

"I accept my punishment. I can never face my father and guardsmen again."

Ruari drew his sword and stalked to the fallen man. "Yer punishment is death."

"No!" Esme, helped by the farmer and his wife, rounded the cottage. "His punishment will be to live with the label of a coward. Ten lashes and tied to a post for ten days in the center of the courtyard will be more than enough. Death would be too swift."

It was evident that, like him, Keithen struggled to do as Esme asked. Ruari gritted his teeth and finally lowered his sword. "If ye even look at my wife, I will not hesitate to run ye through."

"Get up!" Keithen ordered and prodded him with the tip of his sword. "Mount. We are returning to the keep immediately."

The farmer and his wife knew better than to intervene. "Thank ye for sparing his life," the woman said to Esme when Ruari neared to fetch her. "Ye are merciful."

"She may be, but I am not," Ruari told the couple who nodded in understanding.

Ruari lifted Esme into his arms and carried her to the horse.

"I can ride," Esme said, but he shook his head, quieting her. "Ye remain pale and unstable on yer feet."

He lifted her to his horse and mounted.

Esme relaxed against him. "I am also at fault, for not paying closer attention to my instincts. I felt something was wrong when they spoke to me and I ignored it."

"It will be best for ye to rest and not think of it," Ruari replied, unsure of what to say in that moment. His voice wavered at the last two words and Esme turned her head and laid it upon his shoulder.

"I knew ye would come for me and I was prepared to fight until ye came."

He chuckled. "Ye hit me pretty hard."

A shiver went through her and he knew she was considering the possible outcome. The two men meant to kill her and he knew that although they would think to have the light punishment of lashes, it was not to be.

UPON ARRIVING BACK at the keep, with both guards in tow, they were allowed through the gates. Keithen instructed for the prisoners to be kept in the courtyard, while Ruari carried Esme inside.

She looked over his shoulder to the courtyard. "I do not wish to witness their punishment. I know it is customary, but I will not do it."

"I insist ye remain in our chamber. Ye should bathe, have something to eat and rest. I will come to be with ye once this is all done."

Her mother rushed to them upon their entrance. The poor woman looked about to faint as tears streaked down her face. "Thank the heavens ye are alive," the woman wailed, hurrying to keep up with him as he climbed the stairs and up to their bedchamber.

He kissed her gently on the lips and lowered his wife onto the bed. She was immediately surrounded by her mother and other women who began to pepper her with questions.

"Allow her time to rest. She was taken by guards who are now facing punishment," he informed the women.

HE RUSHED BACK down to the great room just as Laird Fraser rushed out to the courtyard and Ruari followed.

In the center of the courtyard, both men were on their knees, hands bound behind their backs.

Ruari stood beside the laird who'd stopped and looked down at the men, both hung their heads, not daring to look up.

"Ye're cowards and there is no place for ye in my clan." The laird looked to the rest of the guards who were lined up and silent. "If any of ye ever dare to do anything against my family let this be a warning to ye."

He drew a jeweled dirk and stalked to the already bleeding man whom Keithen had shot with an arrow. Grabbing the guard's hair, he yanked the man's head back. "Ye are a coward and meant to kill my daughter." The cut across the man's throat was clean and swift. There was a shocked expression upon the man's face just as he fell face first onto the ground.

"Ye promised to let me l-live," the other blubbered. Ruari didn't wish to hear the squalling of a grown man. He went to the man and did as the laird had done, pulling the man's head back by the hair. "I never did. However, ye did take an oath to protect the laird and his family."

Seconds later, the man joined the first, their blood seeping into the dirt. A cart was brought, and the bodies quickly loaded onto it.

Several men neared with buckets of water, pouring it over where they'd bled. Soon after, it was as if nothing had occurred.

Keithen, Ruari and the laird went into the great room. They settled at a table and immediately were served ale.

Laird Fraser met Ruari's gaze. "Ye are a good husband to my daughter."

Unsure about what to say, Ruari remained silent, considering what to say if the man once again repeated that he and Esme should go live on Ross lands. He mentally prepared to argue against it.

"Perhaps it was a good idea that ye remain. Although I hate what Esme went through, I am glad to know the truth of what happened to her in the forest."

"They were wrong to be hunting without permission, and that is probably why they made such a horrible decision to leave her there to die," Keithen said.

"Fools," Ruari added.

The laird drank deeply from the cup and refilled it from a pitcher left on the table. "Ye are welcome to remain here if that is what ye wish." The man met Ruari's gaze. "I fear that my wife cannot withstand another blow at the moment. She is fragile from all that has happened and Esme leaving could kill her."

For the first time in his life, Ruari felt the fullness of his responsibility to a wife. He was to care for her and ensure that she would always be well and provide for her security and safety.

Glancing to the stairwell, he wished nothing more than to be with Esme. But first, he would go to the nearby creek and wash away the dirt and blood.

As they finished the ale, only he and Keithen at the table, Ruari met Keithen's gaze. "Why did ye not kill him at the farm?"

"I did not want his mother and my sister to see it."

Ruari nodded and stood. "Ye are a good man."

When Keithen's gaze met his, there was pride. "I am honored to have ye as part of my family."

CHAPTER EIGHTEEN

I T HAD BEEN several days since her harrowing experience and Esme was back to her routine. Putting down her sewing, she stood and stretched. Catriona sat in a chair by the window, but her gaze remained fixed downward. Shoulders rounded, her hair pulled back, she looked to have aged ten years.

The normally vibrant woman seemed to have lost all caring for life, her outlook as bruised and ugly as the bruising marring her face.

"Would ye like to go out for a walk?" Esme asked, forcing a bright tone. "It is a beautiful day. We can have a picnic."

"No. I would rather remain here." The reply was as lifeless as her friend. "Ye do not have to stay here so long. Go, please."

Esme settled into a chair and lifted up a basket. "I have been avoiding sewing and mending. It's best I do it while there is plenty of light. Would ye like to help?"

When Catriona looked to the basket, a spark of hope showed. But it was quelled when she turned to look back toward the window without reply.

The woman was broken, both physically and emotionally and there was little Esme could do. No matter what she tried, it felt like Catriona had died inside. Whoever this was that returned from being held captive was not the same vibrant and always happy person that had been there before.

"We have both been through much in the last weeks. Although I suspect yer injuries are much greater than mine," Esme said.

A single tear trickled down Catriona's cheek but, like usual, she remained silent.

The door opened and a maid entered with a tray. Upon it were glasses of honeyed mead, cheese and bread. Esme knew how much Catriona loved freshly baked bread, heat from it softening the cheese.

"Yer favorites," Esme exclaimed, instantly feeling foolish. "I am famished. How about ye?"

Catriona sighed heavily and accepted the small plate that Esme offered. "I told cook to send bread up as soon as it came out of the oven."

When Catriona took a bite of the bread without the cheese upon it, Esme wanted to scream in frustration. Instead, she ate from her plate and sipped the mead.

"I think walking outside may be good for me actually. I believe Keithen plans to go to the village today. I may go along. Or perhaps ask to take his place. Ruari and I can go. Although I am still quite sore and riding may be a bit too jarring."

As she talked, Catriona listened and ate the rest of the food on the plate. Being she'd barely eaten in days, Esme was glad to see it.

She continued talking after placing more bread and cheese on Catriona's plate. "I have decided it's best not to free Dot but to allow her free roam within the keep. I was going to release her and the little darling seems to realize it and has stayed in the corral for days. She spends so much time with the horses that she seems to think she's one of them."

Catriona didn't smile as she usually did when discussing Dot. Instead, she placed the plate on the nearby surface with food still on it. "Can ye call a maid to help? I need to lay down for a bit."

"I can help ye." Esme reached for her arm.

Upon touching her, Catriona recoiled. "Ye are hurt and sore. I prefer it if ye call someone else."

Frustrated and wanting to groan in desperation, Esme stalked to the door instead. She peered out and waved a maid who was sweeping the corridor to come. "Can ye help her? Remain here until someone else comes. Do not leave her alone no matter what she says."

Esme couldn't help the tears that rolled down her face. She went up the stairs and into the sitting room where Catriona's mother and hers sat. "We must appoint someone to remain with Catriona at all times."

Catriona's mother's eyes widened. "Did something happen? Why are ye crying?"

"She is the same," Esme replied, wiping the tears away with the back of her hand. "It hurts to see her so broken. I am worried. Her countenance is like that of someone who's given up on living."

"I feel the same," the woman replied with a sniff. "Her father returned home, but I asked to stay. I cannot bear to see her this way and will not leave her alone."

Lady Fraser patted Catriona's mother's hand. "We will find someone to remain with her. A cot will be set up in the room so that she is watched at all times."

"I will go see about it myself. There are several women from the village in the great room for hearings. I am sure one of them will know someone perfect for it," Esme told them.

Esme went back down the stairs. Her side ached a bit. She flinched at recalling the arrows piercing her body. On instinct, her hand shot out to the wall so that she could steady herself. If she reacted to injuries in that manner, how much harder would it be for Catriona, who Esme was sure had been beaten and raped by the guards at Mackenzie Keep.

The horrible man had released her to the guards without regard for her life. Why hadn't he kept both her mother and Catriona together? Although her mother remained shaken, it was obvious she'd been treated with a lot more care.

With careful steps, she descended to the ground floor and into the great room. Her father and brother sat at the high board and oversaw requests and issues brought to them by the clanspeople. There was a larger gathering than normal, most seeming to be there to observe. It was expected since they'd just been attacked. People were anxious to know if they were safe, to then return to the village or farms and spread the word.

At a table near the back was a table of all women. Leaving whatever issues brought them there to their husbands, fathers or brothers, they sat together and talked.

Esme neared and immediately everyone looked to her. One woman smiled widely, showcasing several missing teeth. "Ye are a hero. Bless ye, Lady Esme."

Another nodded with enthusiasm. "Truly a blessing from God. Ye save my husband's life. I am sure of it." The rest of the women nodded enthusiastically.

"I did what the rest of the guards and archers did," Esme insisted, not used to so many compliments.

"My Fergus says ye have the eye of an eagle and struck men down as soon as they stepped foot inside the gates," another woman said, looking toward a man who watched from a few feet away. "He says ye never stopped even after yer fingers bled."

It was a bit of an exaggeration, but Esme let it go, deciding it was best to let them speak and then changed the topic. "Thank ye for all the compliments. I am grateful for the brave Fraser men." She waited while the woman agreed.

"I am looking to hire someone as a lady's companion. Not for me, but for Catriona. Is there someone, one of ye know, who needs work?"

LATER THAT DAY, Ruari guided her past the kitchens and to the garden. Esme wondered what he wished to speak about, deciding to remain silent until they finally came to a bench.

"Ye should sit," he more ordered than asked. "I have seen ye going here and there for hours. Ye are not fully recovered as yet."

It would be easy to agree as it had only been three or four days, she wasn't sure which since her harrowing experience at the hands of the men who meant to kill her. Later, she'd found out they'd been executed in the courtyard. She was still angry at her brother for that. He'd seemed to have agreed with her request they'd be lashed and bound.

Esme glared at her husband. "I would like to go to the village. I need to see about the people. I must speak to several women about coming to work. Catriona requires a companion. This is not a time to be idle."

Instead of a reply, he sat on the bench and pulled her down to sit on his lap. When he wrapped his arms around her, it became impossible to move despite the loose hold.

"Can someone else not be sent to the village?" His indifferent tone grated on her already fragile nerves. "There are plenty of guards and others about. One can be sent."

She turned in his arms and, despite her annoyance, could not resist admiring the bright hazel eyes. "I wish to do it myself. They will not be able to know if the woman's temperament is what Catriona needs."

His hair had grown considerably since his arrival, now resting on his shoulders. She wondered if he preferred it long. Upon meeting him, it had been sheered, the brown waves tamed. Now they were wild, framing his handsome face without apology.

"Do ye prefer yer hair long?" she asked. By the lowering of his brows, the off-topic question had surprised him.

He shrugged. "I do not think about it."

"I see." Esme studied him. "I do not wish to be angry with ye.

There are things we must discuss. Can ye take me to the village so that we can have time alone to talk?"

He glanced around. "We are alone now. If we go to the village, I will insist on an escort."

It was understandable. The air still smelled of blood and battle. The threat of attack was still fresh and within the realm of possibility that it could happen at any moment.

"My friend needs help," Esme said, laying her head on his shoulder. "Why do I feel as if ye are unhappy right now?"

Ruari tightened his hold on her. "I am not unhappy with ye. I am frustrated at all that has happened. Despite the truce, we are all aware that a threat remains. I am angered that I was not able to protect ye from being taken. Ye could have died." His voice grew hoarse and he let out a long breath.

When she lifted her head and looked at him, her chest constricted. Ruari felt that he'd failed her, and it made her mad. The men who'd tried to kill her had caused damage to not just her physically, but her husband as well.

"I am glad they are dead then. Because ye are very important to me." Her breath caught at the words escaping.

The expression on Ruari's face was a combination of surprise and confusion. "Do ye mean that?"

"Aye," Esme said with a nod. "I care for ye, Husband."

He cupped her face and kissed her hard, his mouth hot and demanding. When he stopped and met her gaze, there was a softness to him she'd never seen. "Ye mean so much to me as well. When they took ye, I felt as if my world would end if anything happened to ye. I am thankful that ye are my wife, Esme."

Esme leaned forward, kissing him with the fierceness of claiming him. This strong, brave man was hers. He belonged to her, body and soul. And her entire being was his for life.

The feel of his body against hers was comforting and, at the same time, alluring. She pushed back and smiled at him. "Ye must come to bed early tonight. I do not wish to fall asleep without ye next to me."

Ruari nodded. "I am anxious to join ye, minx."

"Take me to the village, please." Esme slid off his lap and stood. "If we go now, we shall return in time for last meal."

"There is no talking ye out of it, so then we go. Allow me time to get a guard escort." Ruari pressed his lips to hers. "Go and fetch whatever ye need. We will take a wagon."

Satisfied, Esme rushed back inside to inform her mother and Catriona's mother. Since her father and brother remained engrossed in clanspeople business, she continued past the great room and up the stairs to find her mother.

After informing them, she stopped by Catriona's room once again. Her friend would never be the same. Of that, she was sure. But Catriona was strong and would recover. A part of Esme wished for a way to enact revenge, but this one time she feared her mother was correct. A woman had to know her place.

THE RIDE TO the village was uneventful. The perfect weather helped her spirits lift. Esme took a deep breath and looked to Ruari. "This is how our life should always be. Peaceful. Why is that horrible man so intent on destroying it?"

"I do not know. Men like him need no reason other than their need to be powerful."

Hatred raged inside her and Esme shook her head. "If he were to win, what would happen to my clan?"

Ruari's expression was grim. "I imagine he'd expect yer people to pledge allegiance or go. I suppose yer parents and brother would have to go live on Fraser lands across the river."

The fact that it was a possibility infuriated her but Esme decided to enjoy the moment.

When the village came into view, it was a pretty sight. Shops and homes lined up, people meandering about, some with baskets or carrying bundles of purchased goods, while others stood empty-handed, chatting in groups.

Shingles outside shops announcing what was sold there swung in the breeze as children raced in circles, playing games.

"Seems all is well here," Ruari said.

"Aye, it does." Esme motioned to the right. "We can leave the wagon there. The blacksmith will keep an eye on it."

Ruari assisted her down and she spoke to the blacksmith, introducing Ruari to the gruff man who managed a smile at her. They made their way to the village square.

"I must see how everyone fares." Esme hurried down the street, excited to see fresh faces after too many days at the keep.

Several vendors greeted her with enthusiasm. Once again, people repeated that she'd been a hero for protecting the clan.

At a stand where a woman sold beautifully embroidered linens, Esme lingered while picking several to purchase. The woman was quiet and gracious. "Thank ye, Lady Esme. This will help me feed my bairn and mother."

"Do ye not have a husband?"

The woman took a shaky breath. "He was one of the guards killed. Now, Mother and I are left alone."

Esme studied the pretty woman who wiped at errant tears. "How old is yer bairn?"

A smile stretched across the woman's face. "He is almost a year."

"Would ye and yer mother be interested in moving to the keep? We are in need of a companion for Catriona. The work would be simple and ye can eat in the great room daily."

The woman's face lit up. "I would very much appreciate it. I barely sell enough here to eat."

"What is yer name," Esme asked.

"Flora," the woman replied. "Flora Hay."

"Very well then. I will instruct guards to fetch ye when ye are ready." Esme looked to Ruari who remained a distance away and was inspecting other wares. "I am glad to have met ye."

"I as well." Flora reached for Esme's hand. "Thank ye."

"Do not thank me. Ye are doing me a great service. I was afraid that I would not find someone today and the need is dire."

"We shall be ready today then. Just allow me to pack these up and I will hurry to fetch my family."

As the woman hurried to do as she stated, Esme spoke to a guard who assured her that he and another would remain to assist Flora to travel to the keep.

She went to stand by Ruari, who'd purchased a dirk from the blacksmith's son. The small blade was beautifully crafted and fit in the palm of his hand. He handed it to her. "For ye."

Although it was a thoughtful gift, it reminded her of the need for protection that was necessary now. She smiled at him and sighed. "Ye are so kind to me."

They strolled to another stand, her arm through his and Ruari leaned close to whisper, "I wish to be more than kind to ye tonight."

A peal of laughter escaped her, making several people turn to look at them. Several people smiled toward them, approving of their light spirit.

Just then, shouts rang out as a man tried desperately to control the horses that pulled a large wagon. The beasts had been spooked and did not heed his commands. The large farming horses' hooves pounded the ground with force, sending vibrations as they headed in the direction of the square.

People scrambled to move out of the way as Ruari ran straight toward the wagon.

The surroundings lost their color, everything turned black and white and Esme lost her sense of balance. She fell backward, her newly purchased linens and dirk dropping to the ground beside her. Terror seized her as she grabbed the dirk and crawled to hide behind a water barrel. Her heart pounded and all she could hear were the echoes of screams and moans.

Still, nothing came into focus. Had she gone blind? Esme tried to scream for Ruari, but her voice caught. The only sound that came out was like a hoarse moan. Closing her eyes, she curled into a tight ball and waited for whatever was going to happen to end.

"Esme. Ye're safe. Ye're safe." Ruari's soothing voice permeated the fog in her mind and she began to sob as he pulled her up from the ground and held her up in his arms. "Ye're safe," he repeated again.

Feeling stupid at her reaction, she pushed her face into the base of his neck, not wanting to see how people were reacting to her hysterics. "I am so foolish."

Someone neared and whispered soothing remarks. Then another voice said something, but she could not make out what they said, too busy trying to get her thundering heart and sobs to slow.

"They wish ye well and say ye are very brave." Ruari's words made her cry harder until she could barely breathe.

"Look at me," Ruari said after placing her in the wagon and climbing up into it with her. "Esme," he said in a stern voice. "Stop at once."

How could he speak to her in that manner? She glared up at him but stopped crying.

With brows furrowed, he returned the look. "Ye cannot be upset over what happened. If ye wish to cry about being scared, I will not stop ye. But to cry because others see ye being scared, I will not allow it."

In truth, she had been upset over what others thought of her, instead of accepting that indescribable terror had gripped her.

"Do not tell my mother about this. She will worry."

Ruari nodded and helped her down from the back of the wagon and onto the seat. Once she was settled, he went to speak to the blacksmith and to pay him a few coins for looking after the horse.

164

Back straight, Esme sat with her eyes ahead until someone tugged at her skirts. A young, handsome boy held up her linens and the dirk. "Ye left these, Lady Esme."

Somehow she managed to smile and accepted the offering. "Thank ye. I did not realize that I had left even the dirk behind. I must have dropped it."

His cheeks turned pink as he met her gaze. "I wish ye well, Lady Esme."

Watching the slender young man walk away, she prayed that he and others that were not old enough to fight would be spared if ever the Mackenzie attacked.

The ride back to her home was vastly different. Instead of noticing the beauty of the surroundings, she was vigilant and tense.

Unlike her, Ruari seemed at ease. He handled the reins with ease, gently urging the horses forward, his attention ahead.

Then she noticed something. There was a pattern to his movements. Every so often, he would look to one side of the road and then to the other. He scanned the surroundings but never once changed his mannerisms. Outwardly, he seemed calm and unbothered, but if one looked closely, he was on guard and prepared. He sat tall with his sword within reach, back straight and gaze moving.

Seeming to sense her perusal, he looked at her for a long moment. "A warrior never leaves the battlefield without scars. Killing, even when defending yer home, leaves deep scarring that take longer to heal."

Esme swallowed and turned her attention to the road ahead. The truth of his statement fell over her.

>>><<<

THE CALMNESS AND normality of everything struck Esme as they entered the courtyard. Everyone went on with their chores and duties, the familiar happenings continued despite death and war. She squeezed Ruari's upper arm. "Remember not to mention what happened. My mother tends to worry, and she has been through a great deal."

Her husband nodded, his serious gaze traveling over her. "As have ye."

Leaning into him, allowing his strength to seep into her, she sighed. "And with ye at my side, it helps me feel stronger."

Once inside the great hall, she was greeted by the sight of her mother, Catriona's mother and her aunt, sitting at a table chatting. Lady Fraser waved her over. "I was worried about ye going off to the village. Honestly, Esme, ye need to remain home where it is safe." There was sadness in her mother's face that made Esme want to hug her tightly.

Instead, she smiled and spoke in a bright tone. "I felt a need for fresh air away from here. All is well in the village. I purchased these beautiful linens." She held the cloths up ensuring to keep the dirt-stained side away from their gazes.

Her aunt studied the cloths. "Indeed, they are quite lovely. Who made them? Was it Flora?"

"It was. And because she's recently lost her husband and is struggling to feed her bairn and mother, I asked her to come to be a companion to Catriona."

"Splendid idea," her aunt said.

Catriona's mother, although solemn, managed a warm look. "Ye have always been such a good friend to her."

"What if we plan a small celebration?" Esme's aunt exclaimed. "We have yet to observe Esme's marriage and there is the fact we won against that horrible man."

The last thing Esme wished to do at the moment was to host festivities, but she remained quiet to see what the other women would say.

Her mother leaned her head to the side in thought. "A small one of course, aye. I do think it would be good for us at the moment. We can invite a few people, mostly family." She smiled at Esme. "Ye do deserve a wedding celebration."

Everyone looked to Catriona's mother, who replied, "It may be just what is needed. Some levity. I agree."

When Esme remained silent, they waited. She let out a breath and nodded. "Of course, I would love a wedding party."

"Splendid!" Her mother came to life, jumping to her feet and turning in a circle to inspect the great room.

At the front of the room, her father, who'd been sitting with several council members in discussion, looked over at his wife with curiosity.

Lady Fraser motioned for several maids who were cleaning to come over. "Sweep up all the rushes and fetch lads to scrub the tabletops." When the maids hurried off to do as told, Lady Fraser then turned to the trio of women. "How many days will we need to be prepared?"

Her aunt tapped her chin while considering. "Five."

To hold back a chuckle at the arbitrary number, Esme pressed her lips together and shrugged. "Sounds perfect."

"Very well," her mother said and hesitated for a moment. She then came back to life and announced, "I will send someone to the village to fetch the seamstress. Esme requires a new gown."

As her mother and aunt hurried to the kitchen to give instructions for the meal that would be served, Esme sat with Catriona's mother. "I will speak to Catriona now. Explain what is to happen. I do not wish her startled or scared."

"Thank ye." The woman sighed. "I hope that, by then, she will be well enough to attend."

"Esme, what is going on?" Her father neared. "What has come over yer mother?"

"She is planning a wedding celebration," Esme replied with a smile. "There is nothing anyone can do or say to stop her."

He watched for a moment as additional maids walked in with brooms and buckets. "I am aware that once she sets things in motion, nothing will stop whatever it is she plans." Laird Fraser shrugged and returned to the men who waited with obvious curiosity.

Moments later, when Esme entered Catriona's chamber, she found her friend curled up in her bed, facing the wall, her body shaking, heart-wrenching sobs filling the room.

A red-faced maid rushed over. "She will not allow me near."

CHAPTER NINETEEN

MUSIC AND SONG competed with conversations during the marriage festivities. The great room had come to life with flowering branches over the entrances and on surfaces. Ribbons had been fastened to bouquets that were placed atop the high board. Women wore adornments in their hair and had taken extra care with their appearances.

Ruari, along with many guardsmen, had gone to the creek to bathe. Many of his men were anxious to meet single women from the village and other areas nearby.

As much as he wanted to celebrate, a part of him wondered if it was an opportunity for Mackenzie to infiltrate. Not even a season at his new home and, already, he constantly thought of ways the enemy could cause harm. It wasn't something he was used to. At Ross lands, he was part of a large and powerful clan that was rarely threatened. The last battles that had involved his clan, they had been the aggressors.

This experience was completely different. The burden of keeping a wife and her family safe weighed heavily on his shoulders.

"Is something wrong?" Esme asked as she studied him intently.

He shook his head. "No. It is nice to see everyone's enjoyment."

"Do ye dance?" His wife took his right hand with both of hers. "Dance with me."

The center of the room had been cleared for dancing and, currently, there were so many dancing that it would be hard to find a space. Ruari was glad for it as he'd only danced a few times in his lifetime. Only when around his family at Dun Airgid did he give in to prodding and join in reveling.

Unlike him, Esme moved fluidly, her feet in perfect time with the tune. As she whirled, he held her waist, enjoying the feel of her body between his palms. In that moment, both allowed themselves the freedom to enjoy themselves. Neither thought past that night and what it would bring. It was, after all, a celebration of their union as husband and wife.

Ruari nuzzled Esme's neck when she collapsed against him, breathless. He took her hand and led her to the side of the room to escape outdoors.

The cool air felt wonderful against their heated faces, but Ruari didn't take time to relish it. Instead, he pulled his wife against him and took her mouth with his. Esme wrapped her arms around his neck and when he deepened the kiss and cupped her bottom, she moaned.

"I want ye," she whispered breathlessly. "Make me yers, here, now."

There wasn't much privacy, but Ruari wasn't about to argue. He walked her just a few feet away into the shadow of a small tree. Once there, he lifted her, and she wrapped her legs about him.

Somehow, he managed to free himself while holding her against the keep wall. "Be still," he said when Esme wiggled with impatience.

Guiding his hardness, he thrust into her and she let out a loud gasp. "Oh."

While holding her in place, he moved his hips back and forth, sliding in and out of her as she nibbled at his neck. Her bites and nibbles made it hard to focus past the need to crest. Ruari wanted to stay alert to ensure they were not discovered. Anything more than what happened between them was forgotten when she flexed around him, her body constricting and loosening around his shaft.

"Mmm," Esme exclaimed. As she climaxed, she bit into his neck, the pain sending him to join her, his legs barely keeping them upright. Flashes of light formed as everything turned dark around them. It took Herculean effort to keep quiet as a second wave hit him so hard that, this time, he stumbled.

"Do not fall," Esme said as she attempted to put her legs down. But he held fast, still inside her.

Once again, he pressed against her and took her mouth as the last shudders of release ebbed. If he lived another century, he'd never tire of the way his wife managed to take him to realms he'd never known before.

Ruari broke the kiss and looked into her beautiful, brown eyes. "Ye are beautiful, Esme."

Her eyes widened and her lips curved, giving her the appearance of a satisfied kitten. "I…"

"Is someone there?" a woman's voice sounded.

Ruari withdrew and pushed Esme to stand in front of him while he fastened his breeches.

"It is Ruari and me, Aunt Dahlia," Esme said while smoothing the front of her gown. "We needed…fresh air."

The woman came into view, her gaze moving from Esme to Ruari. "I see. It is quite…pleasant out tonight." She looked up to the sky and Esme took the opportunity to run her hands over her hair.

"Yer father is about to toast to yer marriage before sending ye both off to bed." Esme's aunt gave them a dubious look. "I presume the wedding night may have already begun."

"Ah," Esme exclaimed and looked to Ruari who shrugged. "We were just…"

The woman chuckled. "I have lived long enough to know when a couple has just had a moment of enjoyment. Come along. I suggest ye take a moment to run yer fingers through yer hair, young man." The woman gave Ruari a pointed look.

Ruari couldn't help but grin as he did as he was told. Indeed, his hair was quite disheveled. "Let me look at ye," he said to Esme. Her cheeks had brightened to a hot pink. "Ye look perfect."

"I do?" She obviously didn't believe him. "Goodness, what if everyone suspects when we walk inside?"

"We have been married for more than a sennight. No one will be shocked that we enjoy each other."

With a huff, she whirled around. "I will enter first. Please wait a few beats before appearing."

"I did not know that I married such a pious young woman," Ruari teased.

Esme shot him a warning look over her shoulder and stalked toward the great room.

As instructed, he waited a bit before entering. When he joined Esme and her brother, Keithen's eyes were pinned to Ruari's neck. He then turned to Esme. "Ye should not bite him so hard when joining."

Ruari bit his bottom lip to keep from laughing when Esme's eyes grew wide and her face turned a startling shade of red.

"Honestly, Keithen, could ye not have said that in private?" she hissed and then elbowed Ruari. "Cover it up."

"I am not sure where it is. How, exactly, am I to do it?"

"Ugh!" She took his hand and pulled him toward the high board.

Cups where pushed into his and Esme's hands. The laird held his tankard up and spoke of marriage and vows.

Everyone toasted and the musicians began to play again.

"Thank ye, Father," Esme said and hugged the patriarch.

"I wish ye a life of happiness," Laird Fraser replied and then turned to Ruari. Like Keithen, his gaze focused on Ruari's neck. "Ye bit him quite hard."

Esme yanked at the neck of his tunic, but soon gave up. "Why can't ye cover it?"

⇥⇥⇥⇤⇤⇤

THE NEXT DAY, they woke entwined around each other. Bereft of clothing, Ruari slipped from the bed and washed his body from a basin thoughtfully left by maids along with drying cloths.

His head swam when considering how much life had changed. He'd opted for a simple life, choosing to live in rooms he'd built near the stables and spending most of his days training horses.

Now, a beautiful woman slept in his bed, a laird's daughter no less. Their bedchamber consisted of two rooms, each one easily larger than the two together that he'd lived in at Ross Keep.

The furnishings were beautifully crafted, the bedlinens soft. Although admittedly, he preferred Moira's cooking back at Clan Ross, the fare at the Fraser's home was good.

After dressing, Ruari went down to the great room to eat. His stomach grumbled with anticipation. Indeed, the night's activities had left him with little energy and much need for sustenance.

It was very early. A few revelers remained sleeping on the floor in front of the hearth or along the walls to keep from being tripped over.

At a table near the kitchens sat Laird Fraser and one of his council members.

The laird motioned Ruari over. "Join us. Break yer fast."

A maid rushed over and placed fresh bread and sliced meat before him.

Ruari ate while listening to the laird and the elderly man discuss what had to be done to move past the attacks. Listening to them, it was evident the laird was aware another attempt to invade was inevitable. It saddened Ruari that the small clan had to live under threat because of a ruthless power-hungry man.

"Are there other clans that are close who would form an alliance with ye?" Ruari asked the men.

"We have considered it. I plan to send messages to three others. But even combined, we are still not a match for the Mackenzie," Laird Fraser said.

The other man nodded. "The smaller clans prefer to remain on the outskirts of this. Two have but a handful of guards."

With a sword slung across his back, a guard approached. "There are Mackenzies outside the gates. They claim to have a message for ye," the gruff man said in low tones to not be overheard by those sleeping near.

"Call Keithen," Laird Fraser instructed as they stood. He then responded to the guard. "Keep them outside the gates until we are all outside."

The guard went back out and Laird Fraser met Ruari's gaze. "It will not stop, ye are aware?"

"I am." Ruari wasn't sure what the laird wanted to hear. That Ruari had made a wrong decision in keeping Esme there or that he wanted more support from Clan Ross? Perhaps both.

It wasn't long before Keithen appeared. Along with Ewan and the council member, they stood at the house's entry.

The gates opened to show a team of about twenty men. Only three rode through the gates. Surrounded by Fraser guards, the men dismounted and walked to the laird.

"Laird Mackenzie sends his congratulations and has sent a wedding gift to Lady Esme and her husband," the guard said in an even tone. The other guard lifted up a rolled tapestry, which Ruari took from him.

Upon meeting the man's gaze, there was only flatness.

"Is that all?" Laird Fraser asked, also in an even tone.

The guard shook his head. "He requests to meet for a discussion. Neutral territory three days hence."

The laird remained silent, considering the words. Keithen, however, took a step forward. "Why does he wish this? We want nothing to do with yer clan." His face twisted with fury. "Ye took innocent women and mistreated them. Ye took my mother. Why would we want to meet yer laird?"

The guard's face turned to stone. "I am here to give a message. Not to speak on behalf of my laird."

Keithen stood a hairsbreadth from the man's face. "Were ye there when Mackenzie guards attacked a defenseless woman?" He pushed his chest against the man's. "Were ye one of the group of cowards?"

"Enough!" Laird Fraser pulled Keithen back and looked to the guard whose face had reddened with anger. It was obvious the man fought hard not to argue with Keithen.

"Tell yer laird we will meet him at the appointed time." He then gave a specific destination. Ruari noticed the other men scanned the courtyard and he wondered if they were searching for someone in particular.

It was only after they stood atop the keep and watched the Mackenzie contingent depart that the laird seemed to relax. He'd sent a messenger to the other council members, the new constable and his brother, to come at once.

"We will have messengers prepared to go to the other Frasers at the ready," he said to no one in particular. "I know it may seem like a fruitless effort as they cannot continue to be at our beck and call. However, I am not sure what else can be done."

"Have one at the ready to travel to Ross Keep as well," Ruari said. "Perhaps we can seek assistance from the Grant?"

"He has remained neutral and I doubt there is anything for him to gain from joining forces with us. We are a strong clan and, combined, are strong enough to hold him off. Right now, it is a challenge for the Mackenzie, but I do not think he is willing to lose men to conquer us only to gain enemies that will constantly challenge him."

What the laird said made sense. Ruari wondered if perhaps after weighing the options, the Mackenzie sought a way to have a truce that would work to his advantage and not make him look weak.

THREE DAYS LATER, Ruari, along with the Fraser and several hundred guards, arrived at the appointed location. Both lairds had agreed to no more than two hundred warriors. From atop the ridge where they came to a stop, the opposing clan appeared. It seemed the Mackenzie had kept his word, his contingent the same size as theirs.

As customary, both parties advanced until the lairds were a few yards away. Then, along with four escorts each, they rode closer until they were able to speak.

Ruari, Keithen and two guards accompanied Laird Fraser.

The Mackenzie's shrewd gaze pinpointed Ruari for a moment before moving to Keithen and then meeting Laird Fraser's. "I bid ye good day."

"Ye as well," Laird Fraser responded. "Are we here to speak of a way to keep peace?" He went directly to the point, taking control of the conversation. It was obvious by the Mackenzie's tightening of his jaw that the move was not appreciated.

"I wish to discuss an equal alliance."

"Yer clan is much larger and more powerful than mine, we both know it. How would we be allies and I am guaranteed that ye would use it as a tool to take over?"

"By marriage. Yer son," he looked at Keithen, "to my eldest daughter. She has recently become widowed."

Ruari couldn't help but wonder if the woman's husband's death was coincidental.

"By yer son being married to my daughter, she would come to live with ye."

Laird Fraser looked at the man and then over his shoulder. "We are a strong clan. Our numbers may not be as great at yers, but we can stand against ye if we have to." He then looked to Keithen, who stared straight ahead, his features hard, the muscle in his jaw flexing with restraint.

Laird Mackenzie shrugged, acting as if he was nonchalant. However, there was steel in his gaze. "My offer will expire in three days."

"And then what?" Keithen said between clenched teeth. "Ye attack us again and again?"

Laird Fraser held up a hand to silence his son. "I must do what is best to keep my people safe..." he stopped speaking and his brow furrowed. "I fail to see what ye have to gain with this marriage."

"I am proving my willingness for peace between our clans. As ye say, yer clan, when combined with the Frasers of the east, is large and strong. I do not wish to continue any animosity between us."

That a change of heart would happen so soon after battle made Ruari suspicious. Like Laird Fraser, he also did not understand why the man was doing this. To offer his own daughter to a clan so small when not joined with the other portion made little sense.

"I will send a missive with a response to ye within three days," Laird Fraser said, meeting his opponents gaze. "I hope ye are sincere in yer offer. However, ye should understand why I cannot promptly give ye a reply at the moment."

The Mackenzie's chin jutted out as he considered his reply. "I have considered, after advisement, that an alliance rather than a takeover would be more advantageous to...my clan."

Ruari wondered if the man had started to say "to me" and realized it would reveal narcissism.

"As I said, a messenger will be sent to ye before the three days are up," Laird Fraser repeated. With that, they turned their horses about and returned to the ridge, the entire time aware that they had given their backs to the enemy. A very dangerous thing.

"WE MUST FIND a way to turn him down without causing a rift," a councilman said upon their return to the keep. They were in the laird's study, ten men sitting around a table. All had gone to meet with the Mackenzie but the conversation between the lairds was not repeated until there was no chance of being overheard.

"I will never marry a Mackenzie," Keithen said. "I do not care how much ye discuss it. Let that be clear."

"It would be best to turn the entire offer down, with some sort of mention of appreciation for becoming allies," a councilmember stated.

Laird Fraser's gaze turned steely when looking to his son. "Ye will do as I say and what is best for the clan. If I decide ye will marry the woman, then ye will do it."

"It takes a day to reach the Mackenzie keep. He chose three days knowing it cut our time to discuss to only two days at most," the leader of the guard stated.

Ruari cleared his throat. "I believe the Mackenzie is trying to save face. He does not plan to attack again. He realizes that we are too far for him to maintain control over even if he wins a battle. However, the man does not wish to appear weak before his people."

"I doubt any of his clanspeople care one way or another," the laird's brother stated. "Most are too busy carving out a living under his stringent rule."

Laird Fraser shook his head. "If the possibility of continuous peace exists, why would we not take it? The Mackenzie is not a sane man. He is always plotting. I do not trust him, but at the same time, if his daughter comes to live here, we can guarantee our people peace."

A loud boom sounded when Keithen pounded his fist to the table. "I refuse."

"I stand with Keithen," Ruari stated. "His offer comes with an underlying threat. Accept or else. Ye cannot allow it."

The laird's face turned red. He swung an arm, sweeping across the table, knocking glasses over as he got to his feet. "Once again, ye speak against me. Again in my home." He glared at Ruari who maintained eye contact. "Ye should leave immediately. I will not allow disloyalty."

He then pinned Keithen with a menacing look. "And ye will obey me. I am not just yer father, but yer laird."

With a hard push from the table, Ruari stood. He grew tired of the laird's constant back and forth of whether he should remain or not.

Fury filled him as he stalked out and into the courtyard, directly to the corrals. The dirt under his feet kicked up as he paced back and forth deciding on how he'd tell Esme he was leaving.

Keithen approached. "Ye should not leave. Allow him time to calm."

"I cannot remain. He has asked me to leave in front of witnesses. I will not take Esme, not at the moment. I must return to Ross lands and figure out what is best. Where we will live. I have land that I can build upon. Right now, I cannot take her with me. There is no time to plan. I will return for her as soon as possible."

Upon spotting him, his cousin, Ewan, came to where they stood. "What is happening?"

"Gather the men. We return to Ross lands immediately," Ruari growled. "We are no longer welcome here by the laird."

CHAPTER TWENTY

E SME STRETCHED. SHE'D been with Catriona all afternoon.
Although she couldn't wait to speak to Ruari and find out the
outcome of the meeting with the Mackenzie, it was best to wait to
discuss it alone once they retired for the night.

Currently, Catriona slept, her friend seeming frailer than ever.
Although she'd begun eating in the last few days, her countenance had
not changed. There didn't seem to be any wish to participate in what
happened around her. Most of the time when Esme spoke to her about
what was happening at Fraser Keep, Catriona would listen, but not
respond. Instead, she'd heave a heavy sigh and would rise from the
chair, limp to the bed, and lie down.

Just then, Flora returned from spending time with her bairn and
eating. The woman looked refreshed. She smiled at Esme. "I will
remain here for the rest of the day and night."

"I will ensure someone arrives early in the morning to allow ye
time to see about yer child and mother."

"Thank ye," Flora replied and went to the window. She pushed
open the shutters, allowing the last rays of sunshine in. "Miss Catriona.
It is time for ye to get up and walk for a bit."

It had been a good choice to hire Flora. She did not shrink from

Catriona's reluctance. Instead, the companion encouraged her to do more.

Once in the hallway, Esme considered whether to go to her chambers and rest before last meal, or to head directly to the great hall and search out Ruari.

Upon entering the great hall, it was evident something was amiss. The room was empty, other than maids who prepared the room for last meal. There were guards at the doorway, but it was strangely quiet.

The guardsmen appeared to be lined up outside and she hurried to the doorway. "What is going on?" she asked a guard.

"A reassignment of duties now that Ross has left with his men."

The words floated in the air, not making a bit of sense.

"What are ye saying? Ruari Ross left?"

"Aye, Lady Esme. He and the fifty men were sent away by the laird is what I heard."

Frozen in place, she attempted to process what the young man had said. Surely he was mistaken. Ruari would not have left without speaking to her and explaining why.

Despite the fact that her brother stood before the guards and was mid-sentence, she abruptly stood in front of him and looked up into his face. "Tell me why my husband is gone."

"Not now." Keithen pushed her aside none-so-gently. "Go inside."

Embarrassed and furious, she grabbed her skirts and raced back into the keep and straight to her father's study.

The laird looked up as she entered, his brow furrowing immediately. "Esme, we must speak."

"Tell me why my husband left."

"I will not tolerate someone undermining me and disrespecting my orders."

Her entire body shook with the realization that what the guard had said was true. Ruari was gone. "So ye sent him away?" She couldn't help screaming the words.

"I told him that I did not tolerate disloyalty and that he should leave immediately. How was I to know his lack of fidelity would include ye. Leaving ye behind only means he prefers to not be tied to our clan."

A ringing in her ears grew so intense that Esme had to shake her head. "I am leaving as well. Ye had never been like this, Father. Ye have always been fair and willing to listen to others' opinions. That ye refuse to now worries me."

"I am responsible for our clanspeople. The burden of keeping thousands of people alive weighs on me and only me."

"Nay. It weighs on our family. We should carry the burden with ye. But as of late, ye are not allowing it."

Her father's gaze moved from her to the doorway. He did not wish to continue the conversation.

Too angry to pay heed, Esme moved closer to where he sat. "If ye continue like this, things will only grow worse. See reason, Father. I am sure Ruari wishes for peace as much as ye. How can ye call him disloyal when he fought alongside our men? He rode with ye to see the Mackenzie and brought his men."

"I remain standfast in my decision. He stood against me in front of the council."

"Who else?"

Her father shrugged.

"My brother?"

"He is family."

"So is Ruari." Outraged, she shook her head as words left her. "I am disappointed in ye, Father."

HER MOTHER WAS in the bedchamber placing folded clothing into a truck when Esme burst into the room. "Do ye know what happened? Father sent Ruari away. My husband has gone."

"Of course, he did not. I am sure ye are misunderstanding things, dear." It was almost comical how unbothered her mother was at the news. Just days earlier, they had celebrated her marriage and at the announcement her husband was gone, her mother acted as if she'd just told her the weather was bonnie.

"I just spoke to Father." Esme spoke as slowly as possible despite her ire. "Ruari was sent away because he did not agree with Father."

When Lady Fraser let out a sigh, Esme hoped it was due to disappointment at her father. "Come sit with me," her mother said, placing the clothes down and moving to a pair of chairs.

Once they were seated, her mother took Esme's right hand. "Ye are much too outspoken for a woman. There are things we should not involve ourselves in. I am sure the situation will be worked out between yer father and yer husband. If he is really gone, surely, he will return promptly for ye."

"I cannot remain idle and silent, Mother. Father sent him away…"

Her mother interrupted. "It is yer duty as a Fraser to be loyal to this family. Ye may be a Ross by marriage, but yer loyalty rests here. I tire of yer outbursts and expectations. Allow yer father and the council to work this out."

Esme pulled her hand away and studied her mother. "How do ye do it? Remain so complacent throughout everything. Ye have no opinions other than what color thread to use or which meat is to be cooked. Our world changes around us and ye refuse to see it. Mother, open yer eyes. Please."

Tears trailed down her face as she stood and backed away. "I cannot fathom how ye can stand by and never have an opinion on anything. It is never our place to do anything according to ye."

Her mother stood and pointed to the door. "Go to yer chambers, Esme. Remain there. Ye are upsetting me."

"I am not a child to be sent to my room." Esme stalked from the room, deciding she'd speak to Keithen.

As she walked closer to her bedchamber, Esme stopped abruptly at seeing two guards at the doorway. "What is it?" She hurried closer to the men who gave her apologetic looks.

One motioned to the open door. "Go inside, Lady Esme."

Had Ruari returned? Confused, she hurried into the bedchamber. It was only when the door slammed behind her and the latch sounded that she realized her predicament.

Rushing to the balcony, she looked out. Everything looked normal. Guards were training, others stood atop the gates performing their duties. Maids hurried in from the well with water-filled buckets.

People meandered on the road to and from the village. Her eyes misted at the normality of everyday life. While her heart shattered at Ruari's departure, life outside continued.

Peering down at the courtyard, she searched for her brother. "Where is Keithen?" she shouted at a young lad who carried kindling toward the kitchens.

"I do not know, Lady Esme." He scrunched his face as the sun hit it. "Would ye like me to fetch him?"

"Aye, please. Hurry."

Moments later, Keithen stood outside and looked up at her. "I will speak to ye later. I have much to do." He frowned up at her. "What are ye doing?"

"Father had me locked in."

Keithen shook his head. "I will be there momentarily."

By the time Keithen came to the door, she'd grown tired of pacing. Already, she'd stood at the balcony, calculating ways to scale down and had inventoried which items she'd take with her upon leaving.

Her brother's large form filled the doorway. His dark gaze met hers for a long moment before he walked in.

"Ruari asked me to let ye know that he plans to return for ye."

Breath left her at knowing he did not plan to abandon her. "What else did he say?"

Her brother looked past her to the open balcony. "If ye wish to go to Ross lands, I will help ye. I'll send an escort of men to travel with ye."

Esme didn't need to think on it. "I must go, Brother. I cannot remain where my husband is no longer welcome."

"Ye must understand the burden our father carries. It was an outburst that he could not retract after speaking it in front of the council."

Esme crossed her arms. "So all of this is because of pride?"

"We must stand united. I may argue with him, but I will never go against what he considers best for our clan."

"Even if it means marriage to a Mackenzie?" Esme asked.

"How did ye know about that?"

"Maids hear things."

"I do not wish to marry a Mackenzie. We will find another way to remain at peace with them."

"So ye stand against Father in this." She crossed her arms. "How is that best for our clan then?"

Keithen sighed. "It takes time to find a way, Esme. Our clan's future depends on much. The continuance of our people living in peace is in peril." He went back to the door. "Prepare whatever things ye may need. Not much, as ye must travel on horseback."

"I wish to see Catriona."

Keithen nodded. "I will escort ye."

She studied her brother's handsome face, noticing new etches of worry on the sides of his lips and between his eyes. "Why do ye disobey Father in this, helping me? Then ye will obey him in something that will affect yer life."

There was a playful twitch to the corners of his lips. "Because I love ye, Sister, and wish the best for ye. Yer going to be with yer husband does not affect our clan."

CATRIONA STOOD BY a basin splashing water on her face. Most of the bruising was less noticeable that day. Her friend's beauty was returning.

"I must go," Esme said.

"What happened…" at seeing Keithen, Catriona whirled away.

"I will be outside," Keithen said. "Do not linger."

Esme hurried to Catriona. "I must speak to ye. I require yer help in something."

"What is the matter?" Catriona's eyes widened.

Esme told her about her predicament and plans to leave.

Catriona's breath caught and her eyes teared up, but she did not cry. "Ye are going away then?"

"Please see after my brother. He is caught in a horrible situation. I know ye are recovering and cannot speak to men yet. But please, I beg of ye, allow him to confide in ye."

"I am not sure…"

"Remember how when we were but children, ye and he would spend hours looking up at the clouds and would chatter for long moments? He is still that same person, Catriona. Ye and he are like family."

Finally, Catriona nodded. "Very well." Her friend hugged her tightly. "I will miss ye terribly."

"And I ye. I am sure we will visit each other once things settle."

Her friend's lack of emotion crushed her heart. The bastard Mackenzies had extinguished Catriona's zeal for life.

As they walked back to her chamber, Esme touched Keithen's arm. "Brother, promise me we will make them pay for what they did to her."

Although he didn't say anything, when his gaze met hers, a shiver ran through Esme at the darkness within. Keithen was not himself, either. Her brother was black inside.

They returned in silence until they reached her chamber. Esme took Keithen's arm. "I am not sure I should go. The travel with escort means I take men away that could be here fighting if our clan is attacked."

"Ye should go."

It was to keep her safe. Her brother wished her to be away from what would happen. There was no doubt in Esme's mind that the Mackenzie would attack. Her gut twisted at the situation. How could she leave at a time like this? Even though she was married to a Ross, her loyalty was to her family.

Esme sunk onto the bed. "What will happen to us?"

Her brother sat next to her and stared blindly forward. "We will continue to fight to keep our independence. Find out who is truly loyal to us and ensure to keep our people safe. With ye living safely at Ross Keep, that is one less thing I have to think about."

Leaning sideways, she nudged his shoulder. "Ever the watchful brother. I love ye so much."

Not one for displays of emotion, he stood and peered down at her. "Hurry and pack. We leave just before daybreak."

"Look after Catriona, Mother and Fa…"

At the lift of his right brow, she stopped speaking. Of course, he would.

"Look after yerself," she finished.

Keithen nodded and walked out.

Once she was locked in, Esme fought with the decision of what to do. How could she leave her people at a time like this? Although she couldn't fight, her archery skills were beyond reproach. When the Mackenzie attacked again, every single person that could fight would be needed.

She slammed her fists into the bedding and let out a primal yell. A guard opened the door and peered in.

"Go away!" Esme motioned to him with both hands.

Without Ruari there, the bedchamber felt empty. She glanced about the room, trying to decide what to take. Other than a few clothes, she wanted very little. Hopefully, one day they'd return and she would be able to collect more of her things. For the moment, she would do with as little as possible.

It was late by the time Keithen came to her chamber. She'd fallen asleep atop the bedding, fully dressed in breeches, a tunic and leather boots.

As soon as he shook her, Esme was fully awake.

Much later, the sky grew lighter as the sun rose and she rode away from her home and into an uncertain future.

CHAPTER TWENTY-ONE

"**Y**E MUST RETURN for her immediately," Malcolm Ross repeated to Ruari, who tried without success to eat. Upon arriving, he'd been too angry to eat and now, a day later, nothing tasted good. Not knowing how Esme fared filled him with guilt.

"I should not have left her behind," he admitted. "I will return for her today."

His cousin nodded. "I agree with not remaining there. Although I understand Laird Fraser being angry. Ye are part of his family and came there with warriors to help."

"A wife's place is with her husband's family," Elspeth, Malcolm's wife, interjected. "Otherwise, how is she to learn to become her own person?"

Knowing it was fruitless to argue with the woman, Ruari remained silent.

Malcolm, on the other hand, gave his wife a questioning look. "Her clan is in peril. They are constantly threatened by the Mackenzie."

"It is their battle to fight. However, I do believe the other Frasers should send a large contingent to remain with them. Why have they not done this?"

At her statement, Ruari and Malcolm exchanged looks. Ruari frowned. "Ye are correct. I do not know why they have not. Perhaps some sort of family discord."

"They need to work on it." Elspeth stood and leaned to kiss her husband's cheek. "I best go see what the bairns are up to."

It was heartwarming to note how his usually hardened cousin watched his wife walk away, a slight curve to his lips.

"I will leave now." Ruari stood and stretched. "Yer wife is right. Esme belongs here."

Malcolm nodded. "Who is going with ye?"

"I will take twelve. Although I do not expect any problems, there are always Mackenzies traipsing about. I do not wish to be taken to visit that man by force again."

"Very well. Take two archers. They often come in handy."

"Thank ye." Ruari met his cousin's gaze. "I will have to build a home on the lands left to me by yer father."

"Our father," Malcolm corrected. "He loved ye as his own, equal to Tristan, Kieran and me."

"And I loved him the same." Ruari had to clear his throat. The late laird's death was still too real and raw.

AS HE AND the twelve men crested a nearby ridge, in the distance was a rider, escorted by warriors. Long, burnished brown hair had escaped its trappings and blew around her head like waves. The rider lifted a hand at spotting him and was immediately surrounded by six warriors. They did not fly a banner, nor did they wear a tartan identifying who they were.

His cousin, Ewan, came alongside Ruari. "Friend or foe?"

"It doesn't matter, they are a small contingent. We should probably avoid them."

Ewan shrugged his broad shoulders, the bow and arrows on his back moving with the action. "Fly our banner," he instructed to one of the warriors.

They lifted up the red banner with three lions and rode forward. It was then the lone rider took off, urging the horse to a gallop toward them. The escorts seemed to be caught off guard as they gave chase.

Ruari began laughing.

"What is so funny?" Ewan asked.

"That is my wife and she is furious."

URGING HIS OWN mount forward after asking the warriors to remain behind, Ruari dismounted and waited for Esme to near. He braced himself for what was sure to be a loud, verbal bashing.

She practically leaped from her horse, the action admirable and he would have told her so but the punch to his jaw sent his head reeling sideways and he stumbled, caught unaware.

"I will not be left behind. Ye left without a word!" Esme screamed and swung again. This time, he was able to avoid the strike. "How could ye?" She kicked him in the leg and Ruari bit back a curse.

"Stop hitting me," he snapped. "I was just now heading back to fetch ye..." He stopped speaking when she slapped him so hard his ears rang.

Grabbing her hands, he held her in place. "Do not dare kick me," he warned. "Allow me to speak."

Her eyes were glossed with tears of either anger or hurt. Probably both. "How did ye expect me to remain there?"

"I should not have left ye. I have no excuse for it, other than being angry and acting rashly."

Ruari pulled her against him and held her tight, realizing how being away from her for just a few days had felt like an eternity. "I am very sorry."

Pushing away, she took a step backward. "Escort us to the Ross Keep. We have ridden without stopping and are tired and hungry." Her face remained proud and his heart melted. His beautiful wife did her best to keep from breaking down. He understood. She'd brought men with her who were there to ensure her safety while, at the same time, she was responsible for them.

"Ye have a warrior's heart," he told her, cupping her jaw. She immediately slapped his hand away.

Although they rode back side by side, Esme kept her gaze forward and didn't speak to him.

Finally, Ewan came alongside and gave her a warm look. "How fares yer friend?"

Esme let out a breath. "Much better. She still refuses to leave the bedchamber. She will never be the same, I fear."

"I believe women have a fighting spirit and are stronger than us in that manner." Ewan met Ruari's gaze sending a clear message to give them privacy. Although Ruari wanted to remain next to her, he understood.

For the next hour, he remained annoyed that the conversation between Esme and Ewan continued unabated. They spoke of the area and he explained to her who lived at Dun Airgid. Esme listened and asked questions about the villagers and other things pertaining to life around Ross Keep.

Every so often, she'd peer over her shoulder and spear him with a glare. In turn, he gave her apologetic looks. He'd not continue apologizing. His wife would have to accept it.

UPON ARRIVING AT the keep, pride filled him as Esme's eyes rounded at seeing the massive gates and huge stone building within. Ross Keep was perhaps three times the size of her home and housed many more people.

Men and lads hurried to help with horses. Ewan began instructing the men to see about finding the Fraser guards a place to rest. Everyone was invited inside to the great room where they'd be fed.

He took Esme's elbow and escorted her to the main doorways just as Malcolm and Elspeth appeared.

"My cousin, Laird Malcolm Ross," Ruari said by way of introduction, "and his wife, Lady Elspeth Ross."

Malcolm nodded in acknowledgement. "Welcome to yer new home, Lady Esme."

Unlike her formal husband, Elspeth rushed forward and took Esme's hands. The women were almost the exact same height. "Come inside, ye must be exhausted and famished. I will ensure to have a hot bath prepared for ye immediately. Upon eating, ye must bathe and rest."

"I am very tired and hungry," Esme admitted, allowing Elspeth to guide her inside. The women went into the keep leaving Ruari only to stare at his wife's departing figure.

Malcolm studied him for a moment and chuckled. "By the cut on yer lip, she is not happy with ye."

"Not in the least," he replied, giving his cousin a bland look.

ESME SLEPT MOST of the day with Ruari keeping constant vigil. When night fell and she'd yet to speak to him, he slid into the bed and reached for her.

Although she was half-asleep, she turned away from him. Ruari groaned in frustration and lay on his back, staring up at the ceiling. Once morning came, he'd have a talk with his wife and settle things.

SUNLIGHT STREAMED IN through the window and Esme stretched. She opened her eyes and was immediately confused at the strange surroundings. Her heart settled at recalling she was now at Ross Keep.

How long had she slept?

There was movement as the wind blew the window coverings. Ruari stood at the opening, looking out. He was dressed already, his broad back to her as he studied the view.

Esme couldn't help taking him in. He was so handsome and strong. He moved with the grace of self-assuredness, despite his muscular build.

Instead of raving or yelling, he always kept his voice even. She recalled with guilt having struck him the day before. Instead of hitting her back, which would have been in his rights, he'd restrained her and spoken in low tones.

"What do ye see?" she asked, sliding from the bed.

He turned to her, his hazel gaze questioning and then back to the view. "A large group from the village comes. I assume there is something important they wish to discuss with Malcolm."

"Yer laird is much younger than I expected," Esme said. "Does he carry the burden well?"

Ruari nodded. "Aye, he does. I am proud of him."

When she neared, he instantly put his arm around her and pulled Esme to his side. Together, they looked out and she was astounded by the difference between Ross lands and her family's. There was a large loch to the right, next to it a huge field of colorful flowers. In the distance, farms were visible as well as a thick forest.

"How far is the village?" she asked.

"Not far, just an hour or so," Ruari replied and looked to her.

Immediately, she focused on the cut on his bottom lip. Too proud to admit she'd been wrong to hit him, Esme met his gaze. "I am still angry with ye."

He responded with a light kiss to her lips. "And I am still sorry to have left without speaking to ye."

Unable to keep from it, she wrapped her arms around his waist and placed her head on his chest. "I wish to always be wherever ye are."

He hugged her close. "Me, as well."

"Get dressed, it is late. I do not wish to miss first meal."

Upon entering the great room, she was once again astounded at the sheer size of the keep. There were over ten tables, all with people eating. At the high board, there were three men in addition to the laird. Ruari motioned to the table. "The one next to Malcolm is Tristan, who is second born. The one next to him is Kieran. He is the youngest." Both men were huge and attractive. Kieran however, was astoundingly stunning.

"The older man is my uncle, Gregor, advisor to the laird."

"Do their wives not sit with them?"

"Aye, they do for most meals." Ruari looked to a table on the far side of the room. "They sit over there at the moment."

The women sat around a table chatting and laughing. The laird's wife, whom she'd met the day before, waved her over and she looked to Ruari.

"They are probably plotting something."

Esme nodded at Elspeth to let her know she'd be there shortly.

The strength and power of this clan made her realize the difference between Ruari's family and hers. "No one would dare attack yer clan," she told Ruari "This clan is powerful."

Ruari shook his head. "Power and size do not always mean safety, Wife. Someone killed my uncle despite being escorted by guards and on our lands."

He escorted her toward the table of women. "I am glad to meet the women who live here," Esme told him. It was best she find out what her new life would be like and what duties she'd be expected to perform. Not one to remain idle, she would ensure to do her part as well as continue to maintain her archery skills.

"We shall greet them, but I prefer ye sit with me this morning."

Esme ate with gusto. The food was flavorful and well prepared. When she finished her food, Ruari slid a tray closer, so she could refill it. "The cook performs wonders."

"Aye," Ruari said with a grin. "Moira is one of a kind."

JUST AFTER FIRST meal, Ruari went out to inspect his land. Although his mount remained somewhat rebellious, the beast seemed to accept that Ruari was just as stubborn and kept a steady pace to the land that had been left to Ruari.

It was not too far from the keep and a bit farther from the village. Many of the trees had been cut down as that area had been used to harvest wood for building and fires. It was understood that, one day, it would be built upon, so the clearing would make it easier to do so.

Still mounted, Ruari studied the area, mentally picturing where it would be best to build.

He'd never actually planned to use this land. Although his uncle had always insisted it was his birthright, a part of him wondered that if things had been different, would the land have been his father's instead.

Thinking it was an illusion, he leaned forward at seeing smoke. If someone traveled through and had a fire, then he'd allow it as long as the person or persons did not plan to remain.

An old cottage they'd often used when hunting sat amongst the trees. From the chimney, a thin, wavy trail of smoke escaped. Ruari let out a breath. Whoever was there had to be evicted immediately unless they'd received the laird's approval. Malcolm had not said anything about giving someone permission, so it was probable the person was a squatter.

He rode closer and dismounted. Then taking his sword from its sheath, he approached with caution.

"Who is here? I am a Ross, show yerself," he said and knocked on the door with the hilt of his sword.

There was a cough and shuffling. "I have every right to be here." The voice that replied was hoarse from misuse or being infirmed.

Finally, the door opened, and a tall man emerged. Immediately,

Ruari recognized him. The person's appearance took his ability to speak away and Ruari took two steps backward.

"Ye. What are ye doing here?"

Somehow, despite not seeing the man since he was very young, he knew instinctively who he was.

Everything inside Ruari demanded action. His hand tightened around the hilt of his sword and he snarled in the direction of the man who'd left him and his mother many years earlier. This man had let everyone believe he was dead. His own brother had died without ever knowing that he lived.

"Leave at once." Ruari held the sword up when the man took a step toward him. "Turn around, get yer things and leave. This is my land."

Conor Ross straightened to his full height and gave him an angry look. "I won't allow ye to speak to me…"

At the slash of Ruari's sword too close to his throat, Conor held both hands up and took a step back. "I returned because I heard of my brother's death. I had to see for myself if it was true."

"It is true. Now, go." Ruari hated the trembling of his legs.

So many years of wondering, of not knowing if the man lived or died, only to find the man in the hunting cottage. Ruari had gone so far as to suspect his own mother of killing him. And now the man had the gall to act as if he had rights to the land they stood on.

"I will go. But first, ye must know why I left."

"It matters not. Ye are not my father. I do not care."

"She told me ye were not mine, that ye were fathered by my own brother. Yer mother laid with him." Conor jutted his chin in the direction of the keep. "I confronted Robert and he admitted it." The man spat on the ground. "It was his responsibility to raise ye. That is why I left. I was cuckolded by my own flesh and blood."

"Stop."

Conor shrugged. "It is the truth. I had to leave. It was that or kill my own brother."

The words sunk into him and Ruari's chest constricted. He did his best to swallow past the bile that rose in his throat.

"Liar."

Conor met his gaze without wavering. "It is the truth. Ye are Robert's son. He admitted to it. I could not see past my fury. I wanted to do so many wrong things. That is why I left. Ask her, ask yer mother."

Ruari's hand shook and he considered whether to end the man's life then and there.

Conor held up both hands and took several steps back. "I will leave. I was here only for a few weeks. I had to rest. I've seen ye here and there and have to say, despite yer paternity, I am proud of what ye have become."

Without another word, Ruari spun and went back to the horse. He mounted and rode away, not in the direction of the keep, but north to where his mother lived.

"WHAT AGAIN?" HIS mother gave him a bleary look of someone just awakened. "Go away."

"He has returned," Ruari said, knowing she would understand whom he spoke about. "He is not dead."

Blood drained from his mother's face, her eyes widened, and she gasped. After taking a beat to compose herself, she finally spoke. "Why should it concern me?"

"Is it true?" Ruari's voice shook. "I am Robert Ross' son?"

This time, she let out a hard breath, her eyes bulging. She pushed at his chest. "I said go away!" she screamed. "Go away!" Lifting trembling hands to her face, she rubbed her eyes and turned her back.

The subject would not be dropped until he learned the truth. He stalked forward and rounded her. "Tell me."

"He should have left her and married me. But he did not. Instead, he tossed me aside. Sent me away." It was evident she was not speaking to him, but more to herself. "The bastard should have remained. He should have remained and looked the other way. Everyone does that. Everyone has secrets."

She continued to babble about secrets until Ruari took her by the shoulders and shook her. It was as if he scalded her skin and she hissed, "Do not touch me."

"Is that why ye left me? Because I am Robert's son? A reminder of yer adultery?"

His mother came to life, hitting him on the chest with fists and kicking at his legs. "He knew I married his brother to be closer to him. He knew it and when I came to his bed, he allowed me. He used me. So ye are his. Only his. Not mine."

Although her logic made no sense, Ruari finally understood. It wasn't hatred that his mother felt for him. She did not feel as if he were hers to begin with. For some strange reason, the knowledge settled him.

"I will let ye live in peace and never return." Ruari walked out the front door. For some reason, he was feeling lighter than he'd ever felt.

BY THE TIME he rode toward home later that day, it was dark. He was much too exhausted to continue. Ruari knew Esme would be angry with him, but he couldn't bring himself to face anyone. His mother had confirmed the truth. He and his cousins were truly brothers. It was ironic that he and Malcolm had just spoken about how he'd been like a brother to them.

The true reason must have been that the late laird had not been his uncle but, in fact, his father.

After pulling his mount to a stop, Ruari walked for a while and then lowered to sit with his back to a tree. Overcome with emotions, Ruari ran his hands down his face. Once he rested, he'd return to the keep. Although he would have preferred to remain away for longer, it wouldn't be fair to Esme.

He'd keep the truth of his paternity to himself. Better to leave things as they were. There was no reason to bring up the truth of his birth as it mattered not at this juncture. His cousins had always accepted him, and he was an integral part of the family. For that, he was grateful.

Moments later, the moon helped him stay on the path that lead him back to Dun Airgid, his home.

CHAPTER TWENTY-TWO

I T WAS LATE when he finally trudged into the main house. Very few people were up and about in the great room when Ruari entered. Those who'd decided to remain for the night had found places along the walls and in corners to sleep. Upon noticing light coming from Malcolm's study, he lumbered there, hoping to find his cousin alone.

Luck was with him. Malcolm sat at the table reviewing accounting ledgers.

When Ruari went to the sideboard and poured whisky, his cousin, no, his brother looked up.

"I would like one as well," Malcolm said. "Have I told ye I detest reviewing accounts?"

"Aye, I remember. Ye always made excuses to leave the room when we were tutored."

There must have been a strange timbre to his voice because Malcolm studied him with a furrowed brow.

After accepting the glass, the laird motioned for him to sit. "Where have ye been? Yer wife was worried."

The strong liquid formed a heated path down his throat. "I went to see my land and found the place where I would like build. Someone was there. Conor Ross."

Malcolm's brows flew up. "What is he doing here?"

"Claims to have heard of yer father's death." The words stuck in his throat. It was also his father who'd died.

"Does he wish to remain?"

Ruari rolled the glass between his hands. "I told him to go."

"Father searched for him for years."

"I remember."

"Did he say why he left? Why was he gone so long?" Malcolm asked.

Unable to meet Malcolm's gaze, Ruari focused on the glass between his hands. "Nay, he didn't say why he left. And I don't know why he was gone so long."

His cousin stood and placed a hand on Ruari's shoulder. "I cannot dare to know how ye feel. But know that my father loved ye as his own. Ye had no need for Conor Ross."

"What ye say is true." Ruari let out a breath. "I am tired."

Guilt that was not his to bear made it hard to think clearly. That the man had lost it all, wife, land and clan, because of a betrayal was not fair. Perhaps it was up to him to do something.

"Ye should seek yer bed," Malcolm said. "Yer wife will be glad to see ye."

"I would like to discuss this more in the morn."

Malcolm nodded.

As he trudged up the stairs, his body was heavy with the weight of what he'd learned that day.

ESME WAS INSTANTLY awake when Ruari entered the bedchamber and she sat up. Her husband pushed the door closed behind him and heaved a long sigh.

"I was worried," she began, but stopped at noticing he'd yet to lift his head. "Did something happen?"

Slipping from the bed, she went to her husband.

The expression on his face when he met her gaze was inexplicable, a collision of anger and something else. It was as if he'd seen something horrible. Something or someone that had pushed Ruari to the edge of madness.

"Ruari, tell me what happened?" She gasped when he yanked her forward and took her mouth with so much demand, it took her breath.

"Allow me to fuck ye." His voice was as gruff and coarse as the words.

Need surged through her with force, the foreign sensation sending waves of heat through every limb.

Instead of a reply, she nodded.

Madness circled them like birds of prey. The sounds of harsh breaths and tearing of clothing filled the air to mix with the aroma of arousal.

"Ah!" Esme called out when Ruari bent her over the nearest table. She wasn't sure what he would do, but she did not resist.

"Spread yer legs for me." She did as he commanded, her sex constricting with expectation. When he prodded at her entrance, she held her breath only to let out a cry when Ruari thrust in, filling her with one hard push.

The slaps of their bodies colliding, flesh against flesh and Ruari's grunts were like music notes to her senses. It was all Esme could do not to lose her grip on the edge of the table while not becoming lost in the moment.

On he continued, pulling out and driving in, his fingers digging into the soft flesh of her hips.

With an animalistic growl, he pulled out and then took her into his arms and dropped her on the edge of the bed. "Lay back." His eyes were dark with arousal, his beautiful body gleaming with perspiration.

The sight of his aroused state made her want to touch him, but instinctively she knew it would not be welcome. Instead, she lay back. Ruari pulled her legs over his shoulders and then, once again, pressed against her entrance.

"Take me," Esme encouraged.

The lovemaking was not gentle. Once again, he moved in and out of her, each thrust hard and deep. One plunge followed by the next.

He did not look at her, but straight ahead, seeming lost in the moment, giving his body control.

On the edge of a crest, Esme arched up, her body contorting as she fought not to lose control. It was inevitable and she screamed as waves of darkness slammed into her. Thrashing without a reason other than the climax was almost as terrifying as it was delicious.

Ruari had not stopped the sensual assault. His powerful body now out of control, the drives harder and faster, his groans filling their chamber until he began to shake, his release seeming to be as powerful as hers.

When he fell forward, Ruari was careful not to crush her. Both of them fought for breath, gasping for what little air managed to get into their lungs. Esme's sex continued of its own will squeezing Ruari's manhood as if trying to draw every bit of his seed.

"I cannot breathe," she finally managed to say, pushing at his shoulder.

He moved, barely, his broad back shuddering. Esme began to ask that he move again but then stopped at realizing he was crying.

Unsure what to do, Esme rubbed his back. That her husband had been upset cut through like a fiery blade.

Whoever had done something to wound him would pay. She waited quietly until he blew out a breath and silently moved fully onto the bed to lay on the pillows. She crawled up from the edge and snuggled against him, placing her head on his shoulder.

"Whatever happens, I am with ye." She was glad her voice sounded even, despite the anger at whoever had said or done something that hurt her husband.

"I saw him today," he began. His voice was hoarse with emotion. "The man I thought to be my father."

"Yer uncle's brother, who ye thought dead?" Esme scrambled to remember what she knew about the man. Other than him disappearing and Ruari's mother then leaving him to be raised by his uncle, Ruari had never said anything else.

"Aye. He was on my land. He claimed to be here after hearing of his brother's death."

Esme remained silent, instinctively knowing Ruari was trying to figure out things as he spoke. His voice was gruff, each word tearing at her heart.

"He told me that I was not his son. That I was Robert Ross' bastard. All this time, I thought the laird was my uncle. Now...I am not sure what to think. How to feel. He is dead."

Ruari let out a long sigh and met her gaze. "Do not speak of this to anyone. It is best for my cousins not to know."

"Mayhap he lied. To explain his absence."

His throat moved as he swallowed visibly. "After...after seeing him, I went to speak to my mother. She said it was true. That she'd seduced her husband's brother, slipped into his bed one night when his wife was gone. She admitted to having wished to marry him instead of Conor."

They lay in silence for a long moment while Esme did her best to soothe his pain away with kisses to his jaw and throat. He leaned his head to hers in response.

"Malcolm was right."

"In what way?" Esme asked.

"He told me to come to ye. That ye would help calm me."

Esme lifted and looked down at him. "Just as I am here for ye, I expect ye to be there for me as well."

Ruari nodded and hugged her against his broad chest. The hardness of his body filled her with security and calm.

>>>>><<<<<

RUARI ROSE EARLY the next day. Leaving a sleeping Esme, he hurried down the stairs. After not finding Malcolm in the great room, he went to the study.

Malcolm looked up as he walked in. "I am sending a group of men to ensure Conor Ross leaves."

Just then, Ewan walked in. He went directly to Ruari and placed a hand on his shoulder, a simple show of support that made Ruari take a sharp breath to steady himself.

Malcolm held out what looked to be a coin sack. "Give him this. It should be more than a fair price for his portion of the lands. Tell him never to return."

"I should go as well," Ruari said, but Malcolm shook his head.

"Nay. That man does not deserve to see ye. He abandoned not only ye, but our clan."

Ruari wasn't sure what to say. If he disclosed the truth, that Conor had left after being betrayed by their father, it would only cause pain to Malcolm and his brothers. Nothing good would come of it.

He shrugged. "Very well." Then turning to Ewan, he said, "Tell him I am thankful to have been left to live here with my family."

With a curious look, Ewan finally nodded.

After the man left, Malcolm studied him. "Tis for the best, Ruari. He is no longer part of our clan."

"What if he had a good reason for leaving? We do not know everything. He could have had a disagreement with…"

"We should go break our fast," Malcolm interrupted, obviously doing his best to change the subject. "I am famished. There is much to do today. I require yer help."

IT WASN'T MUCH later that Ewan returned and Ruari braced himself for whatever message came back for him. His cousin seemed nonplussed. His manner was relaxed when he motioned to Ruari to come away from the people who sat about the room. Esme had yet to appear as he'd kept her up most of the night. They'd talked and made love again. The second time had been gentler.

"He wishes ye well. He has a family on the western shore near Dornie. A wife, two daughters and a son."

The news made him feel better. "I am glad for him."

Ewan slid a look to the front of the room. "Are ye going to tell them?"

That Conor had shared the truth with Ewan wasn't surprising. His cousin had a way that made people comfortable.

"No. It is better they do not know about the betrayal. What good will come of it?"

"Ye are their brother. Do ye not think they deserve to know?"

Ruari shook his head. "I have always been treated as such. The knowledge would not change anything. Even the land left to me by Robert Ross is the best on our lands, near water and forest. He may have supposed, of the four of us, I'd be the one not to live here and would need a place where I could sustain a family. My father did his best to ensure I never lacked for anything."

Finally, after thinking, Ewan nodded. "I will keep the secret. But I remain steadfast in the thought that if I were them, I would like to know that I have a brother like ye."

Ruari chuckled. "Are ye jealous, Cousin? Jealous that I am not yer brother?"

"Ha," Ewan replied with a look of annoyance. "It is good enough that we are cousins. I do not care for any more brothers."

CHAPTER TWENTY-THREE

"HOW LONG DID it take before yer husband said he loved ye?" Esme asked Elspeth. Weeks had passed since moving to Ross lands and she'd begun to feel comfortable in her new home.

Joined by Elspeth's friend and companion, Ceilidh, they walked through the flower field just outside the gates.

"I feel as if he does. But he has never said it," Esme continued.

"Men are not vocal about such things as feelings," Elspeth replied.

"Ye should ask him," Ceilidh interjected. "'Tis best to be direct."

Esme frowned. "Ruari and I talk about everything. Perhaps ye are right. I should ask him."

"Is it not strange how we require them to tell us how they feel about us?" Elspeth asked with a chuckle. "Have ye told him how ye feel?"

At the question, Esme tried to figure out if she'd actually spoken the words. "I remember telling him he was more important to me than life."

Ceilidh clasped her hands in front of her chest. "In that moment, he should have responded with a greater declaration."

"True," Elspeth added. "He should have."

"He said he cared for me deeply, as well."

The women's expressions told her they found the response lacking.

After collecting flowers, Esme felt better. She missed her parents and Catriona terribly but could see that living with the Ross Clan meant a life of peace.

And yet, knowing her own clan was under threat made it hard to settle. She looked to Elspeth. "Where is yer family?"

The woman's lips curved. "Not too far from here. They live in a small village, Kildonan." She motioned with her arm past the forest. "In that direction. Ceilidh's family lives there, as well."

Esme frowned. "Mine is so far. I am constantly worried for their safety. If they are attacked, there is no way for us to get there in time to help. Two days' journey without stopping is much too far."

Elspeth studied her for a moment. "Ye should not live in fear. I am sure yer father will have come up with ways to ensure the safety of the people."

"By marrying my brother to one of them," she grumbled. "I hope it does not come to that."

In the distance, a rider approached the gates. After speaking to the guards, he was allowed in. Esme hoped it was a messenger from her family and letters from her mother and Catriona. Yet, she forced a slow pace not wishing to be disappointed, but instead to remain hopeful for a bit longer.

"Two letters for ye," Merida, Tristan's wife, said, motioning to the table where she sat with a babe on her lap. "The messenger is in the kitchen about to be fed."

Unable to keep from it, Esme dropped her flowers on the closest table and rushed to pick up the parchments. She then went to sit by the hearth to read in private.

The first was from her mother. The letter was overly bright and pleasant, which made Esme suspicious. Catriona's letter was a contrast. Her friend told her of the tensions in the keep. How guards were on edge. Her companion, Flora, kept Catriona abreast of all that happened, which implied her friend had yet to leave the chamber.

Esme's breathing quickened at news that Keithen had been gone for two days at the time Catriona wrote. The excuse had been that he'd gone hunting. But like Esme, Catriona was suspicious of her brother going hunting alone when their clan remained under threat.

What if he'd been taken by the Mackenzie? If that horrid man hurt her brother, Esme vowed to kill him herself. It was hard, but she continued reading.

> As soon as I learn more about Keithen, I will send a missive. Although I am hesitant to believe he has been taken, I am fearful of the true reason for his absence.
>
> I miss ye and am hopeful that ye have found happiness with yer new husband and in yer new home.

Esme closed her eyes and considered how different her life was and yet the cloud of the Mackenzie's threat hung over her head even there, from so far away.

Just as she folded the parchment, she caught sight of a maid hurrying to the kitchen and Esme followed. There, in the center of the large room, the messenger sat with a large platter of food in front of him and a tankard at his elbow.

Moira, the cook, smiled widely. "Would ye like some cider, Lady Esme?"

"No, thank ye," Esme replied and looked to the messenger who scrambled to his feet. "Please sit and eat. I came to thank ye for bringing news. Tell me, how does my father fare?"

"He is well, Lady Esme. Of good health."

Despite the urge to roll her eyes at the practiced answer, she smiled. "I am grateful. Did my brother send me any message?"

The messenger shook his head. "No. He was not about when I was sent to come here."

"I was hoping to hear from him. How does he fare?"

This time, the messenger swallowed. "I do not know, Lady Esme. I have not seen him as of late."

Esme let out a breath she wasn't aware she had been holding. "I pray he is well."

"I am sure he is," the messenger replied.

Deciding to allow the man to eat, she turned to the door, but then stopped. "I will be sending back letters as well. I am sure someone will show ye a place to rest and sleep tonight."

Her mind awhirl, instead of turning back toward the great room, Esme headed outside. Once in the courtyard, she looked around until she spotted Ruari at the corral with the beast of a horse. Admittedly, the animal had become tamer, but a barely restrained ferocity was clear in the way it shifted and pawed at the grown.

When Esme neared, the horse's grunting noises were a bit unsettling. "Is the horse considering murder?" She eyed the animal with distrust.

"That is a good assumption. He clearly is not one to ever accept being dominated." As if to prove his agreement, the animal reared up, its huge hooves pawing the air.

Ruari did not release his hold on the strap around the animal's neck. Instead, when its hooves landed on the ground, he ran a hand down the animal's nose, soothing it.

When he untied the strap and loosed the beast, the animal trotted in a circle while shaking its long mane.

Her husband's hazel gaze met hers for a long moment. "I saw a messenger come. Does he bring bad news? Ye are troubled."

It seemed, already, Ruari could sense her moods. Esme wasn't sure how she felt about it. "Not bad news really. Catriona sent a letter. My brother has not been seen in days."

"It is probable he is accomplishing work for yer father."

She'd not considered it. If her father required him to do something, they usually did not inform others. Her mother wouldn't ask and she was sure that Flora, Catriona's companion, would definitely not know.

"I am bothered by the news. I wish to go and see about it."

Ruari shook his head. "Ye will not go. I am not welcome at Fraser Keep and, therefore, ye are not as well. Ye are a Ross now."

"It will always be my home," Esme replied with a set jaw. "I am sure ye and my father will work things…"

"I said no."

Words caught in her throat. She thought of too many responses at once until none escaped. How dare he speak to her as if she were a child? She was not a prisoner to be kept from going where she pleased.

Ruari's right brow rose. "Go inside, Esme. We will discuss this later. I have much to do."

Pushing a finger into his chest, Esme snarled, too angry for words. Then, taking a deep breath, she placed both palms on his chest and pushed hard. It was irritating when he didn't move a bit. "Are ye dismissing me? I am worried about my brother. I wish to visit my family and ye tell me to go away?"

"I did not say go away." Ruari pronounced each word clearly. "There is no reason for us not to speak of it later. The messenger will not leave until morning."

"I will go with him."

"No." Ruari shook his head, this time, his eyes darkening. "Ye will not."

Knowing it was a battle of wills neither would win, Esme turned on her heel and hurried back to the house.

She almost fell when, upon entering, one of the house hounds raced across her path. Esme groaned and continued forth, up the stairs and into her bedchamber.

"What happened?" Ceilidh appeared in the doorway, her blonde hair pulled back into a soft braid, allowing for several ringlets to frame her pretty face. "Did ye and Ruari fight?"

Esme nodded. "Why do men act as if they own us?"

"Mostly out of protection."

"I am not sure I believe it. I think it is because they consider us beneath them."

"My husband has always treated me equally. I am sure Ruari is as fair as Ian. All Ross men hold women in high esteem."

Perhaps Ceilidh's husband did, but Ruari had just dismissed her and ordered her into the house. "My mother always said that a woman must know her place. Father never includes her in any important matters."

"Let us go back downstairs. A bit of honeyed mead will help settle yer nerves."

Once again in the great room, Esme noted some people lingered. This place always had many people about.

"Come." Ceilidh took her hand and pulled her to a table where the other women sat. Elspeth, Malcolm's wife, was joined by Merida and Gisela, Kieran's wife.

After Esme settled into a chair, everyone looked to Ceilidh. The pretty blonde explained Esme's concerns. It was quite interesting when their expressions went from curious to narrowed looks in the direction of the doorway.

Merida huffed. "Did ye kick him in the leg?"

"I should have," Esme said.

"Or another place that would have hurt worse," Gisela said.

Elspeth held up a hand. "Women like us must learn to know our places."

Esme groaned. "I tire of hearing that."

"Our place is to control situations without them realizing it," Elspeth finished, and every head bobbed in agreement.

"I do not understand," Esme said.

"What do ye want?" Merida asked, pushing her auburn locks away from her babe's grasp.

After considering, Esme replied, "To return home and assure myself that all is well."

"Is it wise?" Ceilidh interjected.

"It could be dangerous, especially since ye will ride near Mackenzie lands," Elspeth said next.

Her spirits fell.

"However," Gisela said. "If ye leave, ensuring to be followed closely, I am sure Ruari will catch up in time to keep ye from harm."

They quieted when a guard approached and informed Elspeth and Merida that their husbands were about to travel to the village.

"Will my husband and Ruari remain?" Gisela asked.

The guard nodded and left.

A grin stretched across Gisela's face. "I will help ye."

With olive skin, dark eyes and luscious brown hair, Gisela was stunning. Esme wondered how it was that fate brought two extraordinarily attractive people together. Gisela's husband, Kieran, was the lightest of the Ross brothers, and by far the fairest. At first sight, Esme had been struck silent at seeing him.

Obviously, it was a common occurrence because no one paid attention to her reaction.

"I am not sure what to do," Esme admitted.

"First, ye pack food and a wineskin. Ye hide it by an exit," Merida said and then added, "ensure that Ruari sleeps well by pleasuring him"

Ceilidh giggled, her face pinkening. "Slip out at daybreak."

"Tell the stable lad that Ruari is joining ye shortly while ye saddle yer horse," Elspeth instructed next.

Merida leaned forward conspiratorially. "And then ride through the gates as if the devil himself were chasing ye. Shortly after, Ruari will be roused and follow."

"Keep going until ye are far enough away and refuse to return. He will take ye the rest of the way. Of that, I am sure," Elspeth said.

The plan was easy. Esme could not see what could go wrong,

other than Ruari being roused too soon, which she doubted since there was no reason for the stable lads to not believe her.

"I will do it."

IT WAS STILL quite dark when Esme slipped out and across the courtyard. Her bundle under her arm, she went to the stables and found that everyone was asleep. No one in sight. Glad not to have to speak to a stable worker, she went to a stall and coaxed a sleepy mare out.

Soon thereafter, she rode through the gates unchallenged. Just as she passed, she looked up and one of the guards peered down and stared at her.

Esme lifted a hand in greeting. His was much slower in response.

Satisfied the man would go fetch someone, she urged her mount to a gallop. The mare was not in the mood for goading and instead trotted, then slowed back to a walk.

"Ye have to go faster. At this pace, my husband can catch us by walking," Esme grumbled.

Finally, the mare decided to pay heed and, soon, she was past the village and headed to the path along the river that she knew would lead to her home. Several times, she looked over her shoulder, thinking she heard something, but each time there was no one.

Surely the guard had roused Ruari. If not, then the women would. How long would it be before they were up and checked to see if she had, indeed, gone forth with the plan?

It mattered not. Esme decided to pull a hood over her head and continue her trek, hopefully unnoticed.

It became late in the day and still no one had come after her. Esme was becoming too exhausted to continue.

Ruari had yet to catch up and she was becoming alarmed. If he didn't come, was she brave enough to continue the rest of the way alone?

She dismounted and stretched her arms up and then leaned back to allow her back some relief. At spotting the river, she pulled the mare toward the water's edge. Then she looked up at the sky, trying to figure out what direction would lead her toward home.

Several hours later, as the sun began to fall, Esme was sure she was lost. The sun was now behind her and she realized that for the last several hours, she had been going in the wrong direction.

Pulling on the mare's reins, she turned the animal around. An instant later, the sound of horses made her pause. Could it be that Ruari finally caught up?

Surely, he'd picked up her trail, as she'd not been careful. Being that she'd headed in the wrong direction, however, could have proven disastrous.

As men on horseback crested a hill, she narrowed her eyes and attempted to focus on the riders. They did not look familiar.

Her heart began to quicken and her throat constricted. The men wore Mackenzie colors.

"Oh, no." Esme looked around to see if there was anywhere to hide. They'd spotted her and picked up their pace. Esme urged the mare to go faster, which it surprisingly did. But her mount had no chance against the huge warhorses the men rode.

Finally, they caught up with her and Esme did her best to appear brave as she glared at them. "Leave me be."

One of them narrowed his eyes and then they widened in recognition. "Ye are Fraser's daughter." He looked at his companions and searched the area for others.

"This could be a trap," one of the others said and they all began scanning the surroundings.

"Why would we wish to trap ye?" Esme snapped. "I am heading home. Allow me to pass."

"Alone?" the first man, who was probably the leader, asked.

"I prefer to travel alone," Esme said, looking him straight in the eyes. "I do not think ye would like what would happen if ye try anything against me. I am a Ross now."

The man's eyebrows rose. "And yer husband knows ye are out and about alone?"

It was a dire situation and Esme knew the chances they'd allow her to continue home were slim. "I became lost. My escorts should be along shortly."

"Ye are on Mackenzie lands, lass." A gruff man looked at her with distaste. "Not on the edges, but well into our land."

Her heart sank. "I would like to speak to yer laird then." Esme fought not to cry when one of them grabbed the mare's reins from her hands. The men surrounded her, but none attempted to touch her.

For that, she was thankful.

⤐⥼

LAIRD MACKENZIE WAS not physically imposing. It was his manners and expressions that made him terrifying. Madness swirled behind his gaze as he peered down at her. The low timbre of his voice seemed to reach out and rake over her skin like one hundred fingers.

"Why are ye on my lands? Why alone? Tell me what ye seek."

"I became separated from my escorts during the night. I traveled in the wrong direction. I assure ye, they are searching for me now."

After a moment, he looked past her to someone and jutted forward with his chin. A command of some sort because several sets of footsteps sounded, walking away.

She'd been shoved into a chair in the Mackenzie great room. Only a few guards were about, no one from the village was visiting it seemed.

Not even water had been offered to her since she'd arrived several hours earlier. Instead, she'd been ordered to sit and wait for the Mackenzie to arrive from wherever he was.

Exhaustion and hunger had set in, but she refused to ask for anything. She'd rather starve than beg for drink or food from people who may have hurt her brother.

A woman walked in and, by her age, Esme guessed her to be one of the Mackenzie's daughters.

The woman was about her age and quite pretty. Esme wondered if this was the woman he sought to have Keithen marry.

"Father. May I offer her a meal? She has been here for a long time without drink or food." The woman looked to Esme, who studied her in return. Her hair was a light brown that had been pulled away from her face rather tightly. She glanced at Esme and it was as if she tried to communicate something. However, Esme wasn't sure what to make of it.

The Mackenzie stared at Esme. "Why would ye ride away without yer husband?"

"He agreed that I could visit my family alone as he has duties to see to." Esme wanted to add that it was none of his business. But being she'd been caught on Mackenzie lands, perhaps he had a reason to be suspicious.

"Is my brother here?" Esme blurted.

The man's eyebrows rose. "Why do ye ask?"

Now, she'd made a mistake. "I am aware ye wish to have him to marry one of yer daughters."

The woman glanced at her father, her brow crinkling.

The Mackenzie shrugged as if it were inconsequential and then looked to the woman. "She can eat, but must remain here."

The laird walked out and, soon thereafter, Esme was served stew, bread and drink. The woman sat and began eating alongside her. In her company alone, Esme felt comfortable enough to eat.

"Are ye his daughter?" she asked the woman. The young lady

nodded.

"I am Ava, his eldest."

"Ye are married?" Esme asked, noticing she wore a band on her finger.

The woman met her gaze. She had the palest blue eyes Esme had ever seen. "I am widowed."

Instead of a reply, Esme wanted to ask more questions. "I hope yer father allows me to go. I have to attend to family matters."

Ava shrugged. "It is hard to know what he will do."

"Are ye the one he wishes to marry to my brother?" Esme asked.

"Father does not discuss things with me, but I overheard it. I believe so. Although I am told yer father refused."

"Help me leave," Esme said, pushing her plate aside. "I do not wish to be the reason for another clash between our clans."

Her hopes were dashed when Ava shook her head. "There is nothing I can do."

CHAPTER TWENTY-FOUR

I T WAS NOW the second day and, still, they'd yet to catch up with Esme. It was obvious she'd become lost. Ruari's fears were all but confirmed at a traveler telling them he'd seen a woman being escorted by Mackenzies.

Although he was furious at his wife and at the other women who'd confessed their plan after he'd found her gone late the morning before, Ruari was more concerned.

"Should ye send word to Fraser?" Ewan asked.

He'd already sent a scout back to Ross lands to ask Malcolm to send more men. He rode with only twenty at the moment.

"She is my responsibility, not the Fraser's."

They continued farther into Mackenzie lands, their banner on full display to ensure that they were recognized.

Why had Esme gone to such lengths to return home? Had she planned to return to him?

Did he wish her to? His wife had not considered him upon planning to leave.

If she preferred to return to her home to live, would he allow it?

He would. It was preferable to living in fear that she'd run away again.

His mother had left him without remorse, as a matter of fact. There was nothing to gain in forcing someone who didn't wish to be with him to remain at his side.

It could be that Esme resented him for taking her away from her family. Maybe she had decided she'd rather risk her life than continue to live with him.

Yes, she'd brought up the excuse of Keithen being gone, but it did not justify her actions. Ruari looked to his cousin. "Once I find her, I will allow her to return to her family."

Ewan met his gaze. "I am sure she prefers to live with ye."

"Ye cannot be sure of it. Why then leave as she did?"

His cousin's shoulders lifted and lowered. "Ye heard what the women said. They thought ye would be right behind her. She did not plan to be alone. Surely, she became lost and did not mean to end up on Mackenzie lands."

Annoyed, he raked his fingers through his tangled hair.

A man on horseback appeared. Ruari looked to Ewan. "See him?"

"Aye."

Upon noticing them, the rider galloped in their direction. As he got closer, Ruari called to the guards to lower their bows and swords. It was Keithen.

"The bastard's got my sister," Keithen yelled, his anger directed at Ruari. "Why is she out alone?"

"She left on her own."

The enraged man glared at him. "How is it possible for a wee woman to escape without being seen?"

"She was seen. My keep is not a prison. No one is kept from leaving if they wish." Ruari wanted to hit the man in the face.

Keithen's eyes narrowed. "Why did she ride here?"

"I am sure she became lost," Ruari said. "Ye can ask her when I fetch her."

"The Mackenzie will think it's a trap or trick," Keithen said, his voice still tight. "Why would she do this?"

Ruari gave him an annoyed look. "A letter arrived. She was informed ye'd not been seen for days."

When Keithen's face turned to stone, Ruari knew something was amiss. "Why are ye on Mackenzie land?"

"That is not important now," came the curt reply.

They continued forward and would reach the keep shortly. "Are ye coming with us? If so, we will have to explain yer presence," Ewan said to Keithen.

"I will remain in the forest. Tis best not to complicate things by me killing the bastard." And a while later, as the keep came into view, Keithen disappeared.

"What do ye suppose he is doing?" Ewan asked.

Ruari had wondered the same thing. "I would say he is avenging something. The Mackenzie did take his mother and the woman, Catriona. The woman was horribly mistreated."

They rode to the gates and, although the huge portal was open, they were challenged by guards.

Once disclosing their names, they waited until word was sent to the laird. A long while later, guards rode along their sides as the entire party was invited through the gates.

Moments later, they were escorted into the great room. It struck Ruari as strange that no one greeted them at the entrance as was customary.

Highlanders' unwritten customs were to greet visitors and invite them to eat a meal, whether friend or stranger.

Upon his eyes adjusting to the dimness, Esme raced to him and threw her arms around his waist. Her face pushed into his chest. He could not see if she was harmed or not.

The only other person in the room was a woman who stood by a table, hands clenched in front of her. The woman was silent, her gaze moving from him to Ewan. "Father wishes ye to join him in his study."

It was just like the Mackenzie to use theatrics.

It was only when his tunic became wet that he realized Esme was crying. Ruari took her by the shoulders and moved her back so that he could inspect her. Other than a dirty face and reddened nose, she looked to be unharmed.

"Are ye hurt?" he asked, wishing they were alone so he could console her.

Esme shook her head. "I wish to go home."

Did she want to go to Ross Keep or her childhood home? It was not the moment to ask. "Remain here. I will go speak to the Mackenzie."

After a moment, she nodded and allowed a guard to escort her outside.

He and Ewan then followed the woman down a corridor and were shown into a room where the Mackenzie and several other men were. There was a large table in the center.

"Ensure they are served," the Mackenzie said to maids who hurried forward with a tray of food and another with drinks.

"I am glad ye came to fetch yer wife. I was not sure where to send her."

"If ye would have asked, I am sure she would have told ye," Ruari replied, not sitting.

The Mackenzie motioned to the chairs. "If ye would join me for a drink, I would like to speak about the conflict between our clans."

Ewan looked at Ruari and then spoke. "Is there a conflict between us?"

"Not with Ross, no," the Mackenzie said, waving a hand. And then obviously annoyed, he motioned to the chairs again. "Ye. Yer wife and yerselves came here."

Ruari and Ewan pulled back chairs and sat. The man was right. They'd trespassed on his lands. "My wife got lost and ended up on yer lands. I am here to fetch her and to thank ye for keeping her safe."

"As ye know," the laird began, "I am not on good terms with her father. And so, it was unexpected that his daughter would be roaming about. Especially after several of my guards have gone missing."

The sentence was left hanging, bait for Ruari to take.

"So ye think my wee wife is strong enough to overtake yer men and cause them harm?"

The man's eyes narrowed. "Nay. But ye are."

As much as Ruari wanted to push away from the table and slam his fist on it, he kept his temper in check. "I have no reason to kill any of yer men, nor do I wish to do so. To what end? What purpose would it serve?"

His keen eyes on Ruari, the Mackenzie stroked his beard. "I do not know. I will ask that ye leave my lands and warn her family to keep their distance. There are still matters pending between us that, for now, I will let rest."

⭆⭆⭅⭅

BY THE TIME they rode away from Mackenzie Keep, the sky was darkening. Soon, they'd have to make camp. Esme rode with Ruari, leaning back on him. She was glad for his strength as she could barely keep her eyes open.

"Do ye wish to return to yer clan? If so, I will send ye with escort."

His question caught her off guard. She'd assumed that after all she'd done, he'd forbid it. "Ye would allow me to go?"

Ruari motioned to Ewan and the party came to a stop. "We will return in a moment." Her husband helped her down and dismounted. He then led her a short distance away. "I will not force ye to remain with me. If ye wish to return home to live, I will not stop ye."

Her eyes rounded upon realizing what he had just offered. Heart thundering in her ears, she tried to figure out what to say. Of course, she wanted to see her family, but she did not wish to leave the marriage.

"I only came because I worried about Keithen. I wanted to help find him if it was needed."

"Do ye not think if yer father required help in finding him, word would have been sent?"

Her father would not have asked Clan Ross, not after throwing Ruari from the Fraser Clan. "I am not sure my father would. Can ye understand why I came?"

"No." The blunt answer made her cringe. His face was expressionless, and she feared he preferred her to go back to her family.

"If ye allow me to go, I will. I have to see about my brother." Esme took a shaky breath. "I want to be with ye. We are husband and wife, and I love ye even if ye do not feel as strongly for me." When tears slid down her cheeks, Esme wiped them away angrily. "I will require at least four men to escort me. Although I doubt the Mackenzie will stop me again."

Ruari took her arm to keep her from turning away. "I saw yer brother. He is here."

"What?" Unsure she'd heard correctly, Esme studied Ruari's face. "Ye've seen him?"

He nodded. "He did not tell me what he is doing, but I suspect some sort of work for yer father that they prefer to keep quiet."

Breath left her. She'd been rash and stupid for leaving, openly disobeying her husband. And now he was giving her the option to leave. On the precipice of losing Ruari, Esme wasn't sure how to repair all the damage she'd done.

"I should not have come. It was reckless. Will ye forgive me?"

For what seemed like a long moment, Ruari remained silent, his hand around her arm, gently holding her in place. "What do ye wish to do, Esme? Return with me or go to Fraser Keep?"

"I wish to return with ye."

He'd not said that he'd forgiven her and he did not acknowledge her profession of love. When they returned to the horses, Ewan studied their faces, and waited for Ruari to say which direction they'd travel.

"North," Ruari said and they began the trek to Ross lands.

THEY ARRIVED AT Ross Keep the next morning. Once inside, Esme did not look around, but hurried directly to the bedchamber. Maids were already setting up a bath for her, which she figured Elspeth had ordered. A clean nightgown was laid on the bed and, moments later, Ceilidh entered with a tray. "I bring some warm cider and a bit for ye to eat."

"Thank ye, but I am not hungry," Esme said, meeting her friend's gaze. "I wish to bathe and go to sleep."

"Of course." Ceilidh neared. "We are so sorry. We should have seen to it that someone followed closer. It was late by the time Ruari found out and he was so furious, it was terrifying."

Esme let out a breath. "There is no need for any of ye to feel badly. It was I who went forth without making sure that I followed. I kept going and got lost."

Ceilidh's eyes rounded. "Oh, no."

"I will tell ye more once I rest." Esme undressed, not caring that Ceilidh remained in the room and sunk into the fragrant, heated water. She closed her eyes. "I told him I loved him, and he did not respond."

When she opened her eyes, she met Ceilidh's who gave her a warm smile. "It could be that he was too angry to respond at that time. The moment may not have been right."

Esme felt somewhat better. "Ye may be right."

Moments later, as she slipped her night rail on, barely able to keep her eyes open, Esme considered waiting for Ruari to join her. The draw of sleep was too strong.

THE NEXT MORNING, the silence in the great room was like nothing before. The usual jovial mood when the Ross wives gathered was gone. Servants and visitors had all been told to stay out.

Malcolm stood in front of the gathered group. Next to him stood Tristan. Kieran and Ruari sat in chairs, their expressions austere.

Elspeth, Merida, Gisela and Esme had been asked to sit in four chairs placed in a semi-circle facing the laird.

Although she'd often heard of Malcolm Ross described as a heartless laird, for the first time, Esme experienced a shiver of apprehension. His expression was hard, like stone. His darkened brown gaze piercing as it landed on each of the women.

"Yer advice to Esme, that she leave this keep without escort, could have not only cost her life, but also the lives of many of our men. The Mackenzie is volatile and easy to goad. The outcome could have been very different. Our men are tired of war and to be thrown into another would have been disastrous."

When Merida sniffed, Esme took her hand, but at Malcolm's frown, she released it.

She looked to Ruari for support, but his expression mirrored Malcolm's.

"I am very disappointed," Malcolm added. "I do not care who ye are, I will not allow my clan's lives to be put in danger over a silly game. Am I understood?"

Elspeth, Malcolm's wife, stood. She was the only one brave enough to stand up to the man. "We are embarrassed, all of us. It was thoughtless and a big mistake." She turned to Esme. "We owe ye an apology as well for goading ye to do it."

"I should have known better," Esme replied. "I know firsthand how dreadful the Mackenzie is." She looked to Malcolm. "I will never do anything like it again. I would never wish to be the reason for harm to come to Clan Ross."

When Malcolm remained silent, the properly chastised women got up and went to their respective chambers. Esme needed time away to be alone. Although a bit harsh, what Malcolm had said was true.

CHAPTER TWENTY-FIVE

R UARI WASN'T SURE what to say to Esme. He'd not slept in their chamber for several nights. He was still furious that she'd left without taking the repercussions into consideration. The thought burned through him. As much as he wished to speak to her and accept her apology, a part of him still wondered if she did not wish to remain there with him.

Adding insult to injury, she'd not only apologized, but also professed to love him. Had she done it to ensure he'd not leave her behind?

The night before, he'd barely slept, once again rehashing everything. Had Esme even realized how badly things could have gone?

The Mackenzie could have taken it as a spying attempt by Clan Ross and drawn them into another war.

Not only that, but she'd also put her own father's clan in jeopardy. He lifted up from the pallet in front of the hearth when he heard footsteps approaching.

Malcolm peered down at him silently. "When I didn't sleep in my chambers, I managed to find a more comfortable place than the floor."

Ruari sat up and yawned. "I've slept in worse places. Why are ye up?"

The laird frowned. "I am departing shortly to Fraser lands. With yer marriage, they are our allies. I need to ensure the Mackenzie threat is controlled."

"Do ye plan to visit the Mackenzie as well?"

Malcolm shook his head. "In the future perhaps."

"We are not welcome at Fraser Keep. Why would ye go?" Ruari stood and stretched out the tightness in his back.

"I think ye should come. Bring Esme. Tis best to get the situation controlled. If he stands with the decision that ye are not welcome, then I will break the alliance."

Ruari's eyebrows shot up. His cousin…brother's support touched him. "Ye do not need to do it…"

"Ye are like a brother to me. I will not relent on this." Malcolm walked toward the kitchen. "We leave shortly."

"ESME." RUARI STOOD next to the bed. His wife was fast asleep, her hair, having escaped the braid, forming a halo of brown waves. She was a beautiful sight.

"Esme," he repeated, this time touching her shoulder. "Wake."

Her eyes opened slowly. And then startled, her eyes widened. "Is something wrong?"

So many things.

"Malcolm is traveling to see yer father. We are going, as well."

When she rubbed her eyes and yawned, the enticing picture was not lost on him. Ruari stepped back and went to a chest to pull out a change of clothing.

"Ruari? Why are we going?" She'd slipped from the bed and came to stand next to him. "Talk to me."

"Malcolm wishes to discuss our clans' alliance with yer father."

"Oh." In silence, she padded across the room to a wardrobe where her clothes hung. "Why are we going?" she repeated in a soft voice.

He'd not asked Malcolm what he considered doing if the alliance was broken. There were several options. The marriage could be dissolved if both lairds decided, or they could remain married and Esme would have to break her ties with Clan Fraser.

Unsure if she knew, he decided to be honest. "If the alliance continues, then everything remains as is. Although I am not sure how Malcolm will react if I am still not welcome. He vows to break the alliance if so."

Esme stopped in the middle of fastening her dress. "If the alliance ends, then what will happen to us?"

"The lairds can decide to dissolve our marriage or ye will have the choice to break away from Clan Fraser."

When she gasped, Ruari fought to offer comfort. If his mother had taught him anything, it was that no matter how long and how often one tried to gain affection through actions, it rarely had the desired effect.

"We leave momentarily. I will wait for ye downstairs in the kitchens." Ruari grabbed the bundle of clothes and looked at her. "Bring a change of clothes. I will get some food for us."

Esme took a step toward him, but he turned and walked out of the room.

⫸⫷

THE RIDE TO her family's lands was at a good pace. They stopped often to allow the horses to rest. It was almost pleasant, as Malcolm's wife, Elspeth, as well as Ceilidh and her husband, Ian, traveled in the group.

There was a large contingent of warriors, Esme guessed it to be almost a hundred. The Ross banner, currently staked into the ground, waved in the breeze.

Esme had joined the other women earlier to relieve themselves. So this time, when everyone sat on blankets that had been spread on the grass and ate, she remained at Ruari's side.

He'd been silent most of the trip, guiding the horses that pulled their wagon with calm precision. In the back of the wagon were thick blankets, clothing and food.

Esme noted that Elspeth and Ceilidh rode in a carriage, since they traveled with children.

When Ruari lay back, hands beneath his head and stared up at the sky, Esme moved closer. "Ye remain angry with me. I understand. Can ye not see why I wished to go and ensure my brother was not in peril?"

Ruari closed his eyes. "This is not the time to discuss what happened."

Unable to keep from it, Esme pushed his shoulder. "If not now, then when? Ye have kept from me for days, avoiding me. I made a mistake. Have ye never…"

He sat up abruptly and glanced around. "Get up." He stood and stalked away from a nearby group to an area where no one could overhear them.

Esme couldn't help but fear the worst. Was he about to tell her that he wished to end the marriage? Her chest constricted and her eyes watered, but she blinked it away and forced herself to remain strong.

Ruari stood straight, arms to his sides in a proud pose that made him seem larger than life. His gaze was flat when meeting hers. "If the Mackenzie would have taken yer appearance as a threat, he could have decided to declare war on either Clan Ross or Clan Fraser. If ye would have been injured or killed by the men who found ye, war would have followed. By honor, Clan Ross would have declared war. Yer little escapade could have cost countless lives."

Esme remained silent, unsure how to reply.

Her husband continued. "I had promised to meet with important visitors that day since Malcolm had to go to the village for an urgent matter. I had to leave my duties to chase after ye, and all this only so ye could visit yer family."

When she started to say something, he gave her a pointed look. "There was little ye could have done if Keithen was in danger. Ye are lucky the Mackenzie did not keep ye as a prisoner, a bargaining tool to take yer clan over." His chest lifted and fell with each word. Although he kept the tone even, the undercurrent of restrained fury was terrifying.

It was the first time someone had been so furious with her and Esme wasn't quite sure what to say or do. He thought her a self-absorbed simpleton. Perhaps she was.

"I apologized. I admit that I did not consider any of the things as ye explain them. There is little I can do now, other than be thankful the outcome was not worse."

Ruari blew out an annoyed breath and attempted to return to where the others were, but Esme blocked him. "What about us?"

There was a flash of uncertainty in his eyes, but he quickly looked away and shrugged. "I do not know. It is as I explained it to ye this morning."

"Do ye wish to end our marriage?" Esme touched his arm. "I do not."

When his gaze jerked to hers, he studied her face and his brow fell. "Why do ye say that? Do ye really wish to remain? Even if it means turning yer back on Clan Fraser?"

"I would never do that, Ruari. Understand me…"

This time, he rounded her and stalked away.

It was enough, Esme lost control and raced after him. She yanked at his arm. "Do not walk away. I listened to ye, will ye not do the same?"

After he let out a breath, Ruari crossed his arms and looked down at her. "I know where yer loyalties lay. There is nothing else to be said."

Esme opened her mouth, but no words came. Could she turn her back on her clan if the lairds decided against an alliance? She was now a Ross by marriage, and she was a proud Fraser by birth.

ARRIVING AT HER home was strange. Entering through the gates, Esme felt like a visitor looking from the cart to where her father, mother and brother stood at the entrance in welcome.

Malcolm and Elspeth were first to be greeted and then Ruari's uncle, Gregor, who'd insisted on attending the negotiations. Being cousin to the laird meant Ruari and she would be greeted after them.

When they approached, her mother hugged her. As happy as she was to see her mother, Esme was more focused on how her father reacted to Ruari being there. The men exchanged cordial greetings, which made it hard to tell what, exactly, was transpiring internally. She then looked to Keithen who gave her a warm smile. Her heart leaped with joy at seeing he was, indeed, alive and well.

As a group, everyone walked into the great room. The entire time, her mother talked about inconsequential things. "Mother, are ye aware we are here to discuss whether the clans will continue in an alliance?"

Her mother nodded. "I heard something about it. Of course, it is nothing for us to concern ourselves with."

For a long beat, Esme considered telling her mother how much of it concern it was. In that moment, she noticed the pasted smile and worried look her mother directed toward her father. For an instant, the truth was revealed. Her mother feared facing reality. Sadness engulfed Esme at the knowledge.

With an overly bright smile, her mother took her hand. "Come along. Let the men do whatever it is they plan. Ye must see Catriona. She is so much better."

"Does she leave the bedchamber now?"

"If she wished to, I am sure she would," her mother replied with a chuckle. "I think she enjoys spending time alone."

CHAPTER TWENTY-SIX

L AIRD FRASER WAITED until they were served and then sent
everyone except for Keithen, Malcolm, Uncle Gregor and Ruari
away. Once the door closed, he leaned forward and met Ruari's gaze.
"Accept my apologies for how I treated ye. I should not have reacted
as I did. There is no excuse for my treatment of ye, as my daughter's
husband and an allied clan member."

Ruari bent his head and then lifted it to look at the laird. "I accept
yer apology."

"Good," Laird Fraser replied. "It gives me ease to hear it. I do
mean it genuinely."

Ruari believed the apology was heartfelt. He'd not allowed Esme
as much consideration. Ruari frowned at the realization. Why had he
not believed it when she'd said words that made sense?

Malcolm spoke next, outlining an agreement that would give Laird
Fraser a right to call upon them if the need arose. Again, it was
reiterated that Clan Ross would act as reinforcements only until the
larger Clan Fraser's warriors arrived.

The agreement was made, and a scribe was sent for. While they
waited, Gregor, Malcolm and Laird Fraser continued the conversation
regarding logistics and such.

"Can I speak to ye in private?" Keithen said to Ruari motioning to the doorway.

"Aye. Of course."

They walked to a small courtyard. Keithen then glanced around to ensure not to be overheard. "Do ye know what I was doing on Mackenzie lands?"

"I believe I do," Ruari replied. "Ye are treading dangerously. It could cause a clan war if ye are discovered."

Keithen Fraser was built for war, with the build of a predator. Sleek and muscular, the air of restrained power surrounded him. Unlike Esme, who had dark brown hair, her brother's hair was sun streaked, the color of sunsets.

"They took my mother and almost killed Catriona. I must make them pay."

"Yer father is not aware then." Ruari didn't state it as a question.

Keithen shook his head.

"Ye should not continue. It is rash and will not change what has happened."

The man's lips curled into a snarl. "What if they had harmed my sister in the way they did Catriona?"

Ruari inhaled sharply. He'd been ready to go to war to save her. That his life could have been in danger had not mattered.

"I see ye understand then." Keithen pulled the door open and went back inside. When Ruari returned to the laird's study, Malcolm looked to him in question.

"I would like to ask something," Ruari told the laird and everyone looked to him. "I plan to give my wife a choice to remain or return with me. Either way, she will remain my wife. I ask that ye allow her to live here if she chooses to stay."

Laird Fraser's confused look mirrored Keithen's. "Women are not to be given such liberties."

"Yer daughter slipped away and was captured by the Mackenzie,"

Malcolm said. "Her actions put our clan in peril of war."

The laird got to his feet. "I must speak to her immediately. Why was I not informed?"

"It is something that I wished to tell ye in person. She claims to have left because of a letter she received," Ruari said. "I would rather she stay here than have another incident occurring with the potential for dire consequences."

A short time later, Esme appeared. Gregor and Keithen left the room so only Ruari and the two lairds remained.

Ruari's heart thudded when Esme looked to them with obvious confusion. She swallowed visibly and then walked to where he was and sat next to him.

"I must tell ye how disappointed I am to hear of yer escapade." The laird's voice shook with fury. "Do ye have any idea how frail the truce with the Mackenzie is?"

Esme nodded but remained silent. Her face, however, turned red and her eyes became glossy.

Malcolm looked into Ruari's eyes before speaking next. "We have decided to give ye a choice in this matter. We cannot risk ye deciding to escape again, so if ye prefer to remain here, Ruari agrees to remain married to ye."

Wide-eyed, she turned to him.

Ruari met her gaze. "It is yer choice, Esme."

"I have already told my husband I wish to remain with him." Esme glared around the room. "I am aware of my mistake and do not need to be treated like a child, punished over and over for it."

"Ye are not being punished," Malcolm stated.

Her father shook his head. "Ye have an understanding husband. Most would end the marriage."

Esme turned to Ruari. "If ye wish to end the marriage, just say so, Husband. I have already repeated over and over again that I wish to remain with ye. I want to stay married because I love ye. But if ye do not feel the same and wish me to stay here, I will. Oh, to hell with all of ye." She pushed from the table so hard, it moved. Then after one more glare, she raced away.

The men remained silent. Malcolm and Laird Fraser looking everywhere but directly at Ruari.

"Mayhap ye should go speak to her," Malcolm finally said.

HE FOUND HER pacing in the same courtyard in which he'd just spoken with Keithen. When seeing him, she turned away, but not before he saw she was crying. "Go away, Ruari. Just leave. I will remain here."

"Ye can return with me." He reached for her and she shrugged away. "The offer was so that ye can be safe."

There was fire in her eyes. "Twice, I have told ye how I feel." She wiped at tears that continued to spill. "And both times, ye dismiss it. I was forced on ye and now ye have found a way to rid yerself of me."

"Esme," he started. "I have hope that we are able to remain as husband and wife."

"That is not how I see it," she snapped. "Ye keep repeating that I can stay here, and I have told ye each time that I do not wish it. It is almost as if ye do not want to hear it."

Ruari was at a loss. As if he were being pulled under water, he struggled to find the adequate words. Why would Esme want to remain with him? The idea was foreign. Nothing formed in his mind other than the thought to get away and return to the simple life of living in the stables back at Ross Keep where he didn't have to fear anymore loss.

"Yer silence makes my decision easier," Esme said. Her eyes filled with sorrow and she shook her head. "I will stay."

For a long moment, after his wife walked away, Ruari remained still. He felt if he took one step, he'd falter and collapse. He remembered sensations that he'd not felt since being left at Ross Keep, both his parents leaving. He struggled to take breaths before he stumbled to a nearby wall and leaned against it.

No longer a lad, but a grown man, a strong fighter, he refused to allow sensations of rejection to take purchase. He struck the wall with his fist, the pain helping bring a semblance of control.

⇥⟫⟫✖⟪⟪⇤

THE ENTIRE TRIP back to Ross Keep, Ruari refused to speak to anyone. After growing tired of the glares from Malcolm and Ian's wives, he urged his mount to a gallop and left the party. Several guards, thinking it a race, followed suit. Upon arriving, he ensured his horse was brushed down, watered and fed and then he went to the rooms just behind the stable.

Had those rooms always been so sparse? A bed, tiny table and a dusty trunk were the only items in one. In the other, there were two chairs and a slender table on one side with the rest of the space empty. The window had no covering and a spider had decided to use its skills to provide one.

"I thought I'd find ye here." Ewan stood at the doorway, making the already small space shrink.

"I prefer to be alone."

His cousin shrugged. "I prefer to be naked with a buxom woman atop me but, yet, here we are."

"What is it?" Ruari gave him what he hoped was an obvious look to leave him be.

Oblivious, Ewan pulled a chair out, turned it around and straddled it. "Ye're running scared."

What Ruari wanted right now was to hit his cousin. "Says the man who has yet to be honest about why he is really here."

The barb hit, because Ewan physically flinched. But he was not dissuaded from the conversation. "Ye are in love with yer wife and are running scared from it. Do not sit there and pretend ye are content to return to this." Ewan swept his hand across the air in the meager room. "She did not wish to stay behind, but ye forced her because ye're a coward."

Ruari shoved the table aside with so much force, it crashed against the wall and flopped onto its side.

When he threw himself at Ewan, his cousin was prepared and fled out the door, laughing. Enraged, Ruari gave chase.

The surroundings turned red and he growled in frustration, unable to catch up with Ewan who was lithe and fast. Finally, when Ewan turned to avoid crashing with a maid hauling a bucket, Ruari was able to tackle him to the ground.

Ewan hit first, the fist to Ruari's face sending his head sideways. Ruari then hit the man with force, satisfied when blood sprouted from Ewan's nose.

"Augh!" Ewan yelled. "Get off of me." He covered his face with both hands.

Ruari was hauled off of Ewan and he swung blindly, not caring who it was. His first punch landed on Tristan's jaw. The second hit sent Malcolm backward.

Guards rushed forward, but Malcolm told them to remain back.

"This is between Ewan and me," Ruari yelled, rushing Ewan who was holding his nose with two fingers.

His cousin was quick, punching him twice, but he barely felt it. They rolled around the ground and when he lifted a fist to hit Ewan, once again he was pulled away.

Chest heaving, Ruari shrugged them off and trudged back toward the stables. He would not fight the three of them. It was obvious they'd put Ewan up to goading him and why they'd interfered.

What his cousin said was not true. That he was in love was a ridiculous notion. Did he even know what it felt like? Was it what he experienced for the men who, up until recently, he thought of as cousins? Was it what he'd felt for his father, who he'd thought of as his uncle? Was it the pain and emptiness that had filled him since leaving Esme behind?

Pressing his lips together, Ruari sat on the cot and closed his eyes. When he touched his face, he winced.

What was he supposed to do now? He'd left Esme behind.

He remained sitting in the empty room without eating for the next two days. He was unable to speak or think of anything more than why he'd allowed Esme to go.

Laird Fraser had been understanding, telling him he was welcome to return at any time. Keithen, on the other hand, not as much, calling him a coward for not fighting for his wife.

If ever there was a time he needed advice it was then.

MORNING CAME AND Ruari could not fight against the pangs of hunger any longer. He went to the main house and entered through the back door. It was late morning, so most of the maids were outside in the garden or had gone to the village to purchase what would be needed for last meal. Moira didn't speak to him. Instead, she placed a plate piled with meat and root vegetables on the table. "Drink this," she said, slamming a cup of ale on the table.

While he ate, the older woman studied him. Ian's mother had always treated him like a son. The late laird's wife, Lady Ross, had always been distant, so all of them had sought maternal guidance from the cook, who had no problem doling out advice and reprimands.

"Ye look horrible. Once ye eat, go bathe."

Ruari nodded and shoved food into his mouth.

"After ye finish washing, pack up and go."

Thinking there was more to the sentence, he looked to Moira. The woman slapped him on the side of the head. "What were ye thinking leaving yer wife behind? Ye took a vow to protect her and she is now part of ye. Go get yer wife or I will never speak to ye again."

"She chose to remain behind. What of her vow to me?"

"Sometimes, a person is forced to make a decision, especially when pushed away."

He ate the rest of the food and then went to the bedchamber to retrieve clean clothing. The interior of the chamber was like they'd left it. A light fragrance in the air was all Esme and he inhaled deeply. Across the bed was a shawl she often used when getting up to cover herself from the chill in the air. Refusing to look at the table that held her belongings, he went to a trunk at the foot of the bed and retrieved a tunic and breeches.

He stopped at seeing a ribbon that had fallen on the floor.

How could he have been so stupid? So utterly, utterly foolish to have allowed his deep feelings for her to scare him and send her away.

Chapter Twenty-Seven

E SME WASN'T SURE how to face every morning in her new role back in Fraser Keep. Although everything was the same, it felt so very different.

Her mother's disapproval of her decision to remain kept them at odds. It was grating to constantly hear that she'd ruined her own life.

Then there were the questioning looks from the maids and servants, who seemed confused about her status in the household.

Her only solace was Catriona, who she spent hours with talking about inconsequential things. Admittedly, her friend was still not the same. Most of the time, Catriona seemed to fade away during their time together, escaping into her own mind.

It was heartbreaking to see the once bright and exuberant Catriona no longer take care of her appearance, wearing her hair in a single braid every day and choosing only dull gowns to wear. Only once had Esme been able to coax her friend out to the garden and, even then, Catriona didn't seem to take notice of the surroundings.

"Ye should make it clear to yer mother that her constant berating is not acceptable," Catriona said, sounding like her former self. "It is not fair to ye."

"I did make the decision to remain..." Esme said and sighed.

"Mayhap it was wrong."

Catriona shook her head. "It was up to Ruari to convince ye to return and not to be so quick to allow ye to remain behind. I am convinced he cares for ye but is too stubborn to admit it, even to himself."

To Esme, it was doubtful that Ruari cared. He was attracted to her, but his actions had been driven by the fact that they were married and not by love.

"Lady Esme," a maid said from the doorway. "There is a visitor here for ye."

If it was someone from the village, Esme was not in the mood for it. "Who is it?"

"Yer husband."

Esme's stomach plummeted, her breath caught in her throat and she looked to Catriona, who seemed to have a similar reaction.

"I will be there shortly."

She looked down at her gown, a simple but flattering frock, and then felt foolish for wanting to look her best.

"Ye look beautiful," Catriona told her with a soft smile. "The color is most flattering on ye."

The pale green did complement her olive complexion and dark hair.

Still, it was hard to make herself stand. Although she was told by her mother that her father had insisted Ruari visit often, she'd not expected it to be more than once every season or so.

Clasping her hands together to keep the trembling from showing, she went to the sitting room where Ruari awaited.

His hair had been shorn and he looked like he had recently trimmed his beard as well. He looked a bit different, perhaps gaunt in the face, but it did not diminish his attractiveness.

When their eyes met, Esme fought to keep an even expression. However, she knew hurt could not be kept from her eyes.

"I did not expect ye to come so soon," she said, motioning to a chair. She lowered and, once again, clasped her hands together on her lap. Esme kept her gaze forward, refusing to look at him.

When he lowered to his knees in front of her, she leaned back.

Ruari then grasped her hands and looked into her eyes. "Forgive me."

Struck silent, she could only stare at his large hands. When she met his gaze, there was determination.

"I am a coward to have left ye. I came to ask that ye return to me."

Esme wanted to, her entire being missing him, but she pulled her hands away from his. "Give me a good reason."

"Because I love ye and vow to never allow fear to separate me from ye again." He cupped her face. "I love ye, Esme."

His words fell over her, tendrils of warmth fanning. They were only words, she told herself. Something that could be easily swept away by a strong wind.

"Ye made vows before and it did not matter. Ye left me behind."

"I am a fool."

Certainly, she would return with him. This wasn't her home anymore. The hollowness in every part of the home kept her cold and distant. It was not who she was, and she refused to become that woman that kept everyone at a distance.

"Do ye trust me at all?" Esme asked. "Do you believe that I have learned from my mistakes and will not do something so rash again?"

"I do," he replied. "Return with me, Esme. I cannot live without ye by my side."

His declarations were foreign, although he'd said he cared for her in the past. Even during lovemaking, Ruari never spoke of emotions or feelings.

Esme didn't expect it when his lips touched hers, but she accepted the kiss, her eyes falling closed at the familiarity of her husband's touch.

More than ever, she wanted to be his, to feel protected, secure and comforted. Although tingles of fear prodded her, she pushed them away. She was, after all, the daughter of a laird, a brave archer.

"Ye must remind me regularly of this," she said. "I wish to hear daily and in different ways how ye feel about me. I need it, Ruari."

He seemed puzzled, but then nodded. "I promise."

"I wish to be beside ye if ever there is a need to protect our home. I am a warrior, a fighter who will not hide and simper when enemies approach."

"I am aware of it," Ruari said. "Ye may not be beside me, but I do expect ye up on the ramparts with that bow and arrows of yers."

She considered his words and acquiesced. "Very well."

"Does this mean ye will return to Ross Keep with me?"

Her lips curved at his expectant expression. "I will return with ye."

A fortnight later

HER ARROW HIT the center of the target and Esme grinned at her husband who, in turn, frowned.

Although he was an intimidating fighter, his archery skills were passable at best. Ruari lifted his bow, pulled back the arrow and concentrated on the target. Esme stepped behind him and blew into his ear.

The arrow flew into the air, much too high and impaled into a nearby tree.

"That was not fair. Were ye scared I would best ye?"

Her laughter was bright. "Not in the least."

"Come with me." Ruari took her hand and led her toward the house. Together, they raced up the stairs to their bedchamber.

There was a mischievous gleam in his eyes. "Ye can best me any-where ye please." Pulling her against him, his mouth covered hers, his arousal evident by the hardness that prodded at her lower abdomen.

When his hand slid down her back to cup her bottom, she moaned into his mouth, molding her body against his.

She then pushed back and gave him a playful look. "Take yer

clothes off now."

Ruari's lips curved. "I will."

Moments later, they tumbled onto the floor, both completely nude and breathless. The feel of his skin against hers never grew old. It was exciting to know that anyone could open the door and happen upon them.

Ruari rolled onto his back, pulling her over him. She pushed up, straddling him, then slid her sex against his.

Her husband grunted with pleasure, his jaw flexing.

The view of the man, unmade by her, was a most alluring picture.

When she guided him to enter her, both of them groaned at joining. Immediately, Esme began to move, taking him deeper and faster until everything disappeared. All that remained was the two of them, their bodies taking and giving and the beautiful sounds of their exclamations.

Two days later

Esme sat in the bedchamber re-reading Catriona's latest letter describing the sheep outside her window, knowing the animals were always brought to the closer fields when the weather would grow cooler. Shepherds were offered warm places to sleep when not caring for the flocks and it was easier for the guards to keep watch for predators.

From the balcony, the large field just past the gates at Ross Keep was empty of flowers now. In the distance, the sounds of sword practice rang in the air. Soon, it would be time to head downstairs for last meal, but she relished the quiet time alone when not having to be around so many people.

She leaned forward at seeing a man walking to the center of the field. It looked like her husband.

Going to the open window, she leaned out. From the second floor, she had a clear view of him as she was sure all the guards did, too.

"Esme! Esme!" Ruari yelled and held his arms out.

"Yes? What is it?" she yelled back.

From the other balcony, Elspeth and Ceilidh emerged. "What is he doing?" Elspeth asked.

"I do not know," Esme replied and then looked to Ruari. "What is it?"

Several of the guards stopped and were now watching as her husband began to undress.

"Has he gone mad?" Ceilidh said with a chuckle. "I must admit I like the view."

"Ruari, stop at once," Esme yelled.

The guards goaded him, the deep laughter making her shake her head at how easily men could be entertained.

"Come inside now," Esme called out.

Tunic already gone, Ruari removed his britches next and stood as bare as the day he was born.

"He must have been drinking too much whisky," Ceilidh remarked with a giggle.

"Esme!" Ruari repeated, holding his arms wide. "I love ye. I belong wholly to ye. I am reminding ye of how I feel."

Despite the ridiculous form of expression, Esme began to laugh, her heart light and happy. The guards atop the gate did the same, some whistling and cheering now.

"I love ye, Esme!" Ruari screamed and then ran toward the loch.

"What are ye waiting for?" Elspeth said with a wide grin. "Go get him."

She flew down the stairs and out the front gates to capture her husband.

The End!!!

About the Author

Most days USA Today Bestseller Hildie McQueen can be found in her overly tight leggings and green hoodie, holding a cup of British black tea while stalking her hunky lawn guy. Author of Medieval Highlander and American Historical romance, she writes something every reader can enjoy.

Hildie's favorite past-times are reader conventions, traveling, shopping and reading.

She resides in beautiful small town Georgia with her super-hero husband Kurt and three little doggies.

Visit her website at www.hildiemcqueen.com
Facebook: HildieMcQueen
Twitter: @HildieMcQueen
Instagram: hildiemcqueenwriter

Printed in Great Britain
by Amazon

46630403R00145